HAWAIIAN TABOO

THE SPIRIT OF OHANA CRUISE SHIP SERIES, BOOK TWO

LANEY KAYE

ABOUT THE AUTHOR

Laney Kaye spent her youth in the rural areas of South Australia and seeks to recreate that lifestyle as an adult—apparently mainly by homing a ridiculous and diverse number of animals.

A qualified professional counselor with a keen interest in the empowerment of women, she enjoys messing with heads by day and imaginations by night.

Under her 'real name' she pens award-winning young adult titles and women's fiction.

www.laney-kaye-author@weebly.com

Copyright © Laney Kaye 2019

ASIN: B07QGPSLJG

ISBN: 978-0-6486584-2-9

Cover Design: Black Bird Book Covers

CrossWorlds Publishing Australia / United States

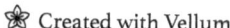 Created with Vellum

For Taylor,
Who never harbors doubt

ALSO BY LANEY KAYE

THE LURE OF THE MER SERIES

Hook

Line

THE SPIRIT OF OHANA SERIES

Hawaiian Hurricane

Hawaiian Taboo

CAT SHIFTERS OF AAIDAR SERIES

(co-written with Christina Wilder)

Escape

Engage

Ensnare

Endings

BENT, NOT BROKEN SERIES

Malicious Desire

1

The cotton of my cargo shorts snagged on the studs of the upcycled denim-jean cushion as I wriggled farther back on the stool. My Vans swung two inches short of the narrow steel bar of the footrest. "So, I'm struggling here." Not only with my height disadvantage. "Remind me why the heck I'm going?"

Suzee made a three-course meal of licking salt from a peanut, and I didn't need to check our artfully-lit surrounds to know my friend had found an audience to play to. She had a sixth sense for knowing when eyes were on her.

Well, eyes were always on her, so I guess it wasn't so much a sense, as an expectation.

The grungy-meets-trendy Sydney bar vibed with an after-work influx of business types and a smattering of well-heeled tourists. Considering we were in The Rocks, scene of the meet-cute between an Australian commoner and a certain Danish prince quite a few years back, most women there were probably on the hunt. They'd sure dressed the part. No one else wore shorts. Or trundled a suitcase.

But, unlike them, I was done kissing frogs.

The pub wasn't my usual haunt, but as my regular came with a side of Damien, I'd deal.

"Why are you going?" Suzee repeated. She opted for a mercy killing, flipping the peanut into her mouth, then speaking through the shards. "Let me see. Sidestepping your obvious need-to-please-mommy issues—because there's no way we've time to crack that can of worms—you need to find a guy to check your dark, damp spots for funnel-web spiders."

"Jeez, Suze!" The crisp Sauv Blanc she'd chosen was supremely less appetizing as I spluttered it over the bowl of complimentary bar food. "Keep it down." I'd rather have a conversation about my mother than discuss my lack of a sex life. At least, not here.

"Sorry, chick." She didn't look the least apologetic, keeping up a blue-eyed survey of the cocktail-sipping crowd. "But elevator pitching is my God-given, remember? I may as well use my talent for good not evil. And I nailed it, right? Frick knows, someone sure needs to take you in hand." She lowered a hundred dollars' worth of Russian Princess extensions in a slow wink. "Pun unintended, but nonetheless, remarkably good."

She flashed me an unrepentant grin, then turned the killer-wattage toward a guy in a pinstriped suit at the far end of the bar. "Hey, how about him? He's overdoing the man-spreading, it looks like he's laying the Crown Jewels out on display. And I'll bet we're talking zirconia, not diamonds. But still, you've time for a quick practice before you go."

At least she'd dropped the decibels, though her husky voice didn't carry. It was modulated to make men lean toward her.

However, as she spoke, she lifted her chin, boobs, and

eyebrows toward the guy. Suzee didn't do subtle. "Go on, at least glance his way, Melissa," she urged.

Ignoring her, I methodically folded a burgundy napkin and blotted at the slab counter made from repurposed wharf pilings. God only knew what lived in the two-hundred-year-old crevices in the wood. I paused with my hand extended above the bowl of nuts. Nope. Stirring the bacteria around wouldn't see the nibbles magically redeemed to acceptable food safety standards. "I thought your specialty was magazine placement, not pimping."

That wasn't entirely true. Suzee had tried to hook me up even when I had been *technically* hooked up—or garroted, tangled in a noose, choked by the hangman's knot—or whatever it was that Damien's seven-year hold over me had constituted.

Oblivious to the saliva-infused wine splatter, Suzee grabbed another handful of nuts. "Multi-tasker. I'll do whatever floats your boat. Or, preferably, rocks it. In any case, my fear of cobwebs on your behalf is entirely justified."

A guy leaned across her, far closer than necessary, on the pretext of reaching for the nuts. I lurched forward to warn him off them but stopped myself. What the heck, I wasn't responsible for everyone. "Fear of spiders, you mean. Arachnophobia."

Suzee swirled the wine around her glass, squinting through the viscous film toward the man at the end of the bar, as though the filter would soften the angular planes of his face. Because, yeah, I'd checked him out. No harm in looking. That was all I ever did, nowadays. "Not my type, Suze," I cautioned.

Her long hair swayed with her exaggerated sigh. "Yeah, but what is your type? Until you nail that, you can't nail him."

I knew my type all right; he existed on a computer screen. Nice, neat, safe pixels. "I meant more of the I'm not *his* type. You know...." I admiringly outlined her silhouette with one hand, then jerked my thumb back at myself, pulling a disparaging face.

Suzee shook her head despairingly. "Sweets, I love you to death, but you have a totally fucked-up idea of self. You give any guy in here a chance, and he's going to say you're a wet dream come true. I keep telling you, I'll take you home myself."

Yup, she did tell me that, every time we got a bit tipsy.

Suzee tossed back her drink and tapped the rim of the glass. Despite the crowd, a bartender rushed to do her silent bidding. "Anyway, just because you hang around with creeps, don't correct me on my creepies, Miss Bee-Ess-Cee." She spelled out my qualification. "I definitely mean cobwebs. You've got parts more thickly festooned than teen Spiderman's bedroom ceiling the first time he jizzed."

"Suzee..." My groaning remonstration was pointless. As usual, Suzee was flying, high on life. "Remind me why we're even friends?"

"Because you lovee me. Everyone lovees me."

"Truth." Suzee could leave this bar with any man or woman of her choosing. And, despite hanging out for years, not one speck of her confidence or sexiness had rubbed off on me.

She toasted the bearded hipster barman over the edge of her brimming glass. We all knew she wouldn't be paying for that drink. "You do understand that re-virgination is a scientific phenomenon, Melissa? The hymen grows over, and you're all shiny brand new again. Except for the cobwebs, that is." The tip of her tongue caressed another peanut.

I rubbed my temples. Suzee's teasing wasn't helping my

pre-flight nerves, and neither was the wine. "Could you just stop with the nuts for a moment—?"

Suzee snorted. "Can't say I've *ever* had that request before." She flicked the peanut into her mouth, crunching it between her back teeth.

The stool alongside me creaked as its occupant stiffened. Hopefully, just his stance. I edged away from him. "I'm serious, Suze. I can't do this. I've got stuff to do here, I can't afford to take time out for this." My hand waved toward the suitcase pulled up between our barstools, as though the fluttering motion would add merit to my avoidance.

Avoiding a holiday, avoiding my mother, avoiding my extended family. And avoiding temptation.

Suzee twitched her stiletto-tipped finger from side-to-side, and I followed the movement like a hypnotized cobra. One glass of wine was definitely my limit. "I'm calling BS on that one, Melissa. You've got more time-off due than you'll ever manage to take because you never leave that underground lair of yours. I wouldn't have a problem with that if you were holed up with Batman—or should I say, had Batman in your hole—but I know it's just you and jars of pickled fish."

True enough. But my lab, my desk, my familiar windowless office, were all safe. Nothing ever turned to shit while I was in there, with my focus on measurable constants and empirical data. Information uncontaminated by emotion and human fallibility: aka, Damien's lies.

Well, technically, I guess maybe my life did turn to shit while I was in there; but buried beneath my work, I never had to acknowledge the issues. The lab was my safe space, my cocoon.

And I should have spent a couple more hours there, instead of sitting here with my swinging legs cutting off the circulation in the back of my thighs. Which sucked on so many levels; if the Universe was at all fair, my extra padding would protect my arterial network from being compromised and crimped.

I cringed as Suzee's tongue probed the recess under her acrylic nails. "You know a blacklight swipe of one of those nuts would illuminate an entire suburb, right?"

"An all-night bug rave? Cool."

"No joke, Suze. I'm talking E-coli, Salmonella, Shigella, Clostridium, Campylobacter, Staph..."

"Aww, how cute, you know all the little guys by their first names. Guess it's lucky I like purple then, my nerdy germo-phobe friend." She wiped the excess salt—*germs*—onto a napkin, then nodded toward my suitcase. "Nice ribbons."

"Yeah, Mom's idea. To make it easier to spot my luggage."

A perfectly arched eyebrow disappeared beneath Suzee's bangs. "You really don't get out much, do you?" I lifted one shoulder and she shook her head. "Your mom's a freaking genius. Is that where you get it from?"

Sarcasm? I'd tossed back my wine too fast to now be capable of deciphering Suzee's tone. In any case, she probably wasn't making sense given that she had, as usual, matched me three-to-one in the drinks department. "You know, Suze, your boobs are truly a miracle of modern medicine."

"Random, but thanks." Suzee cupped her silicone-enhanced attributes. "Worth every dollar."

I shook my head, then immediately wished I hadn't, as the room continued the movement long after I was reasonably sure I'd stopped. Maybe I could get a grant to research whether it was possible to ingest sufficient quantities of alcohol through the skin for it to have a discernible effect. Despite frequent swipes with the hand towel the bartender had tucked down the front of his jeans—undoubtedly a less-than-hygienic locale—the stickiness of the bar indicated a build-up of residue. Not that I'd leaned on it much. More used it as a launchpad to help me levitate onto the stool.

Enunciating with on-the-way-to-being-wrecked clarity, I tried to sound logical. "No, I mean, how is it you can keep downing drinks with no effect? The secret has to be in the boobs. Camel hump storage abilities. They should be scientifically assessed. For use in, I don't know, the space station. Or...something," I finished, waving a vague hand at our noisy surroundings. A band had cranked up in the adjoining room, through a narrow doorway lined with dark beams that looked like they belonged on a ship. Though I couldn't make out an actual tune, or even rhythm, the bass thumped through my head.

"Sweet, you're not exactly lacking in the boobage department yourself. So maybe it's more to do with silicone? Perhaps it absorbs alcohol. In any case, locked in a spaceship full of astronauts? I'm in. Anything for research." Suzee glanced at her phone, which lay on the bar. Sighed. Waggled a long finger in my face. "Time for a serious talk."

The slurred 's' made incoming wisdom seem unlikely.

Suzee leaned close, overbalanced, and slapped a hand on my knee. "Whoa, nearly an early dismount there. Can't be having that."

"Serious, huh?"

Suit guy craned forward to check how far Suzee's hand crept up my thigh. Suzee flipped ash-blonde hair over her shoulder, grinned, and slid her palm higher. "By the way, his suit is a Zegna. And the watch is Rolex. Predictable, but are you sure you don't want to go there? You've done your time with leeches."

"Doesn't mean I'm going to be the leech."

Suzee looked momentarily affronted. "Accepting gifts is a long way from leeching."

"Yeah, I'm sure that's how Damien chose to view it, too. Anyway, I wasn't having a go at you. You're independent, Suze. You work, you have your own place. You don't need a guy."

"Nope. I don't." She drew herself up straight and looked smug. "But I'm going to give it to you straight, Melissa. You do. Need a guy, that is. You're going to Hawaii because revenge is a dish best served tropical-heat hot. And, let's not beat around the bush here—though a bit of that might actually be good for you, if you know what I mean?" She hooted at my scowl. "Too much? Okay, then, I'll lay it on the table."

I rolled my eyes. "You're the queen of shite innuendo."

"Australia has run out of men. At least, as far as you're concerned."

I slapped Suzee's hand off my leg. "That's not even remotely close to true. A handful of Tinder fails hardly constitutes running out."

"Sorry, sweets, but it's a fact. I could hook you up with every Hemsworth brother, individually or as a group—which would be my personal recommendation—and you'd still find fault. Because no amount of dating is going to work when you're running scared and afraid to climb back on that horse." Suzee planted her Manolos on the rung of her stool, lifted a couple of inches, and slapped her own tight ass to punctuate her point. To a man, the patrons ranged along the bar froze, mouths hanging open.

"Trust you to mangle metaphors." And find a way to mention her exceedingly tenuous—and completely unproven—connection with the Hemsworth Hunks.

Suzee dropped back onto her seat, her eyes glittering

with triumph as her gaze skimmed her audience. "Melissa, it's going to be spinster city for you, if you stay here. Let's face it, you're gorgeous, but your fashion sense already screams more of a *run thither* vibe than *come hither*."

I pulled my shirt free of my shorts, suddenly aware that it'd folded into the crease of my waist. To be fair, these were my casual, comfortable, traveling clothes. If I'd been going to work, I'd have worn...well, much the same, probably. And a lab coat.

"In a couple more years, you won't have any of *this* going on to rescue you." Suzee waved a hand down my five-foot frame, then fake-groped my boobs. "Those girls will be tucked into the waistband of your mumsy stretch pants, and you'll be begging Dickhead Damien to come back."

"Like hell, I will. And single is the new married, anyway."

She looked at me pityingly.

Yeah, one glass was definitely my limit. I tried again. "There's nothing wrong with being single."

Suzee snorted. She'd hadn't been single more than three consecutive days since she turned fifteen. In fact, she generally had multiple guys racked up, so I guess they covered for the odd dry day.

"Spinsters can be sexy." My dwindling defenses sounded increasingly lame, and I hoped the guy behind me, practically breathing down my neck, couldn't hear.

"Sexy spinsters? Are you for real? Hate to say it, Liss, but you are spending too much time on your computer."

"Yeah, well, work—"

"Porn, I mean."

"Slander." I dashed a hand across my face, trying to cool the sudden burn of my cheeks.

"Sure. Or, y'know, a pretty accurate assessment. In any

case, real spinsters are *not* sexy. You know they don't actually have the messy bun and horn-rimmed glasses thing happening, right? More like a house full of cats and lint-ball festooned tweed skirts. And I'm telling you, Liss, end up like that and you can kiss goodbye to even Tinder hookups."

"I don't want a Tinder hookup," I yelped. The protest too fast and too loud, I hunched a shoulder as the guy next to me shifted his coaster along the bar, trying to edge into our conversation. Without even checking him out, I knew there was no point allowing him in. Within five minutes he'd ask about my salary, homeownership status, and what I'd love to cook him for dinner. Because that's the way it went for me, every darn time.

A bellow of male laughter across the room caught Suzee's attention. When she swiveled back, she pinioned me with her gaze. "Of course you want a hookup, Melissa. Do yourself a favor, stop holding out for a mythical Mr. Right. All men are going to fail, at least in your eyes. You've got a self-protection mindset happening, you're terrified that you're going to get stuck with another Damien, so you're marking all guys as duds from the outset." She palmed my cheek, tapping a little harder than necessary, as though really, she wanted to slap some sense into me. "So, you know what you have to do? Change your target. What you *need* is a Mr. Right-Now to blow your cobwebs away. Get back in the game and have some fun."

I leaned my elbows on the bar, staring into the wishing-well of my wine. "Great plan. If I could even remember how to play the game. But you forget I seem to be a magnet for the emotionally needy. That's not exactly my fault."

"Pfft. *Emotionally* needy? Puhleese. Your swipe-right game is seriously messed up. All the guys you pick are after a sugar momma. You need a fucker, girl, not a fix-upper."

"Not arguing with you." I'd been so damn careful in my selections on the dating apps—which I probably had shares in by now—yet my profile matches were always after promises and paychecks. "It might be sexist, but I thought women were supposed to be the gold diggers. I mean, look at Mom."

"Have you thought about getting a puppy?"

"Say what, now?" Suzee's tangents could be hard to follow at the best of times. Add alcohol and noise, and I was lost.

"Well, you do have a knack for choosing dogs." Suzee tucked hair behind one ear, making sure the best of her perfect profiles was on display. "I mean, Damien? Don't even get me started on him."

Yeah, please don't. Neither of us wanted to go there.

Yet, apparently, we were...

"I warned you about putting up with his crap, yet still it took you *how many* years to kick him to the curb? You were so intent on being empathetic and the *nice* girl, you didn't even see his un-fucking-believable bullshit coming. Hell, you didn't even see it when he laid it out for you."

Sure, I'd tried to be understanding toward Damien—but I wasn't as altruistic as Suzee seemed to think. I had long ago figured I'd be better off with the devil I knew.

Or so I thought, until a couple of months ago.

Suzee blew out a sharp breath and held her flattened palms above the counter, stroking the air and seeking her Zen. With her breasts heaving out of her top, which was not helping anyone else's chill. "Anyway, Damien is water under the bridge, crap through the sewer pipe, diarrhea down the drain—"

"You're magic with words. I can see why you're in advertising."

Her finger jabbing toward the suitcase, Suzee ignored me. "It's time to move on. Plenty more sperm whales in the sea, you just need to cast your net a bit wider. Hawaii should do it nicely. No risk, no reservations. No need to pre-judge the guys or play it safe. You'll never see them again."

The bartender replaced my drink, though I didn't recall signaling for another. I probably hadn't. He'd no doubt heard—along with two-thirds of the bar—about my non-existent sex life.

I tossed back a good swig of the pity-plonk. "Except I'm not going there to look for guys."

Or was I? My head fuzzier by the swallow, Suzee's suggestions were taking root. *Ha.* That was the only kind of rooting I'd been getting for years.

Yet...what if I *could* find a Hawaiian hookup? Suzee was right, that would be the ultimate in no-strings sex. Thousands of miles from home there could be no risk, only the chance to discover whether a guy could want me solely for my physical assets, rather than my financial ones.

I shook my head and scrubbed a hand across my eyes. What kind of loser traveled five thousand miles to build their self-esteem by getting down and dirty? I wasn't that desperate.

Was I?

Like a schoolmarm ticking off a naughty student, I made my point with my index finger. However, either my finger or my vision wasn't to be trusted, wavering like a poorly focused microscope slide. "I'm going for Mom's wedding, remember? Though why I should, when she's not bothered coming back here for nearly five years..."

Of course, there was the other reason I was going, too. The one no one knew about, the one I barely dared give thought to, because it loosed a flock of butterflies in my stomach each time. It was a mad plan. Irrational. Totally flew in the face of my need for familiarity and safety.

Suzee crossed one leg over the other, angled so the guy to my left copped a lot of thigh. Not a slightly chubby, possibly dimpled thigh, but a sleek, long, golden limb. If she wasn't my best friend, Suzee would be scary easy to hate on.

Her hand trailing slowly up from her knee, like she modeled silk stockings, Suzee pulled on the hem of her short skirt—not so much to tug it down, as to draw attention. Like there was a chance the guys were looking anywhere else. "Yet, you're going. Ever the dutiful daughter. I'm not even going to bother faking sympathy for you, chick. That's reserved for friends who don't get a guilt trip that includes paid flights and an island cruise."

"Otherwise known as forced proximity with Mom and the step-sibs. Playing Happy Families."

"Small price. And just think, now you get to go without... baggage. You can go be whoever you want. Do whoever you want. Just think of all the hot guys you'll come across." Suzee's pomegranate-shaded lips curved, her laughter cascading like a magpie's warble. "Yeah, I said it. Hey, did I tell you about my vacation in Greece, summer before last?"

"Yep. In pornographic detail."

Suzee dismissed my reply with a flick of her wrist, launching into a lurid recount of her favorite holiday memory of a father-and-son tag team, much to the enjoyment of her unofficial audience.

I zoned out, staring at my suitcase. Maybe she was right. Half a world from home, no one knew anything about me. Least of all, Mom. If I reinvented myself, started fresh, maybe even changed my name a little—*Lissa*—could I magically erase the last seven years? Or was that notion simply the alcohol talking?

I startled as Suzee tapped the back of my hand, looking at me questioningly. "Earth to Melissa. So, what do you reckon?"

About her ménage? "Uh, cool?"

A lot of exposed, tanned skin flashed as Suzee slid gracefully from the stool. "Excellent. I'll set that up tonight, then, while you're winging your way over to hot-Yank land."

"Set it up? Wait, what?" A threesome? I gracelessly fell-clambered from my stool, then glowered accusingly at my wine glass. It was always the last drink that snuck up on me. That, and the first one. I generally didn't have any in-between.

"I'll organize the sheets."

Sheets? Threesomes? Why had I risked zoning out around Suzee?

Hand under my elbow, Suzee steered me through the bar. "Uber texted. He's outside. I ordered a hot driver."

So, a threesome with a hot driver who carried sheets in his car? That sounded like the setup for a bad sitcom, a lousy murder mystery, or even worse porn. Whatever, I wasn't about to star in it. I swiped a hand through my hair in a vain attempt to clear the mental fog. "I have to get to the airport, Suze."

Suzee cut her eyes sideways. "Uh huh. Hence the Uber." She snapped her fingers impatiently, the deep red polish glinting as we neared the neon-enhanced door. "Honestly, you might have rounded out those luscious curves a bit since Damien, but you're still such a lightweight, Melissa. You only had a couple of drinks. I was saying, I'll set up a conquest spreadsheet. Ten days, you have ten sexual conquests to make. Ten tasks. Starting with kissing. No, I'll make it easier, you're so out of practice. Starting with looking, then flirting. Ending with...how good's your imagination?"

Pretty darn good, considering that's all I'd had for years. That and the internet, anyway.

"Consider it an experiment," Suzee continued, adjusting her boobs and almost causing a traffic accident as we stepped out into the early-summer evening. "I know how you love them. An experiment into what it takes to persuade you that you're desirable and that not all men are after the same thing."

The reliability of the result would most certainly be in question, but a spreadsheet? I dealt well with logic and procedure. Suzee could be on to something.

As we wobbled down the three rough-hewn sandstone steps to the waiting Uber, I sniffed at the surprising ozone tang of approaching rain.

Maybe the drought was about to break.

2

One more wrong choice and they'd probably cart me off in handcuffs. Not the fluffy pink-feather trimmed variety, either.

I scrubbed sweat-slick palms on the sides of my shorts, then hauled another suitcase from the overloaded airport carousel. No wonder Suzee had sneered at Mom's 'idea' of tying ribbons to my luggage. Not only were two-thirds of the cases and bags similarly decorated, but there must have been a sale on azure-blue, one-inch wide satin.

I leaned the case against my leg and flicked the ID tag over. Heaved a sigh of relief. Third time *was* the charm. With the *Me* scratched out, only *Lissa* remained on the nametag. Which was kind of fitting; losing *me* to become someone new, like that was all it took to change who I'd always been.

I tented my cotton tee between thumb and forefinger, pumping air down my front. Maybe not so much of a tent; like all of my clothes, the shirt strained to cover my questionable assets.

The terminal teemed with people and noise, the frenetic

pace of the pulse vibrating through the soles of my feet and feeding my panic with an almost overwhelming urge to about-turn and board a flight back home.

Back to Suzee and the threesome-that-wasn't, yet still left my brain slightly addled. Eleven hours in the air hadn't helped with that.

Concentrating on deep, calming inhalations, I scanned the huge concourse. No sign of a welcoming committee of lei-bearing maidens. Or, even better, hot Hawaiian guys in traditional grass skirts. That's what the travel brochures mom sent had promised. Pictorially, anyway. I'd spent a fair few lunch breaks—and perhaps a little lab time—ogling the bronzed gods, imagining a tropical breeze stirring the fronds against their muscular legs...

Researching. I'd spent a lot of time *researching* Hawaii. As would any intelligent twenty-something whose smarts had failed to save her from being manipulated into traipsing halfway across the world.

The multitude of scrolling panels above me provided directions in more languages than I could recognize. Even forgiving the lack of hot guys—not that I was ready to— Honolulu International Airport fell somewhat short of the brochure representations. A halfway-decent PR company had managed to put a hell of a spin on reality; here, the only hint of tropical joy emanated from travelers prematurely decked out in floral shirts and Bermuda shorts and hyped on holiday excitement.

Or, possibly, buzzed on the complimentary in-flight drinks.

Music burst from a speaker hidden between the leaves of a potted palm, the dull roar of hundreds of people speaking *quietly* joined by the twanging notes of a ukulele. My hips swayed involuntarily, and I snorted at the irony;

after whining to Suzee about being obliged to take the tropical vacation, here I was, instantly seduced by quasi-Hawaiian canned music and dancing like a chubby dashboard hula doll.

Well, if I was going full-on tourist, hopefully I'd be able to bring myself to embrace other forms of seduction, too. I firmed my grip on my backpack strap; in there was my laptop, hopefully with Suzee's ten-point task sheet waiting in my emails.

Without instructions, I was lost.

The man zombie-shuffling ahead of me scowled over his shoulder. Either my brief dance had intruded on his ownership of thirty-square-centimeters of polished cement, or he'd missed out on his share of the free mid-air booze.

Though a contrite smile plastered automatically across my face, I bit back the urge to apologize. Instead, I mentally high-fived myself. First outing and my new and improved version of self, Melissa without the *Me*, already kicked ass.

I could totally do this.

Ten days, ten tasks.

Starting with looking.

Either I had a pulmonary embolism, or nerves clenched an imaginary fist around my lungs. Realistically, probably the latter. I'd have to look at real people, not screens.

Suzee hadn't said I had to make eye contact, though, right? At least, not straight up. I could ease myself into it. Ten days, more than enough time to get to...well, whatever base I got to.

One step at a time.

As recycled air snagged my throat I coughed, then clenched my thighs. After the embarrassment of trying to maneuver my carry-on into an overhead locker evidently located for giants, I'd spent the flight curled tight into my window seat, reluctant to disturb my fellow passengers. Now, if I didn't find a restroom soon, it wouldn't be sweat making my flip flops slippery.

I stumbled as the guy behind me in the slow-moving queue pressed close. Any closer and I'd be sending out baby shower invitations by the time I got home.

I clenched my fists; perhaps he was hot as hell. And eager to be the first tick on my spreadsheet.

I should turn around.

Check him out as, his breath warm on my neck, his iron-hard length rode—

What? I lurched forward. How the heck had that escalated from me being too chicken to turn around, to full-on erotica? In reality, that scenario would be creepy as hell. Plus, the brief fantasy set off a tingling in my loins, which most definitely did *not* help with my bathroom issue.

Suzee was right. Too much internet porn. Despite which, hot or not, I wasn't turning to make eye contact with the guy.

Great. I'd never tick off day one on the spreadsheet.

This was going to be a lot harder than two glasses of wine had made it seem.

The sign above the bank of desks we crept toward came into focus. Customs. Thirty meters to my left, a restroom symbol called to me. Taunted. Promised immeasurable relief. My fingertips drummed the top of my suitcase. I jiggled from one foot to the other. Mashed my lips together.

The woman queued alongside shot me a quick smile of commiseration.

My gaze settled on her. Beigely trustworthy and nondescriptly average, maybe she'd mind my luggage for a minute?

I reached toward her, then snatched my hand back with a cold flare of realization; wasn't such stupidity precisely what drug cartels based their business model on? Weak-bladdered women, desperate enough to leave their bags unattended at the airport. Mom would love it if I kicked off the vacation by headlining the evening news as the latest unwitting Aussie drug mule.

I dashed my palm across my sweating brow, even though I'd not had a chance to pick up hand sanitizer. Five more minutes, and I'd be leaking top *and* bottom. This was ridiculous. Surely this kind of thing didn't happen to adults? But what the heck was I supposed to do? Taking the bags with me to the restroom wasn't an option, either. Thanks to Damien, I was going to have enough trouble clearing Customs without having them suspect I'd dashed to the loo to offload contraband.

I slouched to one hip, crossed my ankles and tried to project *relaxed*. A couple of Kegels—about as much of a thrill as anything down south ever got—and I clenched my teeth and held my breath. Like either of those things would help. I squeezed my thighs together. Not that they required much squeezing, with thigh-gap barely a thing anymore. Cheers for that, too, Damien.

In response to the customs official's summons, I hobbled to the counter and slid my open passport onto the desk. A pinch-featured blonde stared from the photo, my narrow face framed by the asymmetrical blunt cut Damien insisted on.

The officer did a double-take between me and the passport. "Pull your hair back, please, and face the camera."

Now they'd drag me off to a side room for questioning. A room with no toilet.

Travel-crazed copper waves bunched in one hand, I sucked in my cheeks—if that evaporated twenty pounds, I'd discovered the secret to making my millions—and tried to recreate the icy expression of the woman on my passport.

A different woman with a different life.

Either the customs officer had experience with radically changed post-break-up travelers, or his camera boasted state-of-the-art facial recognition technology, because he handed back my documents with a smile. "Thank you, Miss Holbrook. Welcome to Hawaii." His voice lilted pleasantly on the triple vowel, running an odd thrill through my stomach. As though I'd arrived somewhere *different*. "Follow the walkway to exit the building."

As the automatic doors sucked me from the canned air of the terminal, the humidity dropped a wet blanket over me and I staggered to a halt. The right side of the customs desk for escape, but the wrong side for a restroom.

I swiveled urgently, surveying my surroundings. A wide, immaculately clean, covered walkway stretched both left and right. Immediately in front of me, a large bank of potted hibiscus offered distinct *oh-my-god, I'm totally-out-of-options* potential.

Maybe it wouldn't come to that, though; overhead signs indicated the commuter terminal a short distance along the concourse. With Kegels and a fast waddle, it might be doable. Maybe. If no one got in my way.

The suitcase wheels a flamenco dancer's castanets chasing me, I scurried toward the smaller terminal, skirting groups of less-desperate tourists. I barged into the foyer, skidding to a halt as I scanned for the restroom. How could it not be neon-lit, heralded by a choir of angels and—most crucially—serviced by an express automated walkway?

The automatic door closed behind me, then immediately whooshed open again, a billow of warm air wreathing me in spicy cologne, hot cotton, and fresh sweat.

I stilled.

My nostrils flared, a hunter stalking prey, as I snatched at the unmistakably male scent. Desire hooded my eyes, narrowing my vision. My pulse ramped up. Liquid warmth flooded the pit of my belly. Spread lower, lubricating and swelling. My hardened nipples pulsed a frantic tempo and — what the heck? I'd zoned out on a smell and started cataloging the effects? Who even did that?

Suzee would no doubt have an answer for that; a spinster librarian-cum-scientist who was beginning to actually look forward to her next pap smear.

The fragrance intensified as two men in military fatigues strode past, headed toward a small counter advertising expedited service for uniformed personnel.

Considering how long it'd taken to clear Arrivals, I needed to get my hands on some camo before I flew out or I'd never make it home in time for Christmas. Not that I had much planned for the holiday season. I'd catch up with a few pals for a meal out, part of the pathetic I-had-nowhere-to-go-but-the-pub crowd.

His broad shoulders tapering to a narrow waist, the taller of the two men rocked a perfect inverted trapezoid. His tight butt punched against the green and brown splotched cotton pants tucked into polished, well-worn black boots. Nice. I wouldn't mind getting my hands on his camo.

Whoa! I lurched back. That was taking the whole new-Lissa thing about ten steps too far, too fast. These guys were real, not the safely untouchable images on my laptop, pixels easily dismissed at the press of a key.

Though at least I'd proved myself still capable of a damp-pantied, ovary-exploding reaction to a real man. While Suzee's hyped re-virgination was scientifically implausible, I had been a little concerned that too much porn may have desensitized me.

However, unlike most everything else in my life, science proved beautifully reliable; the symptoms of my physiological arousal could be attributed to an habituated female response to the perceived strength of a man in uniform.

Pavlovian conditioning at its finest.

Nothing at all to do with my personal drought. Nu-uh.

Their backs to me, the soldiers probably weren't even particularly hot. I was just darn thirsty. Like, plane-crash-survivor-in-the-desert thirsty. Two years' worth of thirsty. Twenty-six months, during which I'd learned two things:

Relationships sucked.

And seven years wasn't a promise of forever.

Tearing my gaze from the soldiers, I bolted for the restroom. With more stalls than people, finally, the Universe was on my side. I latched the cubicle door, dropping my bag and unzipping my pants in a flurry of movement. Moaned aloud. The rush of relief was so intense, I should be able to check off at least three of the boxes on Suzee's spreadsheet. There was something to be said for delayed gratification. Careful not to let my hair touch the tiled wall, I leaned back and gave it my best Meg Ryan.

By the time I exited the restroom, I felt like a brand-new day should've dawned, with baby deer frolicking in the meadow and bluebirds trilling in blossom-laden branches.

Yet the soldiers still stood at the desk a few meters away.

A clerk fluttered between consulting her monitor and maintaining an animated conversation with them, even managing to pull off a coquettish hand-through-the-hair move as one of the soldiers spoke to her. Whatever he said, chased by a deep rumble of laughter, the clerk's cheeks flushed attractively, her chest heaving beneath the tight white blouse. A swell like that had to be deliberate, and I couldn't tear my gaze away, waiting in wincing, breath-held anticipation for the shirt to erupt open like a jack-in-the-box.

The agent swiveled her screen toward the soldiers, inviting them to lean closer. Her gaze lingered on one of them, darted away, then back. She shifted her hand, so it almost touched his on the desk. The tip of her tongue traced her upper lip.

Classic mating behavior, overtly signaling the male of the species to signify her readiness to breed. Though the non-mammalian creatures of my studies didn't behave in precisely the same manner, comparisons could be drawn. Of course, my own continued interest in the men was purely technical. Fact-gathering and observation only, because I was a long way from being ready to conduct experiments.

Even if my heartbeat did register a little erratic, the pulse fluttering in my throat.

Probably caused by jetlag, or altitude change or...something. If I had my laptop handy, I'd research the symptoms.

Or log in to check the requirements on Suzee's spreadsheet.

My fingertips tingled with nervous energy just at the thought of the tasks ahead. Nope, I wasn't ready for that step. No point checking the rodeo eventing sheet just yet. I needed to sidle over to the horse and pat it for a while before I could even consider saddling up.

And maybe I preferred motorbikes, in any case. There was a lot to be said for mechanization. Particularly battery operated.

The soldier rested his forearms on the counter, leaning into the clerk's workspace. She smiled encouragingly.

My lips twisted wryly as I watched the mating dance. If I

tried that move—not that I could, my boobs would be in the way—but if I crossed the imaginary line separating client and clerk, security would be all over me.

My gaze drifted to the soldier's webbing belt. Did military personnel carry restraints? Because maybe I wouldn't need to lodge a complaint at the Consulate if *he* slapped cuffs on me, tossed me over one of those broad shoulders, and strode off into a Hawaiian sunset.

Heat flooded my face, and I glanced around, as though somebody could have tuned in to my thoughts. Suzee was right, I did need to back off on the erotic romances. Problem was, the pages of a book or the anonymous world of the internet offered the only safe places to indulge my desires.

Not that those desires rated as particularly aberrant or abnormal. Had science not been able to allay my fears, the magazine quizzes I completed could; my physical reactions were entirely healthy for a young woman, my urges normal. But my experience? Well, that's where I was screwed. Or not screwed, more like. Unless I counted a couple of backseat blow jobs before I met him, Damien had been—damn, still was—my only lover. Now, once a guy's hands went down, my knees came up. Locked. No entry, no way.

Because I couldn't trust men not to expect more than I was willing to offer.

Fucking Damien. He'd broken me. Not that I wasn't into guys anymore; I had all the thoughts, the desires—the insatiable horniness—but I couldn't allow any of it to translate into action, because what if I screwed up again? What if I wasted another seven years with a guy whose true desire was for free rent?

The only thing worse than being alone forever would be allowing someone to get close to me again.

Suzee was right; I was going to become a lab-coated

version of a spinster librarian. One of a half-dozen flea-bitten rescue cats curled in my lap, licking at its nether regions, I'd read erotica hidden between the pages of Darwin's *Origin of the Species*. The Bunsen burner on my lab bench would provide the only heat in my life, warming my knees which were permanently cemented together by the treachery Damien hid in his promise of commitment.

The taller of the two soldiers picked up his papers from the counter, flicked a casual salute to the clerk, and turned my way, all in one smooth motion.

A smooth move that didn't give me time to collect my wits and look away.

Not that I wanted to look away, because *holy crap*.

It was like watching the spawning of the sea coral: beautiful, majestic, flawless, untouchable. Compelling.

His bicep flexed as he ran a hand through cropped hair, the brown streaked with the blond memories of surf and sun. Impossibly broad shoulders balanced his height—what, six-two, six-four? And—oh, come on, Universe—didn't a jaw that square exist only in superhero comics? Yet, there it was, not ten feet away. Close enough that an urge to stroke my palm over the glitter of golden stubble sighed through me.

Hell, I'd never had this reaction to spawning.

And it wasn't only my palm I wanted to rub against his face. My breathing quickened, nipples hardening at the thought of the exquisite sandpapery torment as he nuzzled at my breasts...

A moan, quickly disguised as a sigh, snuck between my lips.

He was gorgeous. An exemplary specimen.

And looking directly at me.

One side of his mouth quirked in a smile that acknowledged my perving.

Or maybe meant that he read my mind?

No, that was ridiculous. Clairvoyance didn't belong anywhere in the realms of scientific possibility. And, even if he could read minds, my reaction wasn't personal. Nothing but a chemically-driven physical response to pheromones secreted by a member of the opposite sex. Oxytocin release equals hard nipples. Basic biological knowledge.

Still, I should move away.

Should.

Couldn't.

The soldier's eyes narrowed slightly, then flared in sudden...What? What the heck was that look?

A bag hit the back of my knees, and I staggered. The soldier's hand snaked toward me, dropping to his side as I easily regained my balance.

Seriously? *Now* the yoga classes paid off? Thanks for nothing, Yogini Sasha. If I'd fallen, I'd be in the long arms of the law. Military guys counted as the law, right? With no more weighing up of pros and cons, no checking off of Suzee's list, fate, not poor decision-making, would be responsible for what happened.

The soldier dipped his chin with a slight smile and retreated.

Wait! If I dropped to the floor in somewhat delayed reaction, would he turn back, realize I required mouth-to-mouth? Perhaps an external heart massage?

Fingers clutched at my elbow. "I'm so sorry. Are you alright? Hubby says I shouldn't be allowed control of anything with wheels."

My leg hadn't hurt until the interruption punctured my fantasy. I resisted the urge to rub my calf, dragging the toes of my other foot across the muscle instead. "No worries. Shopping trolleys are generally my nemesis, but it seems suitcases are running a close second today."

As I smiled reassurance at the fluttering, bird-like woman, the camouflage-clad dream vanished from my peripheral vision like the end of a chased rainbow. My stomach plummeted with disappointment. Stupid, because it wasn't as though I'd have actually spoken, like a remotely normal person.

But I *had* made eye contact.

Okay, somewhat accidentally, and maybe even unwillingly, but it was a start.

I squared my shoulders and took a deep breath. At some point during this vacation, there *would* be sweaty, steamy, completely gratuitous sex with a stranger.

After all, according to Suzee's ten-task spreadsheet, I'd come to the Land of the Lei to get Laid.

3

I tumbled into the back seat of a cab, momentarily disconcerted as the driver stowed my case, then appeared on the wrong side of the vehicle.

No, the right side. This could take some getting used to.

He caught my eye in the rearview mirror. "Aloha. Where can I take you?"

Aloha! The flight attendants had used the greeting, but it had sounded rote and artificial. The airport behind me, this was now *real*. I was in Hawaii.

A giggle almost bubbled free, so I buried my face in the itinerary Mom had sent, reading as though I didn't have it memorized. "Um, Outrigger Waikiki Beach Resort, please."

Mom. Snacks and paperwork slithered across the seat as I dug my phone from the backpack, turned it on and searched the contact list. Spoke the instant the call clicked through, like I couldn't wait.

Yeah, couldn't wait to get the call over with. "Hey, I'm here."

The cab pulled out of the airport, past verdant green lawns and beds full of vivid flowers.

A gusty sigh on the other end of the line conjured the image of Mom collapsing into a luxuriously upholstered chair, the back of her hand pressed to her medically-assisted wrinkle-free brow. "Darling, I was getting worried. How was your flight? No problems with customs? Where are you now?" Mom had a knack for phrasing almost everything as a question, yet rarely needed—or wanted—a reply. "You have the paperwork for the hotel? You're sure you'll be okay, darling, all alone there?"

It figured that she wouldn't miss an opportunity to rub that one in. Not bothering to reply, I balanced the phone on the seat and shoveled the munchies back into my bag. The packet crinkled noisily as I peeled open a bag of chips.

Mom's voice came through the cell reedy and accusatory. "You're not snacking, Melissa? You know you don't have the metabolism for that. You *are* alone, right? Damien didn't have a change of mind?"

A change of mind? Mom insisted on referring to the continental drift of our split as though it was a temporary disagreement. Mind, she was also a climate change denier.

More snug than it had been on my left hand, the small diamond ring dug into my finger as I twisted it. I should have disposed of it, not simply changed hands. But then, I'd purchased the ring. I had a right to keep it, even if it didn't make me happy.

Maybe I should tell Mom the details, explain exactly why Damien wouldn't be changing his mind any time soon. *'Thing is, Mom, Dame's really into lingerie. Unfortunately, he doesn't need me in it.'*

No, that probably wouldn't cut it.

Besides, I'd have to swallow the potato chip lodged in my throat and talk quicker than a used car salesman, as Mom barely paused for breath. "I'm so looking forward to seeing you, darling. After my cancer scare, I'm determined to make every moment count. Do you have any idea how something like that can shake up your life?"

A benign mole barely rated as a cancer scare—especially the capitalized, italicized, bold font version Mom managed to convey—but still, she had a point. Every moment should count. God knows I'd wasted more than two years after discovering Damien's secret. Well, after exposing the tip of the iceberg of his deceit, anyway. But, as I'd argued with Suzee more times than I cared to recall, I'd felt sorry for him, empathized with what I interpreted as his sexual confusion.

Funny how that supposed confusion had unfailingly been eased by a flash of my credit card.

Unfazed by my lack of response, Mom continued organizing. "Registration and check-in for the cruise can take a while, so you'll be at the dock nice and early tomorrow?"

As far as I knew, Mom had never been on a cruise. But she could be relied on to speak with comfortable familiarity about anything that gave an impression of wealth. Fortunately for her, Mitch was loaded.

I edged the chip packet away, wincing as it noisily announced my guilt. Speaking loudly, I tried to cover the crime, though, like Mom, I didn't truly want any answers. "Yes, Mom, early. How are your preps going?"

Mom's little-girl inhalation of excitement came with an audible fluffing of blonde hair, and I tried not to grit my teeth. "Oh, darling, everything's going to be so perfect. Just wait until you see your dress."

Crap. Chances were, Mom's love of the eighties would be reflected in the bridesmaids' dresses. Shoulder pads. Taffeta. Salmon and gray. Things that even my dubious dress sense would never have seen me wear if I'd I been around back then. "What about your dress, Mom? Have you decided what you'll wear?"

Silence bristled for a moment, and I cringed expectantly. Checked the screen. Not even two minutes, and I'd put my foot in it. Possibly a new record?

Mom's tone could have frozen the nipples on a polar bear. "Decided? What's to decide? Why would I wear anything but a wedding gown?"

Why indeed? Every second-marriage recommitment ceremony with the protagonists well into their fifties warranted a major production and full-blown haute couture, right? I swallowed the retort, hoping silence would pacify Mom.

Unable to maintain her sulking, given that such a course of action would require an unacceptably long period of not sharing her opinion, Mom thawed a little. "Elle helped me choose the gown. She has such wonderful taste, don't you think?"

A forked tongue was bound to enhance taste. Elle's selection would no doubt be preferable to the meringue concoction my mother would favor, but Mom's words left a cramping pain in the center of my chest. Until that second, I hadn't realized that I'd persuaded myself things would be different now my step-siblings and I were all adults. That, despite my memories, our childish rivalries would be forgotten. But clearly, Elle remained perfect in Mom's eyes.

Nothing had changed since we were teenagers, when my three step-siblings-to-be visited Australia during school vacations. Mom had pulled out all the stops to win over the attractive, confident trio, and prove to Mitch what a fantastic step-mom she'd make.

The taxi dipped into a graffiti-covered underpass, my stomach lurching with the motion. Suddenly the cheese-

and-onion chips didn't taste so great. "Do I have to share a cabin with her?" I scowled at my reflection in the window. Great, I hadn't seen Elle in over a decade, but one mention, and I immediately regressed to being seventeen years old.

Mom's laugh crackled like thin toffee. "Don't be silly. You know Elle has a husband? And I did tell you she's made me a grandma?"

Only like a hundred times. It was hard to believe Mom hadn't attended the birth, considering the contraction-by-contraction recount she'd shared. More than once. My lips shriveled at the recollection of the excruciating details, and there was a distinctive cheese-and-onion flavored reflux event in my throat. "Technically, a step-grandma, I guess?"

The frost returned. Really, there was no cause to be concerned about the polar ice caps melting, with Mom on call. "Well, it seems that's as close as I'll ever get, doesn't it?"

Ouch. Round one to Mom. Aw heck, I may as well ring the bell and call the match over. Mom always won.

It'd been nine years since she and Mitch moved to Hawaii. Mom had insisted the relocation was necessary because Hawaii lay precisely halfway between Mitch's kids' U.S. mainland home, and my life in Australia.

But Hawaii was American soil.

Not Australian.

Not neutral.

So, Mom's true intention had always been pretty darn clear.

I pulled the phone away from my ear, adding physical distance to the emotional. "Okay Mom, I've got to go and sort out this fare. I'll see you in a couple of days. Love ya, bye."

I tossed the phone back into my bag, my cheeks pouching as I blew out a deep breath and slumped back into the seat. One day, I'd remember to have a stiff drink before I spoke with Mom.

The semi-industrial surrounds that had flickered past as I'd talked—listened—to Mom were unrelentingly grim. Highways and dilapidated cement-block buildings decorated with litter and festooned in flourishing weeds that attested to a tropical climate. But my attention perked as we wound through an increasingly affluent commercial area.

Palm trees lined wide streets of pristine high-rise buildings, and, despite my disinterest in any form of retail therapy, even I recognized the names above elegant Christmas-themed shopfront displays. Louis Vuitton, Chanel, Prada. Deep arcades wound back from the broad, paved footpaths, magical hobbit burrows framing glimpses of ornate fountains and courtyards filled with bauble-hung trees and giant festive wreaths.

As the car slowed, I stared greedily out of the window, captivated by the blue flash of the ocean at the end of a street that seemed a postcard depiction of Hawaii. Too beautiful to be real.

The cab pulled in to the curb beneath half a dozen tall, slender palm trees sprouting directly out of the sidewalk. "Outrigger Waikiki Beach Resort, Miss."

I gazed at the smooth cream stone front of the building, the vast arched entry portico fringed with planters full of lush greenery. He had to be kidding. Mom had booked me into a hotel on a street that looked like it belonged on a movie set, extravagant yet elegant, sumptuous and stylish? Mitch had money, but...here?

A uniformed porter rushed to open the car door, and I stepped from the cab, into the fantasy.

The correct way to tip should have been built into my DNA, a genetic knowledge, with Mom being American. I frowned at the notes in my hand. The guide books advised tipping porters a dollar or two—but was the porter the guy who rushed to take my bags from the cab, the one who loaded them onto a fancy brass trolley, or the one escorting me into the hotel foyer? And a buck? Enough to buy a Macca's hash brown back home, it seemed embarrassingly insignificant. Particularly given the lavish surrounds of the marble-floored hotel into which I followed the...um, porter.

Had to be a fiver, then. Each. I'd be broke before the vacation truly started.

The porter directed me up a narrow escalator to a vast reception area, decorated in restful shades of green and cream. Chaises and small groups of plush chairs were arranged beneath tropical paintings and carvings, and a table laden with great glass urns filled with ice and floating lemon slices reminded me I'd had nothing to drink for hours and, with the bladder issue under control, I could now indulge.

A receptionist smiled welcomingly from behind the polished black granite check-in desk that stretched almost the length of one wall. At least, I thought she smiled. At that distance, she pretty much needed a semaphore flag or PA system to signal the guests in.

My feet sank into the soft plush of the leaf-patterned carpet as I made my way to the desk and dropped into a huge carved chair opposite a computer terminal.

"Aloha, Miss. Welcome to Outrigger Waikiki Beach Resort. Do you have your reservation confirmation with you?"

"Sure." I pulled my passport and other paperwork from my backpack and slid them across the counter, then wedged the pack between my feet. The hibiscus-wearing clerk

turned her attention back to the computer screen, and I
tried not to gawk at the surroundings.

Discreetly lit by recessed downlights, the elegant foyer
glowed with the warm tones of well-oiled wood and care-
fully-tended foliage. So opulent, I only needed someone to
shake me to prove I was inside a nostalgic handcrafted snow
dome, rich with the promise of yesteryear and the magic of
tomorrow.

I jumped as a hand landed heavily on the back of my
chair, interrupting my perusal. "Seems we could've shared a
cab."

Warm breath against my ear thrilled goosebumps up my
neck. I jerked around, sensations and impressions cataloging with the rapidity of a spinning centrifuge. Green
eyes. Brown hair shot through with blond. Spicy aftershave.
The stubble that'd feel so good against my nipples.

Okay, so my dome was well and truly shaken. I cough-
choked to cover my audible gulp. That guy. The soldier. So
close to me he stole all the oxygen. And his voice...the deep
drawl rippled through me, stirring syrupy warmth in the pit
of my stomach as I oozed into a puddle in my chair.

I blinked rapidly. Crap, I probably should respond to his
words, not sit gawping at him like a stranded fish. "Uh, yeah.
Would've been good."

Closed in a couple of square meters with a guy so hot I
couldn't rationally put the parts of him together in my mind
but had to allow each to separately impact on my brain? It
would have rated somewhat higher than 'good', but it
seemed both my vocabulary and witty repartee had bailed.

"Ah," I cleared my throat again. I needed something
flirty. Memorable. "You could have saved me. This whole
tipping business does my head i-in."

Ugh. With spinster scientist clearly taking control,

maybe I should just wear tee-shirts printed with images of my not-yet-adopted cats. Where the heck had New Lissa disappeared to when I needed her?

A navy outline ringed the soldier's sea-green iris. His pupils flared as I stuttered to a halt. Perhaps he had trouble adjusting to the dim light in here, after the midday sunshine? I was sure having trouble adjusting to the temperature—though the room was nicely air-conditioned only moments ago, now I was melting as that low voice throbbed through me.

"You're an Aussie?" He sounded surprised. "I have a... know a few Aussies. Cool."

I lifted one shoulder. Like a shrug was about as good as coming up with some sexy, unforgettable line. "We're not exactly an endangered species." As the soldier's gaze slowly roamed from my head to my feet, I sucked in my stomach and straightened my back.

He completed his reconnaissance. "The cute ones are."

What? How did I interpret that? Insult or compliment?

One corner of the soldier's mouth lifted, and I tried not to lock my gaze to the fine white scar running diagonally from the cleft in his chin to the edge of his lower lip, stark against his tan. Intriguing. And begging to be touched.

I'd forgotten to speak. Again. I swallowed loudly instead.

The smile lifted. "Given that I have a keen interest in the conservation of endangered species, it seems to me you may require protection while you're here, ma'am." The soldier offered his right hand. "Nate."

Paw. It was a damn paw. I mean, the guy was H.U.G.E.

My breath left in such a rush, he had to hear. If he missed it, the pathetic giggle I managed instead of trading my name clinched my humiliation as his grip enfolded my limp hand. I should have wiped my sweaty palm on my pants, added to the damp spot I was pretty sure already existed there, thanks to *Nate*.

The dark-haired receptionist interrupted politely. "Miss? Your room won't be ready until two. However, if you'd like to head through to Duke's Canoe Club, I'll arrange for a complimentary drink token."

I snatched my backpack from the floor, desperate to escape before the hot flush crawled out of the neck of my shirt and right up my face. "Okay, yeah, thanks. The bar's that way?" I jerked a thumb. Away. It didn't really matter which direction, anywhere that offered a quick exit would do just fine. "Yep? Okay."

Avoiding looking directly at him, I nodded in the soldier's general direction. "Catch you around, then." I slung my pack over my shoulder, grimacing as the bag brushed against him.

Actually, it smacked into him, dragging my shoulder back like I'd slammed a brick wall. Well, it served *Nate* right; he shouldn't be standing so close. Not that the impact shifted him at all.

I hightailed it toward the club, refusing the urge to glance back, to fuel my fantasies with one more peek. My embarrassment needed quenching first, and the island probably didn't manufacture enough ice to achieve that right now. Crap, how could I be so gauche? So much for my cool new persona. If I was going to have any chance of carrying off this flirting thing, I needed Suzee on speed dial.

Not keen on sitting at the bar or advertising my single status by taking a booth alone, I headed out to the pool area. Hidden behind sunglasses, I dropped onto a sun lounge. The small pool was deserted—hardly surprising, given the massive expanse of palm-tree fringed golden beach that curved from view, only meters away. Tinted by chlorophyll, the ocean stretched to the horizon, shading from azure to indigo. The science behind the vibrant colors added to the perfection of the scene. Well, for me, anyway.

Shoes kicked off, I lay back on the striped towel spread over the lounge and tugged my tee a little looser. Suzee was right, I should have lashed out and bought new clothes. Most of the comfort-eating weight seemed to have gone to my boobs and butt. No doubt Mom would notice.

Eyes closed, I tilted my face up to the sun. I would not think about the hot soldier I'd just run away from after he paid me a compliment.

Nope.

Not at all.

No way would I allow myself to dwell on that monumental screwup.

Much.

4

A shadow registered through my closed eyelids. Half asleep, I snapped rigid as something brushed my thighs. My feet slammed to the ground on either side of the deckchair before my eyes were fully open.

Hands raised in surrender, Nate took a half step back. "Whoa there, Freckles. You're burning. I was covering you up." He lifted the corner of a towel spread across my thighs, waving it as evidence.

He wasn't dressed.

Well, he was, but...barely. Cargo shorts. That was it. And that scrap of material left a whole lot of body for me to take in. Which I couldn't be expected to do and hold an intelligent—well, *any*—conversation at the same time.

Nate released the towel, saluting me with two fingers flicked to his forehead. His bicep bulged at the movement. *Bulged.* Like, kinetic perfection, ripped and sinewy, not the steroid-enhanced weight-lifter type of bulge.

Not that I'd spent way too long assessing men's bodies.

One side of his mouth tweaked up, tugging the scar on his chin. "Said I'd protect you, Freckles."

He sauntered around to the far side of the pool—why the heck didn't they have a larger pool here, anyway? Then he dropped onto a lounge, running both hands through the sides of his short hair as he hunched forward to speak to a guy occupying another deck chair.

Adjusting my aviators, I covertly assessed the soldier. Droplets glistened on his broad shoulders and, as he shook his head, his friend raised a hand in protest at the shower. Nate must have swum while I slept.

Slept.

Snored? God no, please not that! Damien swore I snored, but the taunt had been made in bitchy retaliation two years ago when I'd discovered the first fraction of his secret life and kicked him out. Kicked him to my spare room, anyway. Halfway through his third attempt at a university degree— trying to decide where his *passion* lay—he couldn't afford a rental. And I'd been clinging like a baby koala to the safe familiarity of having him around.

Still clinging to hope, too.

Nate sprang to his feet as a waitress approached, bearing a laden tray. He took the tray and turned to place it on the plastic table alongside his chair, revealing his right shoulder and upper arm shadowed by a half-sleeve of tribal tats, dark and dangerous against bronzed skin. A maze I could lose myself in, tracing the labyrinth.

Oh man, look away. Dangerous. Yes, definitely dangerous. That amount of ink in a body was a very bad thing, scientifically speaking. Even if it did look rather awe— Nope, not going there. What time was it? Surely my room would be ready? Because I needed some privacy. Right now.

"Hey, Freckles," Nate beckoned across the pool, his voice

like a handful of gravel washing around the bottom of a goldpan. "Come and join us. The portions here are crazy big, we've nachos to feed a platoon."

"No-o." Fantastic. My voice broke like a pre-teen boy's. "I'm good, thanks."

His grin flashed white. "Not too good, I hope. C'mon, be friendly, Freckles. Otherwise, you're going to have to jump in the pool to save us when we go down with cramps." He jerked a thumb at the guy on the recliner alongside him, who lifted a hand.

Not too good? Did he mean that literally? Was he... coming on to me?

No. Hardly likely. Travel-stained and mussed, I hadn't managed a coherent sentence, never mind the hard-core flirting I'd determined to perfect.

"I...I..." *Damn. I* needed to practice on this guy, get in the mood, because I had only ten days to fulfill my promise, both to myself and to Suzee, who'd be less lenient about letting me off the hook.

Not that 'getting in the mood' was the real problem, that being a pretty much permanent itch I couldn't scratch, no matter how many fingers I used. So to speak.

I peeled myself from the lounge. "Sure, then. Love to."

Under their scrutiny, I trekked around the small pool. Both men stood as I approached.

"Ma'am." The second guy, who I recognized as the other soldier from the airport, dipped his chin.

They really said that, like in the movies? I'd thought Nate was joking when he used it earlier.

"Travis, this is Freckles." Nate tipped his head to one side as he assessed me. "I'm not entirely convinced that's the name her parents gave her but, despite my polite introduction, she's not shared."

"Oh. Uh. M-Melissa." Who stumbled over their own name?

Travis took my hand, a slight frown creasing his forehead.

Another good-looking blond-streaked Yank. Were they all male models around this place? Why the heck had I agreed to come? Hawaii was for the gorgeous few, not doomed-to-be-single, certified science geeks.

Travis released me. "Funny, my—"

Nate whacked a hand on Travis's shoulder. "Melissa? Pleased to finally make your acquaintance."

"Uh, Lissa. Lissa's fine. No one calls me Melissa anymore, except my mother and fianc— ah, a couple of other people." Awesome. Straight from tongue-tied to verbal diarrhea.

Travis appeared stunned by my rapid-fire retort, but a grin carved a furrow in one of Nate's tanned cheeks. "Well, if you can't decide which name, maybe I'll stick with Freckles? Anyway, have a seat." He gestured at the pool chair. "Here, take mine."

What sadistic and potentially misogynistic mind designed pool lounges? To get to the center of the seat, I'd have to wriggle and scoot my butt over miles of white plastic, and there was no elegant way to achieve that. I perched on the edge instead. Gasped as the chair teetered precariously.

"Whoa, there." Nate lunged to steady the chair, then straddled the seat to weigh it down. "Looked like you were about to go for a bit of a ride."

Trying not to stare at Nate's groin as he slid the platter of nachos from the side table onto the seat between us— between his spread thighs—it took me several stunned seconds to formulate my witty and completely impromptu reply. "Probably lucky I like riding, then." Okay, that was not a bad effort. Almost worthy of Suzee, if I could just polish the delivery a little.

Nate licked his fingers slowly, though I couldn't see that he'd managed to get sauce or cheese on them. And I was checking pretty carefully. The green of his eyes changed, darkening to the ocean depths as fine lines feathered around them. "You do, huh?"

"Do?" I could barely breathe, never mind think *and* speak, with the gorgeous half-naked—no, make that two-thirds naked—guy sitting only centimeters from me. Could I snap a picture to send Suzee? Because surely my spreadsheet had a tick-a-box for this, but proof would be required.

And I wouldn't mind having a picture to look at in the privacy of my room later.

Broken into shards by waving palm fronds, the sunlight flickered across Nate's face as he lifted a quizzical brow. "I mean, you do like riding?"

I should pull my gaze from his mouth, stop hoping he'd put his finger back in, lick it sensuously again. "Don't know. I've never ridden."

Nate's lips curved into a grin, the hairline-thin scar straightening, and I cringed as I realized my blunder.

Seated a couple of feet away, Travis leaned between us to scoop up a gloop of meat and sauce. Great, another half-naked, golden body. But at least his interruption stopped Nate from calling out my lie.

"I'm pretty sure we could teach you," Travis said, resting one hand on my knee so he didn't overbalance his own chair. "What do you reckon, bro?"

Nate didn't take his eyes from mine. "I think we could organize something."

Like a tsunami, the blush swept from my chest to my

cheeks. The more I thought about it, the worse it would become. Damn, it wasn't like I'd never flirted before. In fact, I used to be pretty good at it, when I'd had the safety net of being in a relationship, knowing the game could go nowhere, there were no real expectations. But a single email from an anonymous 'concerned friend' three months ago had destroyed so much more than the remnants of my relationship with my fiancé.

The email had contained a link to Damien's Tinder account.

Despite me giving him second chances for more than two years, Damien was advertising his... abilities? services? Not that he had much to offer in either department. But still, the revelation that he intended to cheat on me—no, was actively *trying* to cheat on me—despite our hours of talking, despite his promises, despite my *understanding*, stole the last of my self-confidence. Because, all along, he'd led me to believe that if I was enough, he wouldn't need to look anywhere else.

Pigeons skittered along a balcony behind us, spying the food. I stared down at the amazing unfamiliarity of a man's hand, warm on my leg. Warm on *Lissa's* leg.

It was *Melissa's* self-confidence that had taken the beating. I couldn't allow that to affect me. Not now, not here. What was Mom's new favorite phrase? *Make every moment count.* Well, I had ten days to turn my life around. Ten days to prove Damien wrong, to prove that I could be enough for a man. Just me; not my job, not my income, not my house, not what I could provide.

And I had ten days to prove to myself that there were options other than abusing my internet download limit. That real men were safe.

I took a breath and fought the blush back down. Both

military men were totally hot. Built like brick shithouses, Suzee would say. Nate appeared a few years older than Travis, or maybe just more mature—and he didn't keep grabbing at my knee. Not that I minded Travis's hand on my flesh. Five minutes of his company equated to more physical contact than I'd had over the last few years. Realistically, either of the guys would suit the requirements of my experiment.

I shoved my hands under my thighs, where they couldn't tremble. Tongue tracing my upper lip, I slid my gaze from Travis's hand on my knee, up to his face. Slow and sultry. At least, that's what I aimed for, though it probably looked like I was perving at his near-naked body.

Okay, so maybe I was, just a little.

I held his blue-eyed gaze for a heartbeat and then flicked my eyes to Nate. "So, you're offering private riding lessons? I might take you up on that. But which of you is more...experienced?"

5

N ate choked, though I couldn't tell whether it was on the hot sauce, or at my words.

Travis's hand tightened on my knee, then inched a little higher. "I'm sure we could both be of service. What do you reckon, Nate? Up to the challenge?"

Wait! Did he seriously think I was angling for a three-some? I'd aimed to come across cool and funny, not as totally out there. Dammit, *this* was why I shouldn't flirt.

"Settle, bro." Nate's deep voice rolled through my panic, smoothing it out and heating me up, all at once. "You're scaring the wildlife. C'mon, Freckles, you've barely touched the food."

Not precisely true. I'd always had a good appetite, and nerves only made it worse. Nerves and betrayal. I fiddled with my tee, tugging it over the rounding of my hips.

Suzee said I ate my emotions, along with anything that wasn't smart enough to get out of the way darn fast. She'd been quick to suggest an alternative when I'd buried my humiliation in cookies while sharing the final damning evidence of Damien's treachery "The bastard loves his clothes, right? Then we shred them. Every last fucking item."

In my imagination, I'd leaped onto the coffee shop couch, Tom Cruise-does-Oprah style, brandishing dress-maker's shears and cheering the plan.

In reality, I'd dunked my double-chocolate Tim Tam into an extra-large Vienna latte. "It's a difficult life choice for Damien. I'm sure he's wrestling with his conscience and convictions."

It was more likely he'd been wrestling with how he was going to fund his own expenses for the first time.

Suzee slapped the biscuit out of my hand. "Okay, we stuff the curtain rods with dead fish. You have easy access, right?"

"To both the fish and the rods. It's my place, remember?"

"Well, you have to do *something*, Melissa."

Yeah, I was. Eating.

Nate's voice brought me back to the meal between his legs—so to speak. He nudged the platter framed by his thighs, pushing it my way. "So, spill, Freckles. What do you do when you're not lounging poolside in a tropical love nest?"

The blood rushing in my ears, I tried to focus on the corn chips, rather than what lay barely beyond them. "Marine biologist."

"Biology, huh?" Two drawled words, packed with an impossible amount of innuendo, and Nate had elevated my lab-bound career to Sexiest. Job. Ever.

"Yup." I groaned inwardly. Way to capitalize on the moment.

A burst of laughter from the beach flicked Nate's gaze away from me, and Travis joined the conversation. "So, what brings you here? Outrigger's famous vows on the beach?"

His teasing tone made it obvious he didn't believe I was here to get married. Anger at the presumption flared through me. Stranger things happened. Especially to me. "You almost got it. Recommitment ceremony."

Travis nodded, but Nate's smile disappeared, and he pushed his palms against his knees, leaning away from me. "Really?"

"Sure. But not here. And not mine. My mom and stepfather are being committed." I couldn't hide a quick grin. They could call it a *renewal of vows* all they liked, but I preferred the joke. "On a cruise ship."

Travis's cold beer slopped onto my foot. "No shit? That's—"

Nate's leg shot out, shoving Travis's chair back, the plastic base skittering on the pavers. "Watch your beer, bro. Sorry, Freckles, I haven't even offered you a drink." He indicated the open bar fronting the pool. "What will you have?"

"I, uh, I've no idea." Damien had been into fancy wines, and I drank whatever he poured from my wallet. It was easier that way.

Nate read my hesitation. "How about a Mai Tai? Island specialty."

It would sound equator-level uncool to admit I'd never had a cocktail in my life. "Is it sweet?"

"Rum and juice."

Well, that meant precisely nothing to me. I scrunched my nose and lifted a shoulder.

Nate grinned. "Not a hard-core drinker? You do realize that you are kind of killing the Aussie image there? But I'll take your word for it. Tell you what, we'll get a Mai Tai and a Blue Hawaiian. Try them both."

Middle of the afternoon and he expected me to down

two cocktails while sitting in the sun? Things were rapidly getting out of hand. "No, that's not—"

Travis waved a brightly colored, laminated sheet, then flipped it over to study the other side. "Check this out. There's a specialty cocktail menu. I say we skip the decision-making and order one of each drink. That way Lissa can try them all." He cut his eyes sideways at me, the glint of blue echoing the ocean. "I don't have an issue with sloppy seconds." His gaze shifted to Nate. "I'll take what you leave."

My heart pounded so hard, pumping adrenalin through my body, I was practically hammered before I'd taken a single drink. Inexperienced or not, I couldn't miss the sexual undercurrent here.

My fingers inched toward my backpack. I could really use a dial-a-friend free pass. I needed to sneak off, call Suzee, and beg step-by-step directions.

I started to push up from the lounge.

"Not running away, already, Freckles?" Nate made as though he'd also rise, and my eyes locked to the hard ridges of his torso.

Holy heck, he was the most alpha-male alpha male I'd ever shared oxygen with. Why was I running? After twenty-nine years, I should be able to handle this. While I neither needed nor wanted Mr. Darcy to come and sweep me off my feet, what I *did* want was to learn how to stand on those two feet. I wanted to be able to play fast and loose, have a good time, like a normal woman my age—without leaving myself vulnerable to some guy's asshole moves. Really, I needed to be like Suzee—but with my own tweaks and boundaries. Definitely no dad-n-son tag team action required.

And this was the perfect setup.

The middle of the day, in a sun-drenched, family-friendly area. What the guys suggested wasn't even a date.

Simply an invitation to share a couple of drinks with fellow holidaymakers. Nothing shady.

Though, if I worked up the courage to make it into something more, it seemed clear the invitation was there. From Travis, at least.

So, I'd act like a grownup. Have a drink, loosen up, and practice flirting. If I failed miserably (ninety percent chance) or even more likely, got cold feet (one hundred percent chance, I actually glanced at them to see if they were already blue), I could hightail it. And the best part? No matter how it went, I was guaranteed never to see these guys again.

I deliberately eased the tension from my shoulders and settled more comfortably. As comfortably as possible, while remembering to keep my stomach sucked in. "Sure. Let's do this. Hey, reception gave me a complimentary drink pass; I guess you guys got them too? Let's pool them and hit that menu." There. With a little effort, I could sound badass.

Travis peeled himself off the lounge. "Hang on to them for a bit, I'll shout this round. I need to duck to the head, so I'll order on my way past."

He made toward the thatch-roofed bar that fronted onto the pool area.

Nate squinted after him for a second and then turned back to me. "You don't have plans for the rest of the day?"

I shook my head. "No. I'm boarding the ship tomorrow, but I didn't know if I'd be jet-lagged, so I didn't schedule anything for today." Ugh, I'd suck those words back up like a bottom-feeding catfish if I could. They gave away my inexperience. Not that it mattered, as long as travel was the only area Nate thought me inexperienced.

His thumb rubbed along his jaw. Friction on the golden

stubble that contrasted with his slightly darker military-cut hair created a tiny buzz.

Not the only buzz I was experiencing.

"Overnight flight, what, about ten hours, isn't it?" he said. "Most people manage to sleep through, so no lag. You haven't traveled much?"

"Never been out of Australia."

"And you're here alone? No plus one for the wedding thing?"

My lips pressed tightly for a second as I mulled over the possible replies. "He ended up being more of a minus."

"Ah—" Nate cut off his reply as the waitress approached us with a loaded tray. She leaned down to place it on the low table but angled so that her boobs were at his eye level.

Sweet perfume from her cream orchid lei wafted across me as the waitress waved one hand toward the plate of nachos, still framed by Nate's thighs. "Can I take care of that for you, sir? Or get you *any*thing else?"

How was it that everyone else managed to lace their words with such honeyed come on? I needed to start paying attention, perfect the skill that seemed innate to those who didn't spend their days peering through a microscope's eyepiece.

Nate leaned back in the chair, and I tried not to focus on the undulating ripple of his abs as he dug a billfold from his pocket and slid a note into the waitresses' palm.

Actually, that was a load of crap. I tried not to get *caught* focusing on his abs.

"I think we're good. For now. Thank you, ma'am."

There it was again. The salutation fluttered my stomach. Why did that single word cause such a reaction in me? It sounded somehow respectful and yet commanding at the same time.

Hot. Just hot, that's what it sounded.

Travis reappeared, his hand hovering over the selection of drinks the waitress had slid onto the table. "Ah, good job. Now, let's see. I'm going to guess that you prefer to start slow?" He cocked an eyebrow as he handed me a balloon glass three-quarters full of blue liquid. An umbrella, a straw, and a skewer of pineapple pieces, glace cherries, and thinly-shaved coconut slices protruded from the lagoon.

I frowned at the concoction. "Am I supposed to eat it, or drink it?"

His lounge bowed as Travis dropped back onto it, squinting at me against the sun. "Slurp. Lick. Suck. Whatever does it for you."

It was the acceleration of my heart that caused the buzzing in my ears and racing pulse, making it seem as though my body pumped extra blood. I knew the science.

Acceleration caused by sexual arousal.

Okay, so education wasn't everything, and those kinds of facts weren't the least bit helpful in grounding me.

Travis sat not two feet away, close enough to lean forward and put a hand on my leg, as he'd already demonstrated. Nate was even closer, still straddling the long white deck chair I shared with him. I hadn't been this close to two almost-naked men since...well, I'd never been this close to two almost-naked men. And apparently my brain felt it imperative to keep reminding me of the fact, just in case I was unaware of the novelty of the situation. Just in case I'd been in danger of getting out a semi-intelligent sentence. Just in case I'd not noticed the panty-dampening superfluity of beefcake. Just in case I'd somehow missed the fact that there were only a few inches of tropically-heated air and mere microns of cotton separating my naked body from their naked bodies. Because that's what we all were, under-neath. Naked.

God.

I blew out a ragged breath. Hopefully, the guys would think I was hot.

Heck, I wanted them to think I was hot. In every sense. But I needed to focus my mind on something less...erotic. I planned to be the predator; if anything was going to happen, it would be because I wanted it to.

I willed my heart rate back to something a little less life-threatening, nudged aside the fruit kebab, and put the straw to my lips. Nate's eyes followed the movement and, for a split second, I couldn't remember how to drink through a straw. Hadn't done it since I was a kid.

Oh, yeah. Inhale through the mouth. Easy.

Travis snorted with laughter as I choked. "That's some powerful sucking action you've got going there. Maybe take it a bit easy to start with. Save a little of that enthusiasm for later."

Nate leaned forward, patting my back as my eyes watered. His knee rubbed the side of my thigh and I clutched the edge of the seat. Shit. There it was. Naked on naked.

"Watch it, Freckles," he chuckled. "Sometimes the rum isn't mixed, and you cop it straight."

If the ground could open up and swallow me right now, that'd be real nice, please and thank you. I was so seriously uncool I couldn't even have a drink in a guy's company without screwing it up.

Nate stopped patting and ran his hand up and down my spine, a frisson of electricity following each pass of his palm. It seemed more like he was stroking me than stopping me from dying, but that was okay because at least I'd asphyxiate happy.

His hand dropped back to his thigh, so I coughed experimentally.

No luck, his hand didn't return.

He flicked a finger toward the drink I clutched. "Are you finished with that?"

"Sure." I thrust the glass at him, then licked at the deliciously sticky ooze that slopped onto my wrist.

Nate pushed the fruit aside, locked eyes with me, and took a deep draught through my straw.

Gross. With a swab of enzyme reagent and a swipe of an adenosine triphosphate meter, I'd be able to spotlight the germs writhing on that single-use surface, calculate how many he'd ingested. How did he know I didn't carry some vile disease? Who even used someone else's straw? Like, ever?

And why the heck did such a disgusting action suddenly seem so intimate, so...sexy? I couldn't tear my gaze from his mouth.

He ran his tongue across his lips.

Lips. I had to keep my mind on the facts. *Labium superioris and inferioris.* A necessary part of every body, purely functional in purpose.

These men were my lab guinea pigs, my experimental samples, to see if it were possible for me to attract the opposite gender on a purely sexual basis. Attract and discard, before the experiment became distorted by uncontrollable variables, such as my flooding hormones and the pheromones they exuded.

Of course, as retentive note-taking formed a vital part of acceptable experimentation practice, I'd need to make thorough clinical observations. Maybe starting with those lips...

a couple of shades darker than his tan skin, enhanced by the fine white scar that cut from his chin to the lower left quadrant. The corners curved up slightly and a small crease formed on the right side where superioris met inferioris— he seemed to smile more on that side—giving his mouth a sardonic lift, as though he intended every word to be a tease.

Or a come on.

Moisture glistened on his slightly pouted lower lip. Inviting. I could lean forward and lick it dry, his naked chest pressed against— Whoa! I needed to slow this down. One sip of this particularly delicious poison and I was mentally in bed with the guy? Or, more accurately, humping him on the plastic lounge. Which, considering how it creaked as I shifted, was never going to work as well as it did in the porn videos. Plus, the slatted base had no doubt imprinted a giant tic-tac-toe board on my ass.

Nate's lips curved further—on the right side, of course— and he offered me the glass, a challenge in his eyes.

A dare? Well then, screw the bugs dancing in my imaginary blue light. Maybe the alcohol was proof enough to kill them, anyway.

I took the glass and ran my tongue slowly across the sugar-frosted rim. I actually needed a drink now, my mouth dry, tongue cleaving to my palate.

The fine lines around Nate's eyes deepened as I used the tip of my tongue to toy with the straw, then closed my lips around the shaft. His nostrils flared, and exultation swept me. I might suck at oral flirting, but at least it seemed I could recreate the moves. Thank you, Netflix.

The mouthful of rum hit my belly, hard and fast. Hawaiian courage, not Dutch.

"Try the Mai Tai, next?" Seated opposite me, Travis's hand dropped to my thigh. A whole lot higher than last time, four fingers on the fabric of my shorts, his pinky stroking my bare skin at the hemline.

I'd forgotten about him. Not that he wasn't hot, but there was something about the other soldier, something... mesmerizing. Something that captured my entire focus.

Or something in the darn drink.

I handed the glass back to Nate without looking at him and turned to Travis. "Sure, why not—"

"Trav." Nate cut across my reply

The younger soldier turned his head. "Yeah, bro?"

Nate jerked his chin at Travis's trespassing hand. "Off."

Travis shrugged easily, drumming a tattoo on my thigh with his fingertips, each contact shooting tiny sparks up my leg. "Lissa isn't complaining."

His face suddenly hard, Nate leaned forward. "I am."

As Travis's grip tightened on my thigh, Nate clenched his fists, knuckles showing white.

Travis snatched his hand back and raised it, palm open. "Chill, bro. Sorry, Lissa. No offense intended."

"None taken." Earlier, I hadn't checked out their uniform in detail, more interested in what was *in* it than on it, but it seemed Nate was the senior officer. Why he'd be pissed at Travis for such a minor transgression didn't make sense, though. I felt a brief flicker of pity for Travis—or maybe for myself. It'd seemed for a moment there that I'd have my cock and eat it, too. Oh, oops. Cake. Freudian. But two guys flirting with me a fantasy I'd only ever dared entertain with the lights out, Nate had thrown cold water over the scenario far too soon.

He loaded a corn chip with salsa. "Here, eat before you drink any more."

I crossed my arms over my chest as annoyance flared. He chased Travis off, and now took it upon himself to monitor my alcohol consumption? Hell, I didn't need another mother. Didn't need the one I already had.

I scowled, ignoring Nate's hand extended with the chip dripping goop on the white plastic seat, and reached for the drink Travis still held. I flicked the straw from the glass—which should have been an ultra-smooth move, but instead, the paper spiraled through the air and smeared across the edge of my khaki shorts—then I gulped a slug of the which-ever-color, fruit-flavored, alcoholic, smack-you-in-the-guts cocktail. I raised the glass in challenge toward Nate and planted my free hand firmly on Travis's thigh. Well, maybe not so firmly, because the drink burned both going down and coming back up through my nose. My eyes watered. But I hung onto the mouthful and to Travis's knee.

Nate lifted one eyebrow and the uneven grin quirked his mouth. He pulled the straw from his drink, winked at me, and tipped the glass back, downing the lot. Without choking.

The muscles in Travis's leg had bunched as I settled my hand on his thigh, but he made no move to touch me or to encourage my mauling.

Which was bloody awkward, as now I was ridiculously hunched toward him, in a position which could look neither natural nor sexy. And I was feeling decidedly...not right. Note to self: cocktails are potentially more potent than wine. Never indulge without putting down a good raft of grease and chips, first.

The Wicked Witch's signature theme from *The Wizard of Oz* cut the balmy air.

Travis tipped his head toward my vibrating shorts. "Your cell is ringing."

Obviously. But how did he expect me to answer, with one hand cemented to his warm leg, the other clutching the stem of my glass? "I know. It's Mom." I watched with distant fascination as my glass slowly tipped precariously sideways.

Nate rescued the drink. "Mom? Don't you call her...ah, Mum?"

I snorted back a giggle. He'd hesitated on the word like it was a heavily accented, multi-syllable monstrosity rendered in a foreign language. "Mom's an American. And apparently likes to be called Mom." That came out sour. The fact was, I had used 'mum' for fourteen years, but when Mom met Mitch, she'd raved about how cute it was to hear his kids refer to their 'mom', and how she'd always expected to be a 'mom'.

For a while, I avoided calling her anything. Then I'd rebelled, using 'Carole' for a couple of months, before finally giving in and begrudgingly introducing 'mom' to my vocabulary. Like that would somehow provide an edge in the undeclared competition between me and the step-sibs.

Nate's tattoos danced blurrily as he set the glass on the table. Clearly, he'd had too much to drink. "So, you have a whole lot of family coming for this function with your mom? Brothers, sisters?"

I had to think about that for a moment. Alcohol in the middle of the day didn't agree with me. Or maybe sunshine didn't, there wasn't much of that in the lab where I spent most of my waking hours. Though the sun out here sure felt nice. Warm. Caressing. Made me want to strip my clothes off. "No siblings. Just evil-stepsh. Evil-steps." I took my time over the enunciation on the second try.

Nate waved away the glass Travis held toward me. "Evil?" He purred the word.

I kind of wanted to pout and demand the drink, but my head slumped, heavy and thick. "Evil. Perfect. Fine line, take your pick." My phone beeped as the missed call finally reached the message bank, and I leaned back unsteadily to retrieve it from my pocket. Nate's gaze traveled my body, lingering on my breasts. Darn, if I hadn't had too much to drink, maybe I could've capitalized on the moment.

No, that was bull. If I hadn't had the drinks, I'd already have made an excuse to escape.

My thumb smeared the screen. "Ah, my room is ready." I should have known that, despite the ringtone, the call wasn't Mom. I'd had my quota today.

Nate swung his left leg to the far side of the chair, unstraddling it. "Well, that sounds like our cue then."

Disappointment prickled me. Other than a little double entendre, I'd not managed to convert the encounter to anything more exciting than a friendly chat. Still, if I could manage this much on day one, it made for a promising start to the vacation. I'd have something to report to Suzee already, and, despite being a teeny-tiny bit drunk, I hadn't totally embarrassed myself.

"Don't tip over," Nate cautioned as he stood, the chair rocking without his counterbalance.

I scowled, my stomach knotting with memory. I recognized that sort of sniping, the stealth attack one of Damien's favorite moves, hiding a barbed comment in a pretense of care. "Wow, that's harsh."

"Harsh?" Nate was already in front of me, offering his hand. Those long legs sure moved him around quick. At a guess, I'd need to take three steps to every one of his strides. But, as he was dismissing me, I shouldn't be thinking about his legs. Or any other body part. Particularly the body part level with my face right now. Awkward.

I begrudgingly allowed him to take my hand. "Even after all those nachos, I don't think I'm about to collapse the chair." The annoyed huff in my voice did well to hide the tremor that quivered through me at his touch. Darn, it wasn't like I never touched a guy. Though, excluding today, I couldn't remember the last time I'd initiated even casual contact with male flesh.

Nate pulled me to my feet but didn't step back. My breasts brushed his naked skin. Electricity tingled to my fingertips. Well, more to my nipples, really. I could rest my chin on the ledge created by his pecs. *Must not do that.*

His voice vibrated through me, sending tiny quivers down to my stomach. "That's not what I meant at all. Looks to me like all the curves are in just the right places. But I'd hate to see that cute freckly nose meet the pavers."

Cute? I gulped. Actually gulped. Who bloody did that?

"Now," Nate took a half step back, and I fought the instinctive desire to sway toward him. He leaned down to pick up a cell from the table, and my eyes greedily followed the bronzed curve of his back, the latissimus dorsi muscle flexing with his movement. "It's three. I have a proposal."

My heart stopped. Well, the kick it gave when I sucked in a breath sure made it feel like it had stopped. I jammed my hands in my pockets, because the stubble on Nate's square jaw glinted in the sunlight, and I longed to rub my palm against it, see if it produced the sensation I imagined. Damien was always closely shaven, his skin moisturized. I'd never felt any roughness against my face...or anywhere else.

Nate swiped his phone. "How about you give me your number? It looks like you need to sleep off that, ah, jetlag, right now, but you said you don't have any plans for later? Kalakaua Avenue and the whole beachfront esplanade are closed off for a Thanksgiving street party and parade, tonight." He jerked a thumb over his shoulder, presumably toward the road he named. 'I've been a few times over the years, and they have a pretty cool vibe going on. We can do the touristy thing, cruise the night markets, plus pick up some dinner while we're out. That way, I can keep an eye on you. You know, endangered species and all that."

I sucked in a sobering breath. It didn't work. I'd need a dedicated oxygen tank to counter those mixed drinks. I couldn't think straight. Hawaii Five-o was about the extent of my knowledge of the local crime scene—was Nate trying to warn me that the area was unsafe? "Is it that dangerous here?"

Nate shook his head. "Nope. Not as bad as Sydney, anyway. But I'll pretend it is, if that means I get what I want."

I didn't recall mentioning Sydney, but it was probably pretty safe to guess any Aussie tourist came from there, given that the city accounted for about twenty percent of the nation's population. "What you want?" Great, my voice came out a breathless squeak.

A long finger flicked toward the pocket that housed my phone. "Your number. I'll give you a half hours' notice, then swing by your room to collect you."

"I, uh..." Why was my brain so fried, just when I needed to rely on it? Surely the smart thing would be to refuse? I'd had a bit of fun with these guys, definitely dipped my re-virginated toes into the flirting waters, which had resulted in more than just my feet getting wet. I resisted the urge to pull my shorts out of the damp wedge at the apex of my thighs, though if I thrust my hand into my pocket, it'd help relieve the friction a little. But did I *really* want to ease that friction?

What I needed was to get my mind out of the gutter—my knickers—and concentrate on the conundrum at hand. Should I agree to meet the guys for dinner, or was that courting disaster? Halfway through dinner was generally my cut off, the point at which polite questions about what I did for a living became an interrogation into how much money I made, what I could 'bring' to a relationship.

Except...that couldn't happen here. Nate wasn't inviting me out as a 'date'. He and Travis knew I was only in town for the one night, so clearly, they weren't interested in anything beyond a transitory physical hookup.

Perfect.

Fear and delight shivered down to my feet. Ten days, ten conquests.

Rack up contestant number one.

6

I'd forgotten to close the curtains when I tumbled onto the huge bed, and now the setting sun glowed pink and orange through the balcony window as I stretched luxuriously, reluctant to wake. My phone lay on the side table.

5.45 p.m.

Two hours and no missed calls.

Nate had changed his mind. Disappointment warred with relief in the pit of my stomach. Though there was no denying that both soldiers were sexy as hell, trying to maintain an image of sophistication, allure—or pretty much anything that didn't scream *frigid-mothball-scented-science-geek*—proved hard work. As evidenced by the cotton wool stuffed in my head and a mouth that tasted like the scrapings of a birdcage floor.

I jerked upright, the soft sheets slewing from the bed. The alcohol had given me the courage to flirt, even if it had been a fairly pathetic effort. But how much had Nate and Travis already knocked back while I slept poolside? They were probably half-cut when they'd invited me to join them and, viewed through their beer goggles, maybe I'd seemed worth the effort. Now they'd had a couple of hours to think on it, and sobriety had changed their minds.

I threw myself backward, the pillows closing like marsh-mallows over my head. With a bit of luck, they'd suffocate me. Humiliation chased the vague feeling of relief I'd momentarily enjoyed. So much for turning over a new leaf. This time the guy hadn't even lasted long enough to have a chance to scare me off.

Though, far from scaring me, being around the two soldiers—or, more specifically, around Nate—had awoken reactions I'd forgotten over the years; the tingle of sexual arousal, the breath-holding thrill of the chase, the tanta-lizing insecurity, and the giddy high. The smell of the man, all sun and salt and spicy aftershave, the deep throb of his voice, and his occasional touch had brought me the closest I'd been to a non-self-stimulated orgasm in years.

Oh, actually, in forever.

I struggled upright and fought free of the cascading linen. My legs hanging over the edge of the bed, feet inches short of the carpet, I despondently scrolled through my phone. Multiple texts from Suzee. No doubt nagging me to check in, so she could start the countdown clock she'd been over-eager to set up on my laptop. Nothing like having your bestie charting a visual analysis of your sex life, particularly when it seemed the record was destined to remain blank.

I flicked open a text and pressed reply. The time differ-ence meant it'd be about 10 p.m. back home. Hopefully, Suzee would be out with whoever had earned man-of-the-moment status, and too busy to respond. Then I could grab some room service for dinner and settle in to watch TV.

And not dwell on the fact that I'd already managed to screw up my holiday mission

I took a deep breath and let my thumbs fly over the screen. *'Hey, Suze. I have a name for your file. 'The Vagina's Vacation'. What do you think?'* Hit send.

My phone flashed instantly. *'Ah, she's alive!! I reckon it's lucky I insisted on rejuvenation before vacation. That Downunder topiary work had better garner some interest.'*

I winced at the quick reply. She didn't have a date? *'Ouch. Harsh.'* Actually, harsh had been the triple X wax Suzee had sprung for as a farewell gift. Salons should hand out Nurofen instead of glasses of water.

'Status update?'

Ugh. I'd known this was coming. I should have hedged a bit more, worked out my reply before I texted. *'Preliminary groundwork tackled. Target acquired, but initial mission aborted.'*

'WTF??'

I scrunched my nose. Suzee would never have a career in the military. *'Nothing much to report. Uneventful flight. Checked in. Shared a few drinks poolside.'*

'Shared drinks? With whom, pray tell? This better not be one of those stories where you tell me that you ended up babysitting someone's gross kids while they were off getting wasted.'

Jeez. Once. Just once that had happened. And it had been on a weekend away with Damien and his friends, so it wasn't like I'd been planning a wild time. Come to think of it, it was Damien's friends' kids I'd ended up babysitting, while the other adults had all gone wine tasting.

I shook my head and texted an abridged version of events. *'Met a couple of hot-as military guys. Had drinks. Bit of fun'.*

Even typing that made me feel kind of good, gave me a kick of excitement. Brief though it had been, it *was* an accomplishment, outside the normal routine of a life constrained by work and...work. My thumbs paused. I heaved a sigh. Better 'fess up. '*But the arrangement for tonight fell through.*'

'*What do you mean, fell through? You got cold feet already? Don't tell me I have to come over there and take you in hand... (you know I will :-0)*'

I wish she had been able to come. '*Just fell through. I'm on the cruise tomorrow, in any case, so no point pursuing.*'

'*Er, sweetie, correct me if I'm wrong, but wasn't that the whole freaking game plan? Fuck 'em and fling 'em? No better way to do that, than to have your wicked way with him and sail off into the sunset, yanno. Or sunrise. Whichever. Sure you're not making excuses? I mean, I'm not pointing fingers or anything, but...*' The squiggly emoji was clearly an index finger directed at me.

'*Them, not me. No show.*'

'*WHOA, WAIT, BACK IT UP THERE, SISTER! THEM???? Plural?...I'm scrolling back... You tart, what have I created?*'

Oh, yeah, perhaps I shouldn't have let that bit slip. My teeth caught at my lower lip, but I couldn't stop the smirk that slid across my face as I stared out of the huge picture window at the swirled pastel blues of the tropical ocean. Excitement bubbled deep inside me, a sense of anticipation and adventure, like waking up early on Christmas morning when I was little, knowing the whole day spread before me, full of surprises and fun.

Because, no matter how I looked at it, there had been a *them*. Two guys interested in me. And the only mention of my job hadn't been in regards to my earning capacity, but as an excuse to flirt. Not that Nate needed an excuse.

Sure, I'd screwed up, but next time I'd know not to drink too much. Because, dammit, there *would* be a next time. It was a shame Nate was off my list—such a shame that I didn't even want to let myself dwell on it—but the soldiers weren't the only men this side of the world. Why should I consider myself so easily defeated? In fact, I was totally winning; only a handful of hours into my vacation, and I'd already met a couple of guys, had drinks, a tiny bit of body contact, and a whole lot of daydreaming. Break it down to basic math and, statistically, that had to augur well for the rest of my trip. I was going to find a guy and have wild, passionate sex. No strings attached. I grinned like an idiot as I typed; *'They were my warm-up. You can start playing with my boxes tomorrow. I promise.'*

'Tease. In so many ways. Anyway, come on, it's what, about 6 p.m. there? I expect a report by midnight. And, by the way, I'm alone tonight. Just me, Auntie Flo, and a big-arse box of Ferrero Rocher, so I'm living vicariously through you. Which means said report had better be detailed. And I mean D.E.T.A.I.L.E.D, girl.'

'Pffft.'

'It's that, or back to being a Tinder Tragic.'

'Hell, no. *Every guy I've right-swiped has managed to work* commitment and special someone *into the first date convo, like the words are magical keys to my virtual chastity belt.'* As though I needed to hear more of the lies from which I ran.

'You sure that chastity belt is virtual?'

I snorted and tumbled from the bed, padding across the room and pulling open the bar fridge as I continued reading Suzee's scrolling texts. *'So? What's the plan? Hawaiian hottie, or are you settling for what's on offer here? You know, just because they swear 'truly, madly, deeply,' it doesn't mean you can't jerk them and junk them, Liss. I keep telling you that.'*

Yeah, she did. I pulled a bottle of icy water from the fridge and cracked it. Suzee had no problem acting on her own advice, hooking up with a new guy every couple of months while the old one still languished on her apartment steps clutching a bunch of wilted flowers. But I knew my own failings, my psychological predispositions that were a result of my upbringing. I'd be too easily guilted into a relationship, persuaded I had to stay to make another person happy.

What I *needed* was to be the passing object of a man's lust. The lie of love hurt. Lust? Well, according to porn, that would only hurt in the best kinds of ways.

I rolled the dew-covered bottle across my suddenly over-heated chest. *'I'm on to it, Suze. Land of the Lei, remember? Hot sex, no ties. Chat tomorrow. Love ya. xx'*

The second I typed 'sex' an image of Nate flashed in front of my bleary eyes.

Forget him. The soldiers had been a trial, setup for the true experiment. Which started tomorrow. A cruise ship provided the perfect laboratory to test my hypothesis:

If I act like I'm sexually experienced,

Then I'll attract the right kind of guy.

And the wrong kind of guy—a player—would definitely be my perfect right kind of guy.

The noises of the city buzzing with life around me gradually impinged, and I closed the fridge and skirted an elegant rattan lounge to step out onto the balcony. The buildings pressed close, hi-rises defining the skyline of Waikiki, but the majority of my view was filled with ocean. The last, syrupy sunshine of the day wrapped around me, the air thick with the perfume of frangipani blooms. I'd not smelled them since I'd been in Far North Queensland, years earlier, indulging my passion for active research before I adopted a troglodyte lifestyle in my lab. Now, there seemed to be a message in the evocative fragrance, a *rightness* to the timing of the memory.

Research. Hands-on. That's what I'd truly enjoyed.

But it didn't pay as well as my lab-based job.

Of course, with only myself to support, I could afford to earn half as much money.

My gaze flicked to my suitcase, where I'd stashed the paperwork I wouldn't need until the end of my trip.

Maybe I had made the right call. In a few days, I'd know for sure.

The drowning sun lit a stairway across the surface of the water and haloed the palm trees shading the pool, eight stories below. The pool where I'd sat flirting with Travis and Nate.

Triumph swelled through me. Hanging out with the soldiers had been so far outside my comfort zone or previous experience, yet I'd done it. I had that accomplishment, and I had my plan. *Plans*. I was invincible.

Screw room service. I'd shower and hit the street party Nate had mentioned. By myself. In record time, I'd managed to tick Suzee's first boxes; eye contact and flirting. Even if she had made them deliberately easy, to boost my confidence, in this tropical paradise how hard could it be to tick box number three?

Kiss a hot stranger.

7

Towel wrapped around my torso, I rubbed at my damp hair, leaving the door into the opulent floor-to-ceiling tiled expanse of the bathroom open. My cell winked from where I'd tossed it on the bed. Three missed calls from an unknown number and a voice mail. I dialed the code. Before my brain fully registered the deep voice, my nipples peaked, my knees went stupidly soft.

Nate. He hadn't blown me off. In fact, he'd be here in half an hour.

I stared at the screen in wide-eyed panic.

No, the message logged twenty minutes ago; I had less than ten minutes to get dressed, and it would take longer than that to get my darn suitcase open.

On my knees, I wrestled with the combination. I'd known it was screwed from Damien's solo trip to Thailand, why hadn't I replaced the padlock?

Finally, the tumblers clicked, and I threw the case open, snatching out a short dress and a pair of leather sandals. Cut low and tight on the bodice, the dress enhanced my boobs, and then flared nicely to disguise my stomach and hips. My legs were pretty good, a result of years of yoga, so I didn't mind drawing attention to them.

Heck, Nate could pay attention anywhere he fancied. What was it he'd said? All my curves seemed to be in the right places.

Anticipation sparked and flared in my stomach. No, lower. Somehow, the roller coaster of thinking that Nate had given up on me, then discovering otherwise, lent a whole new level of excitement and possibility to our meeting, almost as though our earlier flirting had been an appetizer. And, as usual, I was all about the food.

Not to mention Suzee's task sheet. Never had I been so committed to anything in my life.

The contents of my makeup bag scattered across the bathroom counter as I fumbled frantically through them. A dash of nude mineral powder to even out my dusting of freckles, and a swoop of bronzer to color my ivory skin. A flick of mascara, then I turned my head upside down, tousling my hair. Hopefully, it would fall into some sort of order, the length helping to tame the wild curls.

Accompanied by a rap, Nate's voice penetrated the door as though he had his mouth pressed to the crack.

Bang. Hot visual, right there. Seriously, I couldn't even keep my thoughts clean for five seconds?

"Lissa, are you ready?"

As I opened the door, Nate gave me a slow once-over.

Slow, as in totally undressing me.

My nipples threatened to rip apart my dress, Incredible Hulk style. I crossed an arm over my chest as his eyes lingered.

Nate rubbed a hand around the back of his neck and then blinked a couple of times, giving a short, sharp shake of his head. "Wow. You look...amazing."

No one had ever said that to me. Literally, no one. And it sure didn't hurt for more than six foot of drop-dead-gorgeous to take my compliment virginity.

"Thanks." Great. I'd actually performed well in English Lit. No one would believe that now, based on my inadequate responses. I should have hit the mini-bar for a bit more of that liquid courage.

Nate didn't seem to notice my lack of conversational skills. "I feel like I should have brought flowers or something."

I smoothed my skirt, willing myself into the role of femme fatale. "I must say, I am disappointed. I expected to get plenty of lei's in Hawaii." *God, the blush already*? More femme fatality, than femme fatale. "The flowers," I clarified, one finger drawing a line around my throat. "You know, necklaces. In the movies, tourists are presented with leis practically everywhere they go. But, so far, nada." Why couldn't I stop talking? Every word made me sound more ridiculous.

Nate stepped closer. His lowered voice oozed through me like molten chocolate. "I'm sure we'll find you a lei tonight."

Damn, this flirting stuff should come with a handbook. And a translator. Was *lay* an Australian-only euphemism for sex? Had Nate even understood my double-entendre? Or, wait...did he tease me deliberately?

He kept a straight face, though the lines feathering from his eyes betrayed him. "Are you ready, Freckles?"

"Sure." I grabbed the denim jacket from my suitcase, revealing the neatly folded *I-plan-to-get-lucky* underwear Suzee gifted me. I had an intense dislike of purchasing lingerie. Far too many of my credit card statements revealed huge accounts run up at online stores for purchases I'd never laid eyes on. The lid snapped my fingers as I slammed it. "Ouch. Is, ah, is Travis not coming?"

Nate's eyes shifted reluctantly from the case, lips firming as he frowned before replying. "Why, did you want him to?"

I shrugged. Yes. And no.

"We'll probably run into him." Nate ushered me toward the elevator, testing my room door as he clicked it shut. "So, are you in the market for some traditional Hawaiian food? Unfortunately, there's no luau tonight. But plenty of street food."

A noisy crowd jostled aboard the lift, and Nate pulled me into a corner, his cologne smoothing across the back of my throat.

The blinking lights on the door panel counted out the two floors it took me to perfect a spontaneous come-on as a reply. I raised my voice to be heard over the throng of holi-day-makers. "I'll try anything you suggest. But there's some-thing I've promised myself to do for the first time. And it has to be tonight."

A hush filled the elevator. Nate's grip tightened and he swayed closer, his presence sucking all the oxygen. Sandal-wood and salt and man drowned out the existence of the rest of the world. I couldn't believe someone this...*fine*...was holding my hand, apparently interested in what I had to say. He raised one eyebrow. "Intriguing."

"I want to try pumpkin pie. And what better time than actually on Thanksgiving?"

The collectively held breath of the elevator occupants exploded. "Ah, you're an Aussie." With three leis around his neck, the guy rocking a white safari suit obviously knew where to hang out. "I heard you guys don't have pumpkin pie."

I shot him a quick smile, though I barely took time to

focus. I'd rather be looking at Nate. "We don't have Thanksgiving, never mind pumpkin pie."

A thin blonde clutched her tote, apparently intent on preventing it from being stolen, along with Thanksgiving. "Are y'all serious?" Her tattooed eyebrows disappeared beneath thick bangs.

"Sure. We go from Easter to Christmas without any celebrations. No Fourth of July, no Labor Day." Everyone looked at me. Crap. Heat bloomed in my chest.

"No. How is that possible?" The blonde sounded genuinely upset, glancing at the other tourists, seeking support for her outrage.

Safari-suit moved his head pendulously from side-to-side, as though he'd challenge my honesty. "But where's your National Pride? Your family spirit? Don't y'all get together to celebrate?" He puffed himself up like a rooster and turned to Nate. "Young man, you need to show your lady friend a good time. US of A style."

Nate's thin-knit polo stretched tight across his chest as he held in a laugh. "I sure intend to try, sir."

Safari-suit squinted at him, probably assessing his bearing and haircut. "You're military, son?"

"Yes, sir."

Safari-suit nodded as though he'd expected no less. "Well, thank you for your service. You make sure you do us proud then, son." He whipped his arm up in a quivering salute, the garlands trembling where they rested on the rounded perch of his stomach.

"Sir." Nate almost dragged me from the elevator as the doors opened. He guided me quickly across the foyer and tugged me behind the full-size outrigger canoe that dominated the reception area. Hands on my upper arms, and clearly unaware that my nipples were brushing his abs—

I

though, God, I was *so far* from unaware—he watched the bank of elevators like he expected pursuit.

As the door closed, he blew out a long breath, a grin lighting his face. His grip eased as he took a step back. "Sorry, I had to get out of there before I lost it. I thought they were gearing up to lynch you for heresy."

Did he realize he'd not let go of me yet? My heart smashed around in my chest, giving competition to the mad fluttering in my belly. Could I speak without my voice trembling? "Yeah, it did get kind of weird." I bit my lip in pretended chagrin. "I guess you're right, maybe I do need protecting."

Nate rumbled with laughter and gestured toward the escalator. "Down another level. But don't rush, I've no desire to run into your new...educators. If they make a concerted attack, I'll not be able to hold them all off."

I'd bet he could.

His hand moved to the small of my back as I made for the escalator on the left. "Uh-uh. Other way around here, remember. Anyway, you said your mom's American? How is it that you've never had pumpkin pie, then?" He gestured for me to precede him on the narrow stairway.

If I was smart, maybe I'd sashay my ass a little. But it'd probably be better if I just focused on not tripping.

I waited until we reached the bottom before replying, so I wouldn't have to risk turning to speak over my shoulder. "Mom never made a big deal about being American. If it wasn't for the accent, no one would have known."

"You didn't pick up her accent, though."

"Funny you think that. My friends reckon I sound like a Yank. Guess I'm a bitser."

Nate looked down at me for a long moment, and I tried not to be too obvious as I inhaled the cologne that spun my head. "You're certainly one of a kind." A frown flickered across his face, then he gestured for me to move forward. "Now, that pumpkin pie. I picked up a pager for the Cheesecake Factory, so how about we have a slice there after we've done the street party? Unless you wanted to experience the full traditional turkey dinner? We could do that, instead. There's plenty of restaurants a block over."

I surveyed the street onto which we'd emerged. Sparkling with the first of the evening lights, it seemed even more like a magical fairyland than it had appeared during the day, if that were possible. "No. My fantasy," I lingered on the word, "hinges solely on pumpkin pie. But, a pager? What does that mean?"

Nate fished a small device from the pocket of his pants. "Y'know, rather than sit outside the restaurant, or propping up the bar, the wait staff will page us when our table comes free."

I stopped midstride. "Seriously? People do that?"

"Do what, wait?"

I swept a hand toward the busy street, though it seemed more high-end fashion shops than restaurants. "Yeah. Why wait on a particular restaurant? Like, why not just go somewhere else to eat?"

Nate lifted one shoulder. "Welcome to America. Lots of hungry people, I guess. Speaking of which, turn hard left."

Left took me through a narrow doorway and into a tiny room wreathed in indescribably delicious smells. Ginger, nutmeg, vanilla, and cinnamon filled my senses. Maybe not quite as good as sandalwood.

"Honolulu Cookie Company," Nate said, then pulled me a little closer to speak more quietly. "Now, the trick is to look like you're interested in the range, but circulate clockwise as quickly as you can."

Actually, the trick was to not quiver with desire as his breath stirred my hair and warmed my cheek.

He guided me around a center display of festive ginger-bread houses, stacks of ornate tins, and boxes of cookies. When we'd almost completed the circuit, returning to the entrance, he paused at a counter full of labeled containers holding fragmented cookies. "Hold out your hand."

The dexterity with which he wielded the steel tongs and filled my palm with crumbled cookies attested to prior experience. He replaced the utensil and hustled me from the shop.

I pulled back, refusing to take another step. "Hey, did we steal this?"

Nate selected a piece of cookie from my cupped hand. Rested it against my lips. "White chocolate macadamia. It's the best one."

I pressed my lips firm, squinting questioningly at him. He grinned. "No, not stolen. They're samples. I haven't led you astray." His eyes narrowed as I retrieved the crumb with the tip of my tongue. "Not yet, anyway," he muttered. Then he tilted his head toward the shop window, his tone lighter, though it sounded forced. "But I've been in there four times today, and the woman behind the counter is angling for either a purchase or a date."

"She's cute and this cookie tastes so good, that sounds like a win either way."

He shook his head. "I'm only interested in the thrill of illicit treats."

"Even when you're onto a sure thing?"

Nate selected another morsel, a brief frown marking his forehead. "Maybe knowing something's a *sure thing* ultimately detracts from the enjoyment. Anyway, hopefully her shift is finished by the time we go back to get our supper."

I massaged my chest with my knuckles. My heart doing weird, erratic things, I should probably find a pharmacy and check my blood pressure.

With the street closed to traffic, tents, caravans, and food trucks lined both the sidewalk and the multi-lane road. Seasonal decorations glittered in the plate-glass windows of brightly-lit shops and swayed from street signs in a balmy, salt-laden breeze that would screw my hair into long, tight ringlets. Fairy lights adorned the smooth trunks of palm trees, twinkling between the fronds, and carols spilled from open doorways, threading through the happy crowd.

Although Christmas was still a full month away—and the flip-flop wearing, tee-shirt and sarong-clad throng heightened the tropical holiday ambiance—the setting exuded an air of festivity and magic that seemed to belong in a traditional snow-bound locale. A fairytale Christmas setting.

"It's so..." I hunted for the right words. "Clean."

Nate halted in obvious surprise, and I waved my hand. "I know, I know. Not the right word. That sounds odd."

"Odd? Not at all. I can see the tourist brochures." He sketched an imaginary banner in front of us. '*Come to Waikiki. It's...clean.*'"

They would probably need to add '*and full of hot guys*' to that banner. Oh, wait; they pretty much did advertise that. I pointed toward the median strip of the street, where several market tents had barely a space between them. "I meant, it's sparkly and fresh and pretty. And not what I expected."

"I can completely see the sparkly and fresh and pretty bit." He sounded unaccountably serious as he broke eye contact and palmed the small of my back to guide me into the center of the street. "And I get the unexpected bit, too.

But what exactly were you expecting? Besides piles of litter and overflowing trashcans, that is."

I mulled it over as we wandered among the stalls in the main thoroughfare of the market. "Call me cynical, but I guess I expected the opposite of the advertising. I thought it'd be busy. Touristy. Dirty. Or at least, tired and run down. Not alive and...and *pulsing*, like this."

"Pulsing, huh?" His raised eyebrow made the word sound dirty in the sexiest way. "Fair to say that you're happy to be wrong, then?"

"Never happier." I shot a sideways glance at him. "Guess I'll have to file that pre-emptive judgment along with all my other misconceptions."

The rainbow-painted menu on the side of a van advertising candied bacon seemed to require Nate's full attention. "More misconceptions? Dare I ask what they are?"

"That I'd be garlanded with leis everywhere I went, and that Americans would be brash and abrasive. Score zero on both counts."

One side of Nate's mouth curved, though he continued to study the menu. "We're brash and abrasive, huh? I guess it's the fault of your evil step-shiblings—I mean, siblings— that you harbor such bias against Americans?"

I was sure I hadn't slurred that badly. Come to think of it, when—and why—had I mentioned my step-siblings were American? That was it, I was sticking to wine only from here on in. "Yes. No. More TV's fault, I guess. But the step-sibs didn't help."

"How so?"

"They were..." I floundered. "I don't know. Cocky? More confident than I expected. Like, when they visited, I thought they'd be shy and try to fit in, given that they were coming onto my turf. Instead, they kind of took over." That was partly my fault. The introversion that dogged me as an adult had been far worse when I was a teen. As my step-siblings lived in America with their mother, I'd only met them a handful of times. Other than a muttered greeting, I'd pretty much hidden in my room, citing a need to study and venturing out only when the 'new family' had gone off to do touristy things. I wouldn't have exchanged more than twenty words with my stepbrothers. Elle, I knew a little better, due to the forced proximity of our shared room, and because she'd visited a couple of extra times.

The trios' self-assurance probably wouldn't have rankled so bad if Mom hadn't obviously reveled in their company. For three years, since Dad's death, I'd had Mom to myself. Then the Americans had stolen her.

Nate gestured at the menu on the side of the van. "Which flavor? I've put in the time and done the hard work, sacrificed my boyish figure, so I can vouch they're all good."

That body looked in no way boyish. "I don't even know what candied bacon is. Whatever you fancy is fine with me." I mentally high-fived myself. Achievement unlocked. Innuendo *did* become easier the more you did it.

Nate stared at me for a beat, clearly trying to work out if I was aware of what I'd said.

Heck, yeah.

He ordered the skewers, and then turned back to me, one shoulder resting against the high counter. "So, there's a horde of these step-siblings?"

"Kind of felt like that, back in the day. But, no. Only the three."

"But all this was what, ten or more years ago? I guess now you're all grown up," his gaze slid down my body and back up again, "Things are different?"

My heart flipped. God, did he even know what he was

doing to me, or was it pure habit? "I guess. Maybe. I moved out of home when I was seventeen, so I didn't see them anymore. And then Mom moved back to the States, so..." I shrugged, not wanting to relive that particular desertion. It wasn't like I'd needed Mom, anyway. I'd been practically an adult, and at college, but it would've been nice to have a relative in the same country. Visiting Dad's grave didn't really cut it.

Behind Nate, the vendor held out spears of sauce-covered bacon. I dug into my pocket. Peered at the handful of notes and coins. "You guys do realize all your money looks the same, right?"

Nate handed the vendor a bill. "Wait until you visit Asia, that's when it gets tough."

"You've been there?"

He waved off the fistful of coins I tried to give him. "Yeah, I've been around."

"Oh, I bet you have." Yes, I was definitely improving. I could barely wait to report to Suzee, though I was in no hurry for the evening to end.

Hampered by the skewers, Nate clutched a fist to his heart. "Ah, wounded. What a thing to insinuate. Here, try my meat."

The blush shot into my cheeks. Okay, so I was nowhere near his level. Baby steps. Concentrate on the food, instead. Which, judging by the first sticky-sweet nibble, would not be hard. "This is amazing. Nothing like regular bacon. How is it made?"

Nate's square teeth yanked the bacon from his stick. "I'm pretty sure it involves disgusting amounts of sugar, so you probably don't really want to know. Here, try mine. I think it's the mango one." He tugged free a strip of bacon and dangled it near my lips. The guy had a thing about feeding me.

Or putting things in my mouth.

He pressed the morsel to my lips. "It's sticky," he murmured, fingertip brushing the pout of my bottom lip.

I reflexively licked at my lips, and his finger tickled across my tongue. I jerked back.

Eyes never leaving mine, Nate transferred the finger to his mouth. Sucked on it. Quirked an eyebrow. "So, do you like that?"

All the blood left my brain, tingling as it arrived far lower. God, I'd be lucky if the bacon was the only thing dripping. I swallowed without tasting. "Yes!" *Oh, the bacon.* "I mean...um, I think yours may taste even better than mine."

Nate grinned, his laugh diffusing the sexual tension as he handed me another skewer. "Okay, Freckles. Let's see what other bits of pure Americana I can find to tempt you with."

I wasn't sure I could handle any more temptation.

8

W e wandered through the stalls, occasionally separating to look at different counters, nibbling at the kalua pig and poke, for which Nate also refused to allow me to pay. "You heard the gentleman in the elevator. I'm to show you a good time. I'd be afraid to set foot back in the hotel if I fail him."

I paused to admire a table filled with carved coconuts and shell trinkets, though it was hard to focus on anything with the tall soldier by my side. I ached for his accidental touch, or for him to briefly take my hand and guide me somewhere. Anywhere. Each time he did, fireworks exploded inside me, leaving me ridiculously shaken and trying to hide my reaction. And desperately wanting more.

Nate's breath stirred my hair. "Don't buy souvenirs here. There's a side alley I want to take you in."

Oh, come on. That had to be deliberate. Didn't it? I sucked in a jagged breath. If it wasn't, my retort could be construed as innocent. "Promise?" I slanted a look up at him.

An uncertain frown flickered across his face.

Shit. My stomach clenched. Had I imagined the come

on? Did I want this—*him*—enough to risk putting myself out there, making a fool of myself?

Yes. I wanted both *this,* whatever it currently was, and I wanted *him*.

All those months of abusing my internet download limit had to be good for something.

Channeling every porn star I'd studied, I locked my eyes to Nate's. Wound a lock of hair around one finger, tracing my lips with the tip of my tongue. If I'd misjudged Nate's banter, hopefully he'd think I was chasing the remnant stickiness of the candied bacon.

A whole lot of stickiness.

Nate's pupils flared, his eyes trained on my mouth. He grunted something unintelligible—sounded like a single syllable curse—then dragged his gaze back to my eyes. "Promise." He drove his hands deep into his pockets. "Later. After supper."

Forgetting to rock the sexy look, I grinned in triumph.

Nate jerked his chin. "Ready to move on?"

"Just a tick." I bent over a tray of tiny pearls threaded onto fine leather thong. Delicate, but not overtly feminine. Damien would love the bracelets. I scooped up three in different shades, handed over a twenty, and strode away.

Nate caught up easily. "Hey, what's the rush?"

"I didn't know whether I was supposed to tip, so I ran."

"Ah, so that's your style. Take what you want and run?"

His words were obviously a tease, but the accusation gouged like a scalpel. It was so far from the truth—and so close to what I wanted to be able to do. Bitterness seeped into my tone. "No. Seems I'm more into the hang-around-and-wait-for-scraps style."

Nate's hand found my waist as he angled me around a

group of tourists. "Hard to believe. Tell me more about this plus-one who now isn't."

A current zipped through me at his touch. I sucked in, as though that'd make a difference to my waist size. "No more to tell. He *isn't*. End of a long story, no interesting bits in the middle. Anyway, about time you dished some mud on yourself."

He ignored the hint, clearly not intending to let me get away without giving more detail. "How long a story?"

"About five years." Why lie? It didn't make the facts, the wasted time, any more palatable. "Seven."

Nate let out a slow whistle. "Seven years. With the one guy? Wow."

I prickled instantly, stung to self-defense. "Monogamy's not exactly unheard of." Except by Damien, maybe. Though he swore he'd never hooked up with anyone, I'd insisted on every STD test under the sun. Twice.

Nate's thumb stroked my waist. "I meant, he's a lucky bastard. So, how long since you kicked him to the curb?"

Lucky he'd escaped? "Why do you figure I was the kicker, not the kickee?"

Nate halted, the hand on my waist pulling me to a stand-still alongside a stall offering SPAM sushi. The slow once-over the soldier gave me was unmistakable. And delicious. And terrifying. "Because no man would be that stupid."

Shit. Like, all kinds of good shit, but still... S*hit.* The words tripped and stumbled as I tried not to make an absolute idiot of myself. "There wasn't really any kicking. More of a mutual slow stagger. A few months, a year, two years, take your pick."

"Huh?" Nate shrugged his incomprehension.

I took an unsteady breath. I hadn't explained this to anyone but Suzee, and the hot soldier probably wasn't the ideal person to start with. "It was a gradual separation. He wanted a lifestyle I didn't agree with. We tried to make it work." This time I shrugged. "It didn't." Damn. Those last words sounded more plaintive than I'd intended, but sometimes it was hard to accept the wasted time. Wasted emotions.

Nate drew me closer into his side, guiding me through the crowd like he realized talking was easier if I didn't face him. "Well, my mom would expect me to make polite noises of commiseration, and say I'm sorry. But that'd be a lie. You're what, twenty-eight? You've plenty of time. If the guy let you go, didn't fight for you, he was a loser. You can do better."

When had I told him my age? God, those cocktails by the pool had a lot to answer for. The government of a number of developing nations would do well to look into mixed drinks, instead of water-boarding.

"Hey, look." Nate's square chin indicated a crowded stall. "Poi balls. These, I know for sure you can't have tried before. Local specialty, I doubt they're available anywhere else in the world. Are you game?"

"Sure."

He looked down at me. "Don't you ever say no?"

"No. I mean, yes." The blush shot up my neck. "Of course, yes. But I don't say no to trying new things. *Food.* I mean food."

Nate's teeth flashed white. "Hey, single for a few months, I imagine there's a whole world of...food...you've been trying."

Even without Suzee here to coach me, I could tell Nate was fishing. But should I play along, or would that make me sound like some kind of nympho? There had to be a pretty fine line between encouraging a guy and scaring him off.

And I had no idea where it lay. So, honesty. "Um, no. I kind of lost my appetite."

"For months?" He sounded incredulous.

Great, wrong answer. Once he realized he was escorting a frigid wannabe cat-lady who couldn't even commit to owning a bloody cat, I'd see how fast those long legs could move him.

Screw it, then. Lay it on the table and get his judgment over with. I squared my shoulders and stiffened my spine, forcing myself to meet his judgment. "For a hell of a lot longer than that. Told you, the relationship died a slow death."

A chime sounded from his pocket, and Nate scrabbled for the pager. Just as well, because it'd looked horribly like pity I'd seen in his eyes.

"Awesome, the table's ready at the Cheesecake Factory. Have you had enough of the appetizers now?"

"Appetizers? I'm about done."

"Oh, I hope not." Nate didn't remove his arm from my waist. Probably so he didn't lose me in the crowd packed into the wide, well-lit entrance of the restaurant, admiring the huge refrigerated cabinet full of delectable cheesecakes.

We followed the waitress through the throng to a small table. She allowed us only a couple of minutes before she bounced back, eager to take our order. Either so they could page the next patrons in or, more likely because she was eager to drool over Nate a little more. Understandable.

"I'll just have the pumpkin pie, please," I said.

"No meal?" Nate waved his menu, as though it'd contain different options.

"Told you, I'm about done for."

"We'll see about that. Pie to share, and a bowl of fries,

thanks." He looked over the menu at me. "Mai Tai? Every place makes them different, so you're kind of obliged to try."

"I'm going to be an alcoholic after two weeks of this." Not to mention those issues with my memory lapses.

Nate leaned across the table, as though the noise from the surrounding tables might impair his understanding. "Two weeks? I thought it was a four-night cruise? You're staying on?"

"Yeah. I have a week or so after the cruise. Stuff to do here." He didn't need to know what. No one needed to know. Not yet.

The waitress flapped her order pad, creating a more effective breeze than the rattan fans managed. "That's all then, sir?"

Nate jerked upright, as though he'd forgotten her presence. "Sorry, ma'am. A Mai Tai and a Bud."

"Sure." The woman dropped napkins on the table.

"Hold on, there." Nate consulted the menu. "Add a classic burger—that's the largest, isn't it? Plus a side of fries, a large cola and a slice of whichever is the most popular cheesecake. To go."

I made my eyes huge. "Seriously? Midnight munchies? You doing something I should know about?"

Elbows on the polished wooden table, Nate hunched toward me, a smile playing at the corner of his mouth. "Figure maybe I'll work up an appetite later on."

Then maybe I shouldn't eat.

My cell rang and I fumbled it out. "Rude. Sorry." I hit the auto-response that appeared on the top of my list. '*Sorry, driving, can't talk.*' Because there was no auto-response that said '*In a restaurant with the hottest freakin' guy ever, and I'm sliding off my chair because I'm pretty darn sure he's coming on to me*'.

The waitress delivered our drinks, and Nate waved off her suggestion of a glass for his beer, concentrating on me. "Your mom?"

Actually, Suzee, which was all the more reason not to answer. She'd be checking that I had taken her direction and gone out to score. "Probably."

"And you dissed her again? Is she that bad?"

"Not really. But I already know precisely how the entire conversation will go, y'know?"

Nate's mouth twisted wryly and he rolled his eyes. "Oh, yeah, I know."

I perked up. "You've got one like that, too?"

Nate's bottle clinked against my glass, and he took a swallow before answering. "You wouldn't believe me if I told you."

The basket of fries arrived, and we steadily demolished the mountain, chatting about the sights and tourist attractions around Hawaii. I had largely limited my research to grass-skirt clad men, but Nate seemed knowledgeable about rather more diverse subjects. He disclosed that he'd been stationed on the mainland but had done several tours overseas and that he was transferring to the Hawaiian military base. He was more reticent when I pushed for details of his service, adroitly changing the subject back to lighter topics.

And not once did he ask about my income.

As the waitress slid a huge plate of pumpkin pie onto the table between us, I eyed the vibrant orange slice dubiously.

Nate edged the plate toward me. "Go on, you promised me you'd try anything." He winked. Actually winked. No doubt about it.

For an unprecedented second, my appetite deserted me. Sure, I wanted him to want me—but was I ready to take the flirtation any further? Or did I still consider Nate my warm up, meaning it was time to start backing off, to make polite excuses to run and hide? Surely the third box on Suzee's chart would only require something relatively light? A peck-on-the-cheek goodnight kiss, tops?

Ten days.

But, Suzee's list aside, I had needs. And right now, I needed something hot, fast, and completely transitory. Damn it, I needed servicing. Nate sure as hell ticked all the boxes on any chart Suzee could come up with. Wham, bam, thank you, ma'am, then he'd be out of my life. And chances were he'd actually say *ma'am*. The thought turned me to jello. Not well-set jello, either. Basically liquid.

I took a tiny sliver of the pie, holding it in my mouth for a moment.

"Well?" Nate's fork hovered above the dessert.

"Wait." I sliced off a larger piece, shoveled it in, and immediately filled my fork again, curling my other forearm possessively around the plate.

"Ha!" Nate seized my hand, holding it captive as he plunged his fork into the pie. "Not good at sharing, huh?"

I tensed. Why did everything have to lead back to Damien? He'd accused me of being selfish.

Cream dripped from Nate's fork, spreading in a pool on the plate. "Hey, what's up? Did I say something?"

I forced a smile. "Nope. Not you at all. Just trying to put you off eating, so I get more."

Nate pushed the plate closer to me and leaned back in his chair, glancing sideways at a sudden burst of noise from a neighboring table. "Knock yourself out. Mom makes the stuff by the ton, so I'm kind of over it. You really like it, huh?"

Nose wrinkled, I assessed my fork. "Truth? It's...odd. A rot-your-teeth-sweet vegetable dessert? I don't know. Like, it's undeniable that the taste is awesome, but at the same time, it's kind of messing with my head, because it seems wrong on so many levels."

Focused on shredding a napkin onto his plate, Nate answered slowly. "Yeah. Funny how sometimes what could work out to be the best thing ever can somehow seem innately wrong. Even when you work through it and understand that there's no logical reason for the conclusion, it's easy to be swayed by common perception of right and wrong."

"Wow. Pretty heavy for a discussion of vegetable versus dessert." The last piece of pie lying in a lake of cream, I searched for a new topic. Still, this was the first awkward pause in around three hours—plus the hour at the pool. That had to be a record. "So, where's your mate?"

The napkin confetti fluttered to the table. "My who?"

"Travis?"

Nate glanced around the room, as though searching for the other soldier. "Oh, yeah. Right. Bar hopping, I guess. Making the most of our leave."

"But no bar for you?" Nothing like stating the obvious.

The naked flames of the tiki torches outside the window guttered in a breeze and then flared, the light flickering across Nate's eyes, making them darker. Dangerous. He lowered his voice, and I leaned forward to catch the deep growl. "I had better things to do. Told you, I'm your sworn protector now."

God, that rumble vibrated right down to my... well, to parts that had no right to be responding to a rumble, though they did like the occasional vibration. I swallowed and forced a light laugh. "Better hope things don't get too freaky when I'm all alone out on the ocean, then." Why did I have to go on that darn cruise?

Arms crossed, biceps stretching the sleeves of his shirt,

Nate leaned back. "Hmm. Guess I'll have to see how far my protector super-powers can reach. Or we could hit the ABC store, and I'll buy you a seasickness band. Do you reckon that'll cover it?"

He inferred that the most action I could expect was seasickness? I bristled, putting out a hand as he took the check from the waitress. "It's fine. I've got this one."

Nate slipped cash from his billfold and snapped the folder shut over both the tally and the money, handing it back to the waitress. Waited until she'd headed toward the register. "Uh huh. And what's the tip rate here? I think it's safer for both of us if I take care of it."

He stood, towering over me as he placed a hand on the back of my chair, waiting to pull it out.

The waitress returned breathlessly. "Sorry, I almost forgot your takeout."

"So did I. Seems I was distracted. Thank you, ma'am." Nate took the paper sacks. The waitress almost tripped as she reluctantly backed away, pausing to fuss unnecessarily with nearby tables, her gaze flicking back to Nate.

At least I wasn't alone in being affected by the soldier's smile. Voice. Presence. Looks. Damn it, everything.

I drew my denim jacket closer as we exited. More to hide my nipples, which had ached with their betrayal over the last three hours, than for protection against the tropical evening. Lifted my chin at the bags Nate carried. "So, will that get you through the whole night, or will you require room service?"

"Room service? Now, that's an interesting thought."

What the hell? How did he manage to make a reply to my innocent question sound like a total come-on?

He hefted the bags. "But this isn't for me. Give me two seconds, okay?"

As we'd entered the restaurant, I'd noticed the panhandler seated on a bench a few meters from the brightly-lit entrance, his gaze on the ground, rather than on the ebbing and swelling tourist crowds surrounding him. A cardboard sign leaned against his ragged track pants. *Hungry. Homeless.*

Nate strode over to him and placed the paper sacks on the seat. "Hey, man. Happy Thanksgiving."

I blinked furiously. Okay, so clearly the combination of jet lag and too much alcohol did not work for me. Because I didn't cry. Not ever. Well, maybe when I watched *Red Dog*. Not otherwise.

Nate held out an arm, inviting me into the shelter of it. Or maybe indicating I should catch up. He flashed his other wrist up close to his face, pausing to read his watch as we passed beneath a street lamp. "We've left our run a bit late, the market shops will be closed, now. I'd better get you home, Cinderella. You have a choice of boarding time tomorrow, yeah? I'll show you where the alley is, you could pick up your souvenirs in the morning."

Despite the cruise venture being almost brand new, Nate was clearly up to date with all things Hawaiian. "I do, but I'll head straight to the dock after hotel checkout. Too hard to explore when I have to cart around my cases." Disappointment shaded my words. Nate had already called an end to the evening and wasn't offering to accompany me in the morning. So much for the need to decide how far I was willing to go.

Nate ran a hand across his mouth, almost hiding his smile. "You know you can leave your luggage with the hotel porter?"

No, I didn't know that. Hadn't stayed in a fancy hotel before. I tried for bravado. "Just figure I might as well make the most of the cruise."

"Your mom's boarding early?"

The porter held open the glass door for us to enter the hotel foyer. "No, she and Mitch are flying in to board at another port. The cruise setup is like one of those perpetual bus loops that you get on or off as suits you. Mom booked me for a short full loop, but she and Mitch are only doing a couple of nights."

Though the elevator was empty this time, Nate stood close. Any closer and he'd hear my heart pounding. I should've watched for shooting stars while we were outside —my prayers for the lift to break down could do with a little celestial assistance.

Nate reached into the side pocket of his cargos. "Close your eyes."

I closed them so quick, the breeze from my eyelashes probably chilled him.

Something slipped over my head.

Warm breath caressed my ear. "I couldn't let you leave Oahu without a lei."

The elevator door swished open at the same time as my eyes, though the perfume from the orchids had already given away the surprise. But did Nate intend me to read more into his words? The thought scared the crap out of me —yet the fear that he might walk away burned stronger.

Taking the key card from my nerveless fingers as we reached my door, Nate swiped it through the chrome slot. "Well," his voice sounded as heavy as my heart. "I guess this is goodnight, then."

So that was it. The night was over, and it was more goodbye than goodnight. He neither wanted nor expected more. I should be relieved.

I forced a smile as I backed toward the door. "Maybe I'll run into you when I get back from the cruise. There's only, like, a million people here, right?" Damn. I tried to swallow the words back; I sounded needy.

Nate lifted one shoulder, the short sleeve of his shirt hitching up a bit further and revealing more of the tattoo inked around his bicep. "A million, plus tourists. But I'll be here. I've two weeks' leave before I'm back on base. Plan to get some surfing and snorkeling in. Anyway, you have my number, now. But, tell you what, wait until after the cruise, see how you feel about catching up then."

Even I could recognize a blow-off. I wrenched down the door handle behind me. "Okay. Well, it's been fun. See you around."

Nate's hands slid up my arms and I shivered at the almost-caress. "Yeah, it was fun." He bent his head, lips briefly brushing mine.

No, too quick! I needed more, this had to last for...God, the way my luck went, probably forever.

Nate took several steps backward, courteously nodded farewell.

Scowled.

"I—" He shook his head, fists bunched at his sides as he stood on the far side of the corridor. "Wait." With startling speed, he strode back toward me. Only a sliver of air separated our bodies. His fingers tilted my chin up as he looked deep into my eyes, seeking permission.

His lips pressed to mine.

Not demanding, but soft and exploratory, moving across my mouth with a sweet tenderness I never could have imagined.

He groaned and pulled away, eyes still closed, his jaw locked with tension. Shook his head again. Turned on his heel, and strode to the elevator without looking back.

9

I looked like I hadn't slept. Because I hadn't slept. Sexual frustration and a deep melancholy made for uncomfortable bedfellows. Even the luxurious linen and a promise of adventure couldn't shake me from the suspicion that last night was as good as my life would get. Nate had kissed me. Then he'd fled. Done a runner. Bolted.

Did I kiss that bad?

Now I had a whole new level of performance anxiety. How the hell would I score on vacation, if I couldn't even kiss a guy? Damn, I wanted a do-over, I was supposed to be the one who got to love and leave them, this time around.

And I wanted a second chance at Nate.

Which was ridiculous. There was no cause to fixate on him, solely because he was more than six foot of muscle-bound lab sample. Who'd paid me attention. Looked out for me. Smelled awesome. Set me trembling with the gritty rumble of his voice. Provided good company, easy conversation. Helped out a homeless guy. Built my ego with his flirting. Sparked fireworks in my stomach with his casual touch.

And left me almost fainting with an inexplicably brief kiss.

Damn it.

The cab pulled into the dock amid a constant flow of vehicles, and I slipped the driver an extra five, not bothering with the calculation. The brochures promised tipping was unnecessary aboard the cruise, so that'd be one less headache. And, man, did my head ache. But I recognized this pain; it had nothing to do with narrowing of blood vessels or strained vision, and everything to do with my world being messed up. Again.

Well, while Melissa might have seen her world destroyed by a guy, New Lissa wasn't about to let anyone, particularly some random intended-but-failed one-night stand, do that to her.

My suitcase deposited in the designated area, I strode toward the check-in. Thick white hawsers delineated the queuing line. Cute. Nice nautical theme, though maybe the lifebuoys, emblazoned with *The Spirit of Ohana,* weren't such a great choice.

Every few meters, hula dancers and the grass-skirted men of my fantasies posed with passengers against backdrops of the ocean, swaying palm trees and golden sand. The men of yesterday's fantasies, anyway. Last night's half-awake dream had been entirely different, consisting of uniforms instead of grass skirts, and inked sleeves instead of leafy armbands.

As a smile twitched my lips, memories of my inadequacy resurfaced. What was the point of trying to flirt, if I couldn't carry off a decent snog? I ducked my head, ignoring the smiling entreaties of the gorgeous dancers.

Parts of me weren't having that, though, and perked interestedly. Apparently, my nipples had no intention of being faithful to any single fantasy. Sweet coconut oil wafted from a warm male body, and my breath huffed out jerkily as I tried to disguise my ogling behind long eyelashes. So much man flesh.

I'd not checked in with Suzee again last night, but no doubt my friend was getting artsy, waiting to fill in my boxes. I snorted; after a promising start, filling my own box was becoming a more distant possibility by the minute. Unless...I eyed off the dancers posing for the ship's photographer, an idea slowly forming. Maybe I could fake it? Photos with hot Hawaiian dudes featured on Suzee's list, but the rules she'd concocted said nothing about the circumstances of the photo, she'd not stipulated that I had to pick the guy up. I could simply purchase a photo with one of the models.

But would that be on par with hiring a male prostitute? Mind, if shit didn't get real soon, that might not be outside the realms of possibility. My boxes had to get filled, somehow. Problem was, Suzee wouldn't fall for the staged photo. My friend had invested a tidy sum in her collection of snaps taken with male strippers—ah, entertainers—and would be sure to recognize the muscle-for-money poses.

Darn it, if I'd had the brains—or guts, but not the variety that muffin-topped my shorts—to take a selfie with Nate yesterday, this wouldn't be an issue. Still, I was planning on counting his brief lip-brush as box number three ticked. Suzee's ten-step virgin rehabilitation plan didn't actually give particulars of the type of kiss, so much as strictly detail what would constitute an acceptable kissee. And Nate definitely met Suzee's prerequisites. He'd tick anyone's box.

But pretending that he was actually a score wouldn't gain me anything other than getting Suzee temporarily off my back. I was here to break the drought.

Oh, and see Mom remarried, of course. With Nate a non-starter, I had to find a new target, or I may as well start Googling animal adoption agencies.

I cast a glance around, assessing my opportunities. Great. Not only did I appear to be the sole lone traveler, but I was a decade younger than the other passengers.

Actually, on closer inspection, make that four or five decades younger than most. And, with the onboard wi-fi slap-you-in-the-face expensive, there'd be no internet searching to entertain me. Of pets, or anything else.

The operator at the check-in counter smiled. "Aloha, Miss. Traveling alone?"

Every person in the echoing cavern of the dockyard terminal froze, staring at the revelation of my pathetic aloneness. Well, maybe they did. I wasn't raising my eyes to find out. "Yes."

"Passport and boarding pass, please."

Kudos to him, the receptionist didn't do a double-take at my passport. Maybe he didn't care; the Hawaiian dancers stood not ten feet away, and his focus seemed to keep pulling that way. With that kind of a distraction, I wouldn't be intent on checking some lonely tourist's ID, either.

"Face the camera."

I grimaced at the flash. Well, possibly before the flash. Having my photo taken rated with having teeth pulled. Another excuse not to have taken a selfie with Nate. *Sigh.* Nate. Why did my mind keep going back there?

The check-in operator waved the laminated card at me, as though I should share his delight in the instantly-produced freeze-frame of my Grumpy Cat impersonation. I'd bury that monstrosity deep in my backpack the moment he stopped flapping it about like he was holding the traces on a pterodactyl.

He attached the tag to a white lanyard printed with yellow hibiscus flowers. "It's important you wear this at all times. It's your pass to re-board the ship when you disembark at a port, your room key, your restaurant voucher, and, most importantly, your bar tab."

So much for my burial plan.

It also didn't escape me that the clerk assumed, as the sole-solo passenger, I'd spend the cruise propping up the bar, hoping to get lucky. Or drowning my sorrows. Well, he was wrong. There was a library on board.

At least, considering the average age of my fellow travelers, I wouldn't be the only one not getting a bit on this updated version of the Love Boat. There would probably even be a scrabble tournament.

The lanyard around my neck and the card turned to my chest, I headed for the embarkation line. An elderly couple held up the process as they posed for a photograph. Gnarled, arthritic hands entwined like teenagers', and their curly gray heads pressed together, they looked sweet. I smiled, forgetting my cantankerous mood.

Until the oldies went in for some tongue action, egged on by a rousing cheer from the onlookers.

Ugh. Apparently, I *would* be the only one not getting a bit.

A steward scanned my ID and dropped a soft pink and white orchid lei around my neck. "Thank you for choosing *The Spirit of Ohana*, ma'am. We now consider you part of our *ohana*, our family, and welcome you aboard. Your bags will be delivered to your room within the next two hours. In the meantime, lunch is being served in the forward dining area, the bars on decks two and five are open for a complimentary happy hour, plus we have a drinks voucher for you to use any time. The library and the gym facilities are also open."

Was that last a hint? I sucked in my stomach, smiled pleasantly and stalked toward my cabin.

Hang on; I didn't know where that was. Biting my tongue, I turned back and asked for directions. I couldn't even make an exit with panache.

AN AMPLE WOMAN huffed into the theater seat alongside me, fanning herself with a brochure. "My, my, my. I can't work out why they insist we attend the lifeboat drill on every single cruise. If they're gonna do that, maybe they shouldn't open the bar first, huh?"

I smiled non-committally. I'd spent five hours familiarizing myself with the layout of the ship, including checking the placement of the lifeboats and even trialing the evacuation route, but still no way would I consider skipping the drill. Preparedness saved lives.

The woman settled more comfortably, the entire row of chairs creaking. "So, where y'all from, honey? No, no, don't tell me, let me guess. Just give me a little something, like your name and what you had for breakfast, and I'll pick it from your accent."

Couldn't they just start the darned drill already? "Uh, Melissa. Lissa. And, um, I guess I had fruit and coffee." Actually, more like a full breakfast, given that it was included with the room tariff.

"Woohoo!" The woman levered herself up, presenting me a wide, dusky pink-shorts clad bottom as she turned to include the brightly-lit, half-full theatre. "Y'all, we got us an Aussie down here. Aussie, Aussie, Aussie!"

"Oy, oy, oy!" The crowd hollered back.

I shriveled inside. Unfortunately, this part of the world had scant chance of rogue icebergs.

The woman dropped back into her seat, platinum blonde hair a halo, as wide as it was long. It seemed she addressed the entire hall, rather than just me. "Y'all can call me Tex. Hubs and I cruise every year, but we've always gone *Pride of America*. Darn love that ship, but thought we should check out the new line, this time." She hefted herself forward to peer at the vacant seats alongside me. "Who y'all traveling with?"

If I whispered, maybe Tex would follow suit. "No one. Just me." I definitely was not a *y'all*.

Tex rocked back, sucker-punched by shock. "Aw, no, honey. Y'all can't be doing that. Tell you what, you'll join Bill and me. We'll show you the ropes. Get it, ropes? Bit of a sea-farin' joke there for y'all." She elbowed the white-bearded man alongside her, who didn't seem to notice, his attention fixed to the stage. "We're at the Captain's table for dinner tonight. Y'all join us, I'll square up with the steward for an extra seat."

A couple of crew members onstage clambered into life jackets, trying valiantly to pitch their instructions over the increasing volume of Tex's generous indignation.

I shrank into the plush seat. "No, really, that's not neces-sary. I, uh, I didn't bring anything to wear for a dress dinner. And I have plans." After the drill, I'd grab an early dinner at the twenty-three-hour diner, before the restau-rants filled with couples and families, then escape back to my room and spend the evening with a book I'd already checked out from the small but beautifully appointed library.

Tex huffed, her bosom swelling to alarming proportions. "No, no. Won't hear of it. Anyhow, a tiny little thing like you can get away with wearing just about anything. Or nothing." She winked, false lashes pressed to her cheeks like stunned butterflies. "And the captain's pretty easy on the eye. Don't ya reckon, Bill?"

Seated alongside her, Santa Claus cupped a hand around his ear and leaned forward, though his rotund belly prevented it being much of a movement.

Tex sighed dramatically and increased her volume so he'd hear. As could everyone in the auditorium. "Lissa's traveling all on her lonesome. We're going to find a man for her. Oh—" she turned to me in a wave of consternation and musk perfume. "Unless y'all don't want a man? That's fine, no judgment here. We'll find whatever flavor you've a hankering for."

My stomach roiled with anxiety and embarrassment, my voice not much more than a mouse squeak. Now I really did need sea sickness bands. "No, a man will be fine." Were they the most ridiculous words I'd ever uttered?

Tex nodded assertively. "That'll be easy fixed, then. Just take a look at the bait." Already hell-bent on her mission, she shifted to the edge of her chair so she could swivel to check the room for talent.

Despite her compliments, I'd make sure to lose Tex after the drill. A quick exit and I'd easily outdistance the older woman, then hide in my cabin. With fifteen hundred people on board, plus crew, what were the chances of running into the overly-friendly Texan again?

As the drill concluded, Tex snagged the ID tag on my lanyard. "Now, let's have a look-see where you're at. We'll swing by and collect you, so you don't get lost. Oh, will ya look at that?" She slapped a hand against her powdered cheek, a stack of bangles so wedged on her wrist, they barely moved. "We're only five cabins apart. Oh, this is gonna be so much fun."

Fun? Regardless of whether it was used as a noun, verb

or adjective, *fun* wasn't the word that sprang to my mind. Hell? Abomination? Torture? Yes, all of those.

But then, who was I to refuse a little help with my mission? Normally I'd defer to Suzee's prodding and match-making—not that it had ever managed to surmount my lock-knee. On the high seas, with what seemed a dearth of likely first-mates, maybe I needed a bit of help setting my jib and steering into the current.

Tex patted my arm with a gold-and-diamond encrusted hand. "Our sitting's not until six-thirty, so you've plenty of time to get prettied up, alrighty? We'll swing by your cabin on the quarter hour."

Though I nodded, my brain was frantically scrolling through the ship's directory I'd memorized. Where was the nearest bar? I still had my free drink credit, and I'd sure as heck need it. I'd dress first, though, to eliminate the possible risk of sobering-up time between bar and dinner.

Suzee had insisted I pack an LBD. Of course, I hadn't bothered trying it on in months. Years. Now the black fabric of the dress hugged my curves a little too snug, and my breasts threatened to spill over the low-cut neckline.

Damn. I had no option but to suck it up. Literally.

Staggering a little as the ship hit choppy water departing Honolulu Harbor, I made for the nearest bar. Perched on a stool at the glossy black counter, I hunched over my drink, trying to minimize my boobs. Or at least prevent them from escaping.

"I guess the 'what's a nice girl like you doing in a place like this' line would be too obvious?"

Shit, how many drinks had I downed? Surely only the one? Yet the voice behind me seemed familiar. I swiveled, grabbing the edge of the bar as I teetered on the stool. "Travis?" My surprise echoed too loud in the genteel hush of the elegant bar, and I lowered my voice "What are you doing here?"

Travis waved his ID tag. Even in the subdued lighting, it

was a decent photo. As were all the others I'd noticed. "Complimentary drink, of course. I'd advise you to make the most of it, they cost an arm and a leg at full tote. The rest of the cruise may send me broke."

"Cruise? You're doing it too?" God, what was the yoga pose called where you shoved your own foot in your mouth? Because I'd certainly perfected it. We were at sea, so the answer was pretty darn obvious. Embarrassment turned my tone petulant. "You never said." Or had he? I peered suspiciously into the glass in my hand. I'd have to give up this shit. It messed with my head. First Nate had known trivial details, like my age and home town, that I didn't recall sharing. Now I had no memory of Travis mentioning he was taking the cruise. Scary.

I thumped the glass onto the counter.

The soldier lifted one shoulder. "You never asked. What are you drinking this time? I'll grab you another." He picked up my glass and sniffed at the dregs. "Still hitting the Mai Tais?"

I tapped the straw. "I can't remember the name of anything else, so this is my go-to."

Travis caught the bartender's attention, held up two fingers, then pointed to my glass. As he slid onto the adjoining stool, his knee brushed my thigh. He jiggled it back and forth, effectively stroking my leg.

I clutched the edge of my chair. Forget my abstemious resolution, I needed a drink, stat. In any case, it was a bad idea to make rash decisions without conducting proper research. I couldn't pinpoint the alcohol as being to blame for my lapses in memory, without further studies. And another drink might settle the sudden arrhythmia of my heart.

Trav couldn't match Nate's too-hot confidence and

innate sexiness. But he sure was cute. And here. And there were only nine vacation days left.

Maybe I wouldn't need Tex's help. "Are you on the cruise for the full circuit?"

Travis puffed out his cheeks and looked bored. "Just the loop back to Oahu, not the next leg. Stuck for four days on the high seas. Because confined quarters is exactly where I'd *choose* to spend precious R&R." He made the cruise sound like penance.

Heck. I was down with that. With Nate's disinterest and the humiliation of Tex sharing my status with an entire auditorium, the vacation had gone from bad to worse before the lights of Honolulu had faded into the dark over the ship's stern. With Travis here, perhaps it could be salvaged. I took a deep breath, said a prayer to Suzee, and turned on the flirt. "You're traveling alone? Or with...someone?"

Travis screwed up his forehead, lifting one hand in confused query. "I'm with Nate."

A piece of pineapple lodged in my throat as I gulped a mouthful of my drink. "Oh. Of course," I spluttered.

Hell, how had I missed it? No wonder Nate looked conflicted when he'd done the gentlemanly kiss goodnight bit. And it also explained his chivalrous behavior, go-nowhere flirting, and the inference that I wouldn't want to see him after the cruise—the cruise he'd known all the intricate details of. He and Travis were *together*.

I refrained from slapping my forehead, basically because I couldn't afford to look any more stupid. "That'll be nice for you, then." God, I sounded like my mom. The drink went down easier with the next massive gulp. Could I pick them, or what? Though, considering the guys' hard-core sexual innuendo toward me, maybe I hadn't been totally off-base.

Perhaps they were looking to add a little variety in the form of a ménage à trois?

As if to confirm my suspicion, Travis's hand slid onto my thigh. "Nice, you reckon? Bonding and all that crap? Not really my scene."

I stared at his hand. The warmth tempted me, but I couldn't handle being with one guy, never mind two. And, while a fling with either of the military men might be commitment free, under these conditions I doubted it would be complication free. "I, uh, I have to go. I have a dinner reservation."

A hand pressed into the small of my back, preventing my escape as a deep voice sent my pulse racing. "So, I brave the wild oceans to protect you, and you're running out on me?"

If I didn't turn around, maybe he'd disappear. Hopefully. Because the sudden realization that I could never have him made me want him more—if that was even possible.

I turned. And nearly slid off the seat. Memory, fantasy, imagination; none of them had played me false. *Shit.* "Nate."

A smile creased his cheek, and he jerked his chin toward the other soldier. "I should have known Trav would find you first. He's like a bloodhound when it comes to pretty girls."

Okay, so that was the clincher. A little late in the day, but I had them pegged, now; they were definitely bisexual, definitely not my thing, and I definitely would not allow myself to be seduced by his cavalier compliments. Definitely maybe.

Nate squeezed into the space alongside me, extending his ID to the bartender. I was sandwiched between them. As Travis's hand slid from my thigh, I swiveled on my stool, scoping for the nearest exit through the growing crowd.

Nate turned toward me at the same moment, his hand

open in invitation. "What are you—" His knuckles brushed my breast, and he jerked his hand back.

Oh, come on, the guy couldn't move away quick enough, but still my nipples leaped to attention? If my dress had been cut a centimeter lower, the men would know all about it. Though, the way Nate stared, maybe I *had* popped out. I crossed my arms over my chest before he could look any more appalled.

Nate dragged his gaze to my face, his pupils enlarged in the diffused light. "Drinking. Uh, what are you drinking? Mai Tai?" He rubbed at his jaw, eyes wandering down again. "You look amazing. How about you join us for dinner? Trav and I are heading to the Chinese restaurant, and then to the welcome-aboard party."

A list of entertainment options lay among the travel brochures in my room. Karaoke in the forward bar, an LGBT meet and greet on the deck, Polynesian culture appreciation lecture in the theatre on level one, and a cabaret in the lounge. Plenty of choice for those brave enough to move beyond their cabins and the library. No suggestions for solo travelers, though.

"Yeah, come hang with us. I promise we'll show you a good time," Travis's tone was all sexy suggestion, and I had no doubt he planned to make good on his promise.

I had zero interest in that, but maybe I should go with the guys? Although they were a couple, I could still claim I'd partied, rather than be forced to admit to Suzee I'd spent the cruise hiding in my cabin.

But would hanging out with the lovers simply reinforce my aloneness, leave me jealous of every woman *and* man in the place? At least, by the time I'd discovered Dame's final secret, I'd been way past the jealousy stage. The only emotions not completely exhausted had been sadness and betrayal.

I couldn't risk opening the Pandora's Box of 'what ifs'. Despite vowing never to be trapped in another relationship, I wasn't immune to envying others' happiness. And danger lay in the temptation to second guess my resolution to never allow anything more than a transitory physical connection. "Uh, thanks, but I'll take a rain check. I'm already hooked up for the night." Great. If I correctly recalled the few conversations I'd had with my stepsister, *hook up* meant something different to Americans. The familiar blush burned across my chest.

Travis raised his glass in a toast. "Whoa, sweet! You sure don't waste any time." He leaned toward me, lowering his voice. "Hey, if that doesn't work out, you can always drop by our cabin. But just so you know, we're sharing…"

Nate shot him an icy glare. "Fuck off, Trav. I warned you."

Travis lifted one shoulder. "Seems the rules should apply both ways, bro."

I'd not said or done anything, yet it seemed my presence caused the air to thicken with tension, the two men squaring up to each other like roosters. Further evidence that *all* relationships were crap. Well, I was out of there. "I'm late, better be off." I slipped from the stool.

Nate didn't step back, sea-green eyes drowning me as I brushed against him. The touch awoke taunting memories of his brief, sweet kiss.

"Wait a sec." He dug into the pocket of his cargos. "Here, I promised you this." A pink latex band lay across his palm. "Put it on your wrist, the metal discs against your pulse. Like this. It engages acupressure points to stop seasickness. Apparently, we're in for a cyclone in a couple of days' time."

My breath hitched as his thumb circled the soft pad of my palm. Damn, it was so clearly a come-on. A revenge move to piss-off Travis? The two men were playing some kind of game with each other, and I had a feeling I was the bait. Or the prize?

Nate lowered his voice, glancing across the bar to make sure he wasn't overheard. "Are you sure you don't want to... come...with us?"

I couldn't go there...could I? The logistics scrambled my brain. Did the two men together represent double the chance of me being hurt, or halve my risk? And how was the math even relevant when, with Nate around, I had no interest in Travis?

Or any other man.

That fact alone rendered the soldier out of bounds "Uh, no, can't do. I'll probably catch up with you guys on some of the tours?"

A crease appeared between Nate's eyes, though he still held my hand.

Travis snorted. "Not a chance. Who goes on a cruise to see the sights? All the action will be onboard, if you know what I mean." He winked, and I smiled brightly, trying to ignore the throb of my nipples as I pressed past Nate.

I wasn't sure how old—or desperate?—Tex took me to be but, though my usual embarrassed fluster meant I'd missed the captain's name upon introduction, I suspected it may have been Ahab. Or Davy Jones. Whatever, he was most definitely *not* Captain Jack Sparrow. Shame. I could totally have gone there.

With only thirty place settings, dinner at the Captain's table should have been a relatively private affair. Navy blue napkins, heavily embroidered with gold anchors, lay in fans on a crisp white tablecloth. Silverware and crystal reflected the chandeliers centered between faux-marble arches, thick burgundy carpet promising to dull the clatter of the other black-tie diners in the spacious restaurant.

Unfortunately, the size of the dining room proved no obstacle to Tex. It took her a single glass of wine and precisely sixteen minutes to deduce I was solo due to a love affair gone wrong. Another two courses and forty-seven minutes saw the information disseminated among the Chinese-whisper filled tables dotting the room.

Though I glued my gaze to the amuse-bouche of smoked salmon pâté and roe, served on a minuscule crouton, I was churningly aware there were at least a hundred people in the restaurant. Which meant one-twentieth of the ship had been advised of my loveless, sexless predicament. Allowing for three meal sittings a day, Tex had enough time to make sure everyone knew my shame before I disembarked.

Worse, as the evening torturously proceeded, I discovered Tex wasn't the only one intrigued and enthralled by my circumstances. Nor was the woman alone in her outspoken curiosity. As Tex worked the room between the squid ink risotto course and the main of venison filet on date purée, snaffling the occasional bread roll to stay the pangs of the starvation she wailed would do her in, other diners showed no reticence in claiming the vacated seat alongside me.

Brief introductions made, they sought to reaffirm the gossip they'd purchased with their bread rolls, murmuring words of sympathy as though I'd suffered a bereavement.

Did I truly come across as that pitiful? Sure, as I was repeatedly reminded, the combination of the holiday season and a romantic cruise around tropical isles made for a shit time to be single. But why did an educated, successful career woman in her twenties evoke sympathy, not a round of applause?

The other patrons—though it was exclusively a female assumption—seemed determined to define me by what they believed I lacked, rather than by what I'd achieved. To them, being single rated as a tragedy. They didn't realize that I was determined to have neither intention nor interest in being otherwise. My only tragedy lay in failing to reclaim my single status quickly enough.

I didn't want a relationship. I didn't need a man. What I did want was hot, uncomplicated sex. To be the predator, not the prey.

Spearing a forkful of drunken fig, I swirled it through the rich cream sauce and glanced up, catching Ahab's eye.

Nope. Not going there. Though the captain had, in a courtly, olde-worlde manner, made his interest apparent, my need was not that dire. I'd left my vibrator at home, knowing I'd be the one person pulled aside for a full bag search by Customs if I provoked fate by packing it. But I still had my fingers.

This vacation had started solo, and it would end the same. Just me, my fingers, and my smutty dreams.

Which currently centered on a completely unavailable soldier.

11

Neurotically early, I queued alongside the bollard displaying the placard for the coach tour, arriving before anyone else had even disembarked the ship.

Though I'd successfully made certain I wouldn't miss the tour, it wasn't my best plan; as others wandered up in groups of two or more, my solo status became increasingly obvious.

No matter. I was here to tour Maui, familiarize myself with some of the Hawaiian localities, not to fawn over some guy. My ten-day target would have to be hit after the cruise because absolutely zip was going to happen aboard.

I adjusted my backpack and tried to adopt a condescending air; at least I was ensuring I'd get more value for my money than the other tourists.

Mom's money.

Ugh. I let my shoulders slump; I only had a couple of days to enjoy the sights before Mom boarded. I'd best make the most of it and at least have something decent in the way of holiday memories to take back with me.

If I went back.

The familiar butterflies swooped and darted in my stomach.

Clipboard wedged against her toned midriff, the tour operator ran her finger down the list of names. "Oh, yes, here we are. Holbrook. I'm sorry, what other name should I check off? It's not been linked on our sheet."

"Nobody," I muttered.

"Pardon?"

Tex's strident voice cut through my fluster. "She's solo." The woman steamed alongside, bypassing the others who'd queued, and hugged me against her ample breasts with one arm. "You can tag along with our group, honey."

My heart sank. Though her interruption saved me from repeating the details, the last thing I needed was an encore of the previous night's humiliation and judgment. I'd sit as far from Tex's group as possible.

Not that it would make any difference; it seemed everyone was pulled into Tex's orbit like we were planets circling her great celestial body.

I climbed the three steps into the coach and took a seat a few rows behind the driver, scrunching against the window. Hopefully, the spot alongside me would remain vacant, and I wouldn't have to make conversation with someone who either knew my story or would discover it within the first few miles, courtesy of Tex.

The coach filled steadily as tourists stashed backpacks and cameras in an excited flurry of conversation and laughter.

"Aloha, ladies and gentlemen. Welcome to Crusoe's Hawaii tour of Maui—" the microphone squealed as the driver tipped it away from his face to speak with the tour operator who'd checked us aboard. "One more? Not booked in?" He shrugged. "Not a problem. Enter it as a late booking, fill in the data when you get back to the office."

The tour operator ducked back down the steps, shifting her clipboard to balance it on one thrust-out hip, and tossing her dark hair as she spoke with someone out of sight.

The driver looked up to the rear vision mirror and smiled as he made eye contact with me. "As I was saying, AAAAALOOOOOOOHA, folks. Now, according to my calculations, we have room for a latecomer. Where are the vacant seats?"

Tex heaved herself up, gesturing to the space directly in front of her. Alongside me. "There's a seat down here, y'all."

I squirmed. So much for distancing myself from my gregarious new friend. And there had to be other seats still vacant. How many people wanted to go see a volcanic crater anyway?

Tex pounded on the back of my chair. "Woohoo, Lissa. Check this out, hon. You done got lucky."

Lucky? Lucky would be if a hole opened in the coach floor. I shifted my bag off the spare seat, trying to squash it in front of my knees.

"How about I put it up top for you?"

The deep voice halted my fumbling and shoving. I slowly looked up. And up. Chiseled jaw, the fine scar drawing my gaze to the firm mouth with the perfect lips. Sea-green eyes sparkling with humor.

Nate.

He seized my pack, tossed it into the overhead locker, then dropped into the seat. "Guess you couldn't reach to put it away, huh, Freckles?"

Tex leaned over from the seat behind, all breathless excitement. "Now what? Y'all know each other already? Ah, honey, that's just too perfect. Maybe things are looking up for y'all, and you can forget about that no-good, two-timing bastard. Drought over." She switched her butterfly-eyelashed gaze to Nate. "This girl could use some fun, young man."

"Ah." Nate seemed momentarily lost for words. "Is that so?"

No hole would ever be deep enough to bury my mortification. I needed to fling myself into a volcano. Fortunately, they abounded on this island.

I pretended to be absorbed in the coach driver's welcoming address as we headed out of downtown Kahului and slowly pulled up the lush green mountains. But it was hard to think beyond the fact that Nate smelled better than should be possible for what seemed to be a mixture of soap and aftershave. Took up more than his share of the seat, though. No way could he and Travis have sat together, their broad shoulders jostling for room.

His firm thigh pressed against my short-clad leg, but he didn't seem to notice, making no effort to shift it. I could probably have squeezed another couple of centimeters toward the window, but why should I? Besides; I didn't want to.

Apparently, the opportunity to gossip held far more charm for Tex than the verdant scenery. She pushed her head between our seats. "So, where'd y'all meet? On the ship?"

"No, ma'am."

Shit. That word. He really shouldn't be allowed to say it.

Nate let a smile crease his cheek. "Freckles and I go way back."

Yeah, like twenty-four hours way back.

Tex swiveled, no mean feat without a neck, to stare accusingly at me. "But you didn't mention this one, Lissa. How's that?"

Wow, the third degree from a stranger? "I, uh, he's not...available."

The bus lurched over a pothole, and Tex plopped heavily back into her seat.

Nate scowled. "Figured that out, did you?"

I shook my head. "Travis told me."

Nate grunted, his jaw firming. "He did? Sonofabitch. He had no right."

My instant urge to defend Travis was probably a relic of shielding Damien against friends and colleagues who'd not understood his choices. Whatever the reason for the instinct, I arced up, shoving one hand against the seat in front as I screwed sideways to face Nate. "I guess he had as much right to tell as you had not to."

Nate's expression stayed hard for a moment, then he nodded slowly, seeming reluctant. "Yeah. You're right. And you're okay with it?"

I shrugged. Funny he'd be the one to ask that. Damien had never bothered, despite the similarities in the situation. "None of my business. I guess, seeing as you're here and Travis is on the ship, it's not a honeymoon or anything? Just a vacation?"

"Not a honeymoon...?" Incredulity warred with Nate's scowl. "What do you mean?"

I retreated, huddling against the window. Clearly a touchy subject. Though Australia had gotten with the program, embracing gay marriage, maybe that wasn't the case here. "N-nothing. I just thought the two of you... Fancy cruise, maybe it was for a special occasion?"

Nate recoiled. "Two of us? What the—? *Us?* Hell, no. You thought *that*? Jesus, no. Not my scene, I don't swing that way."

He couldn't get the denials out quick enough, and I let him go until he stuttered to a halt. Mainly because I didn't know what to say. Or think. "Sorry. I, uh, didn't mean to offend you."

The seat creaked as Nate relaxed, the tension draining from his body. "Not offended at all, just kind of confused. I thought I'd made it clear where my interests lie." He reached above us to adjust the air conditioner vent. "Let me get this straight, though—the *thing* that Travis told you, it was this? Nothing else?"

Sweat prickled my underarms. "I must have misunderstood. I can't remember his exact words."

Nate snorted, though he sounded amused. "Bloody Travis. He would have been messing with you deliberately. He's, y'know, a cocky bastard."

Something about the phrase seemed familiar, but I was too busy pulling the thin cotton of my shirt away from my chest, trying to force a little air into my lungs, to puzzle it out. One thought—no, two, which was way more than I could cope with—hammered my brain.

Nate wasn't bisexual.

And he was here.

He tapped the brochure on my lap. "Anyway, where are we off to today, Freckles?"

I covered the glossy print so he couldn't see it. "You joined the tour. Shouldn't you know?"

His palm pressed over my hand, fingers caging mine. "I've no idea where we're headed." He let the words hang, his eyes stealing the wild green of the thick jungle we wound through, slowly climbing toward a peak. "I totally stalked you. Saw you in the departure bay, raced back to my cabin to grab my stuff, then just made it to the coach in time. The *where* didn't seem as important as the *with who*."

My heart juddered to a standstill, but Nate screwed up his face. "Whom? Is that *with whom*? I never know. Anyway, told you I was here to protect you, Freckles. If you're going to insist on rappelling waterfalls and zip lining from the tallest trees, I figured a more physical presence would be required to activate my superpowers."

I found my tongue. Unfortunately, not in Nate's mouth. So, he was only here in his role of self-appointed protector? "Sorry to disappoint, but I don't think any of those activities are on the schedule today." Or any other day. I wasn't the type to risk life and limb for an endorphin rush. "More like long coach rides and short walks."

"Guess you'll have to find other ways to entertain me, then. Fair warning, I have a short attention span."

I had to stop reading into everything he said. The guy was joking. And he'd just warned he would be easily bored by me. "Well, we're touring the Haleakala Crater today. Looks like it's mostly by coach, though. Shame, I'd hoped for something a bit more active."

Nate raised his eyebrows suggestively, and I pretended disapproval, firming my mouth. And my thighs. Clamping them together. Even Suzee would have trouble deciphering this guy's hot and cold messages. "I mean, some decent hiking. But this reads like it's planned as drive to the photo point, bail out, click, and jump back in. Though there are some walking trails mapped." I tapped the brochure with my forefinger. Couldn't open the pamphlet to show him, because our hands still rested on top of it—and no way in hell would I be the first to uncouple them.

Nate solved the problem, sliding the brochure loose with

his free hand, and awkwardly twitching it open between forefinger and thumb.

He didn't want to let go, either?

He waved the pamphlet. "Have you brushed up on the mythology of the crater?"

I jerked my chin at the brochure. "All in there."

"Yeah, but I like your accent. Tell me the story."

Tex lunged between us, gusting pastry-laden breath into my face. Apparently, I wasn't the only one to hit the breakfast buffet hard. "That accent's too adorable, isn't it? Go on, honey, talk some Croc Dundee for us."

Nate leaned back, his head topping the headrest, hand tightening on mine as he laughed silently at me.

I made my eyes huge in feigned shock. "Women aren't allowed to do Croc Dundee, Tex. It's like playing the didgeridoo. Secret men's business only."

"Really?" Tex sounded thrilled and awed at the same time. "Bill? Did you hear that? I can't do the 'put another shrimp on the barbie' line, any more. Looks like you'll have to do the cooking."

The seat juddered as Nate fought to keep his noiseless mirth in. Eventually, he took a shaky breath, his gaze darting my way. "It's an old movie, but I have a favorite line too."

I rolled my eyes. "That's not a knife." Everyone claimed the same line, whipping out a pretend dagger from behind their back.

Nate moved close, his breath tickling my ear. His voice dropped octaves, and goosebumps shivered through me. "No. It's when the journalist is hysterical, claiming the crocodile wanted to eat her alive. Croc Dundee says 'Can't blame him. Same thought crossed my mind once or twice.'"

Fuck! My labia swelled, pulsing against the tight confines of my shorts, and I shifted uncomfortably on the seat.

Slipped, more like. I had to get a grip. Nate was quoting a corny movie line, nothing more. It wasn't directed at me. The entire coachload of tourists were probably all citing lines at Tex's urging.

But Nate's lips weren't pressed against anyone else's ear.

As though I wasn't open-mouthed with shock, he continued smoothly. "You are aware the coach tours have a pop quiz every hour? You have to pay attention to the guide and the scenery." He waved the brochure toward the window.

Uh, yeah. Right. I turned and stared blindly out of the tinted glass, careful not to shift my leg away from his or lose the casual embrace of our hands.

Within minutes, though, I'd been sucked into the tour, and had to reluctantly free my hand to grab the Nikon hung around my neck. Clicking pictures through the large window as the coach wound up the steep grades, I noted with amazement the rapidity with which the lush vegetation gave way to sparse alpine plants, an invisible line apparently delineating an entirely different microclimate. As we rounded a hairpin bend, climbing into the clouds, the harbor spread far below us like an ozone-encased diorama.

We pulled into the parking lot of the crater, and I glanced at my phone. Did a double-take. Already ninety minutes into the tour, it felt like no time had passed.

Tex dragged on the back of the seat to haul herself upright. "Time for a comfort stop and something to eat, I'd say."

I took the brochure from Nate and flipped it over to the map. "How long did the driver say we have up here?"

"What was that I told you about listening?" he teased. "Forty minutes. Why? What do you have in mind?"

Oh, so much in my mind. And it'd probably take

nothing like forty minutes. Not that I could really remember. "According to the brochure—which *I* did read—there are a couple of shorter trails around the inside of the crater. I kind of feel like burning off some energy. If we leg it, we might be able to do a partial circuit and back."

"Leg it? Is that an Australianism?"

I shrugged. "More likely a me-ism. Anyway, are you up for it?" His gaze met mine, but I didn't falter. I didn't know what game he was playing, but I'd had some time to think, and I was pretty sure I knew what game I wanted to play.

His pupils flared. "More than up for it."

It was surprisingly cold as we stepped from the coach, the balmy air of coastal Maui replaced by the frigid breeze of alpine heights.

I gasped as the wind sucked my breath away. Nate draped an arm around my shoulders like he was my poncho. "Still fancy that walk?"

"Can you suggest a better way to warm up?" I crunched over the lava-strewn ground toward a well-trodden walkway.

"I'm pretty sure I could." Nate pulled me a little closer, pausing as we reached the vantage point, already crowded with tourists taking photos.

Okay. Focus. It wasn't actually possible—or at least, not likely—for my heart to stop. It was simply the chill preventing the beat from registering on my fists, balled up against my chest.

The massive crater, a hollowed-out alien landscape, stretched into the distance, so vast I couldn't make out details on the far side. "There's nothing to use for scale, no perspective." I shook my head in amazement, then pointed at beautiful, multi-hued funnels sprouting from the red earth in the far distant basin. "Those cinder cones could be four feet or forty feet high. Because it's so completely barren down there, there's no way to tell without getting closer."

Nate squinted against the icy breeze that whipped from first one direction, then another, as though trying to steal our words. My hair blew across my face, but his short, blond-streaked crop merely ruffled. "It sure is something. Did you consider doing the sunrise tour? That's supposed to be spectacular."

"I *read* about it." I tried to arch an eyebrow teasingly, but my face was too numb to feel if I succeeded. "I figured if I liked what I saw, I'd do that tour next time."

Nate stood behind me, hands thrust into his pockets to broaden his shoulders and block me from the worst of the wind. Not that he really needed to make himself appear any larger. "And do you like what you see?"

"So far."

"You're planning on coming to Hawaii again?"

"Maybe." I wouldn't know what my future held until next week. Tuesday, at eleven, to be precise. "There's the head of the walking path, over there. C'mon, let's hit that trail."

The altitude thinned the air, so we talked little. Within minutes, I realized we'd have to walk hard if we were to traverse even a tiny part of the tracks, which had appeared ant-like when seen from the rim of the crater, and still make it back to the coach on time. And walking hard ten thousand feet up was not the same as walking at sea level.

I slogged on, trying not to pant. The first section of the path declined only slightly but was made treacherous by the cocoa-colored lava pebbles that rolled and broke underfoot.

As we huffed on down—okay, so only I was huffing—a yodel echoed from the lookout a hundred feet above. I cringed. "Tex. God no, don't wave. It'll encourage her. Make like you can't hear."

"The blood is pounding so hard in my ears, I don't need to pretend," Nate groaned. "I thought this tourist stuff was supposed to be fun, not a workout."

I wheezed as I started up the next gradual incline on a path that was sadistically intent on forcing us to climb *up* to get further down inside the crater. How was it possible to freeze and sweat at the same time? "I thought you military types would be accustomed to this kind of thing?"

I glanced back, catching the sudden somber expression on Nate's face as he paused to gaze across the barren landscape. "The air is a lot thinner here than in the desert."

He kept his reply short, clipped. But then, the guy was on vacation. Who wanted to talk work while touring a tropical paradise?

I pointed at the path. "We need to pick up the pace. Didn't you attend the familiarization talk on the ship? The gym instructor said average weight gain for the short cruise is seven pounds. Have to work it off somehow."

Nate pulled me to a halt, swinging his backpack forward to tug out a water bottle. "I say an extra seven pounds wouldn't do you any harm at all. Let's take it a bit easier."

Even when I'd been stick thin, Damien had nagged about my weight, taunting that the propensity for any weight gain to head straight for my boobs and butt made me a Jessica Rabbit caricature.

Maybe Nate liked rabbits.

He offered me the water bottle, taking a swig after me.

Not a good time for my knees to go wobbly. It was the exertion.

He wiped his mouth on the back of his hand, recapping

the bottle and swinging the bag back over his shoulders. "What happens if we don't get back to the coach in time?"

"I'm guessing they leave without us."

"And we'd be stranded on a deserted tropical island together."

Sounded like the opposite of a problem to me. I cupped my hands over my face, breathing into them to cut the cold, my eyes watering as I squinted up at him. "Totally ignoring the deserted bit, and can't say I'm getting much of a tropical vibe in the world's largest dormant volcano crater."

Nate pulled me against his chest, chafing my back. "Ah, so you really did do your homework? Just as well. I heard they throw us off the coach if you get it wrong."

Walking buddies. It wasn't an embrace or anything. Was it?

He released me and gestured at the zig-zagging path. "Alright, then, if I can't tempt you to be the Wilson to my Noland, better get a move on."

"*Castaway*, huh? You're really into those old movies. How come I have to be the ball?"

Nate watched me in silence, drawing the moment out until I realized what was coming, and the blush crawled up my chest. His eyes glittered as the sun broke through the clouds. "Because then I get to play with you."

Okay, now I wasn't the least bit cold.

Twenty minutes later, we collapsed into the coach seats. I drained my bottle, then groaned. "My buscles are going to kill me tomorrow."

Nate held his water bottle toward me. "Here, finish it. Buscles?"

I waved away the offer. "Pretty sure I owe you drinks. Butt muscles. Buscles."

"Ah. Buscles. I like that. Them." A smile tweaked the corner of his mouth. "I'm sure they'll respond to massage. Anyway, about those drinks. I think, in light of the aspersions you cast on my masculinity today, you do owe me something."

I lifted an eyebrow. Not that I could manage much more. I wasn't entirely joking about the buscles.

"Promise you'll come to the toga party tonight."

I cringed. "Toga? Seriously? In the Hawaiian Islands?"

Nate tucked the bottle into his backpack and stood, swaying with the motion of the coach. "Yeah, defies logic, I know. Mind, if there hadn't been one, I'd pay to have them put one on. You'll look spectacular in a toga." He shoved the backpack and our jackets in the overhead locker, his long-sleeved, slim fit Henley riding up to expose an inch of taut stomach.

Excitement sparked through me. Yeah, right. Excitement. How about I call it by the right name? Lust. Desire. *Need.*

I licked at my lips, trying to find a little moisture in my mouth. "Can't do. I didn't bring gear for any of the themed parties." I'd deliberately avoided looking at what was on offer, actually.

Hands planted wide against the locker, Nate looked down at me. "Well, you not wearing anything would suit me just fine. But if you insist on conforming, there's a rental place in the mall on the ship. They'll be expensive, though." He snapped his fingers. "Hey, did you tip your cabin steward with your usual generosity? If you did, he'll probably find some linen you can cut up..."

I wrinkled my nose. "I left a tip in my room when I went for dinner last night. When I came back, my bed was turned down."

"That's part of the service."

"Uh huh. There were also two towel animals."

Nate chuckled as he dropped back into the seat. "Seriously? Oh, that's priceless. You definitely over tipped."

I rolled my eyes. "Yeah, well I kind of figured that. But now I have two problems; I don't know how much to tip the steward today, because even though it's discretionary, I can't really reduce it, right? And I can't shower, because I can't bear to pull the elephant apart. I already dismembered a penguin, and I feel like a murderer."

"Oh, then you are going to be a dirty girl—"

Unembarrassed to be caught eavesdropping, Tex butted in. "Honey, the solution to both of your problems is simple. Change rooms."

"I...can't?" I threw a questioning look at Nate, who hiked a shoulder. Surely Tex realized I was joking about the towels being an issue?

Tex's red-tipped nail tapped my forearm. "Sure, you can, hon. Share a room. I've been watching you two." The finger waggled admonishment. "And to think you had us all feeling sorry for you after that dirtbag cheated on you. Just looking at this one—" she did exactly that, a slow burn up and down Nate's length. "I can tell you've upgraded."

My cheeks flamed, but Nate leaned close to me as Tex fluffed her hair and sat back with an air of satisfaction. "I don't know about you, but I feel like I've been molested. Hold me?" He made puppy-dog eyes of fear.

I patted at his leg. Limited myself to two touches. Maybe three. "Oh, there, there, you poor sensitive thing."

Nate captured my hand on the third pat and pressed it down hard on his thigh. Slouched in the seat, he put his head on my shoulder, pretending to sniffle. His warm breath bathed my nipple, and I gritted my teeth, trying not to scream with the exquisite sensitivity.

Heaving an over-engineered sigh, as though he'd been wracked by tears, Nate slid a hand to my stomach and nestled in closer to my shoulder.

To my breast.

I tensed my abs and held my breath.

"Nice pillow," he mumbled and promptly fell asleep, his breaths long and regular.

THE INTERCOM CRACKLED TO LIFE, startling me awake. "Please have your ID and passport out for the security officers to check. Thank you for your company, and aloha from beautiful Maui."

I'd slept the entire trip back to the ship, missing not only the scenery but two hours of Nate's company. How could I have wasted so much time? The exhaustion had to be a side-effect of the lack of oxygen at higher altitude. And, somehow, we'd changed position; I was now nestled into the crook of his shoulder.

I shoved myself upright, swiping at my mouth to make sure I hadn't drooled in my sleep. Because my salacious thoughts had most definitely been drool-worthy.

Nate smiled down at me, not lifting the arm around my shoulders, his fingers tickling my upper arm. Had he actually slept, or had it been a ruse?

Why?

Because he didn't want to talk, or as an excuse to cuddle up to me?

Hell, he didn't need an excuse.

I'd already decided. With only three nights available for *us*, this man was perfect in every way.

This was it.

I was letting go of my self-doubt, and totally going for it.
Going for him.

12

Nate was right, the costume shop charged like a high-end divorce lawyer. However, my toga did look pretty good. But short. Awfully short.

I turned side-on to the cabin mirror. Held with a clasp on one shoulder, the toga left my other shoulder bare. I hadn't brought a strapless bra—didn't actually own one—so the girls would have to roam free tonight. A gold cord belted the white fabric in tightly beneath my breasts, then the material draped in soft folds, falling to high-thigh. I pulled my long, dark hair forward to curl over my naked shoulder.

Before Damien and I split, we'd dined out two or three times a week. As I spent long hours at my desk or lab bench, and it was easier to agree to his frequent suggestions of a night out than have to come home and organize a meal. We'd meet our friends at one of the intimate restaurants in Kings Cross—well, they'd been more Damien's friends than mine. Still trying to decide what he wanted to *do* with his life, he had a large social circle from University and plenty of free time. I relied on work colleagues for friendship but had enough cash for Damien's mates to mooch drinks from me. After dinner, Damien would invariably guide our group to Darlinghurst to catch a favorite show. The drag queens' routines and jokes were all comfortably familiar, and that fit our relationship, which had become more habit than fun. The entertainment option only varied when one of the Lady Boyz shows came to town.

Naive, lazy, busy; whatever the excuse, I'd missed so many red flags.

My phone beeped, and I snatched it up. Nate said he'd text me when he was dressed.

Mom. *'Boarding tomorrow. Early dinner, then bridesmaids fitting at 6 p.m.!!!!!'*

That much enthusiasm, not to mention the exclamation point abuse, should be illegal. I glanced in the mirror again. Shame we couldn't wear togas for the wedding. Mom's undying love for the 1980s had extended to trying to persuade me to wear a flouncy pink dress with capped Cinderella sleeves for every school formal and first date.

My hand stilled as I tamed a wild ringlet. Would Mom bring *the* actual dress?

Surely not. Even she couldn't be that cruel.

The phone beeped again. *'Deck 7. Darn breezy out here. Waiting for you...or would you prefer I collected?'*

Oh, he could collect anytime he wanted. I blew out a long breath as my stomach jittered like I'd downed a pound of sherbet. God, my skirt was seriously short.

I flicked my hands, trying to dispel the tension. My legs were good. Focus on the legs. Not the other *blobby bits,* as Damien called them. Nate had made it clear he liked what he saw.

And I sure as hell liked what I saw when I looked at him.

Okay, I had to calm down, channel some Suzee. I tapped out a reply. *'I'll be there in five.'* Then I flicked up Suzee's number. *'This is it. Going in. Or down. Tonight's the night.'* The drought-breaker.

I bolted from my cabin without waiting for her reply.

I'd thought my legs looked okay, but Nate's...wow. No wonder he'd said it was breezy on the deck; his white toga wasn't a lot longer than mine. But where I had smooth, pale skin, his tanned legs were burnished with golden hairs, his thigh muscles cording as he strode toward me. Because, yep, thighs. That's totally all I was staring at.

I should have researched—were togas the Roman equivalent of kilts? What did he have on underneath?

His gaze slid appreciatively over me. "I had hoped you'd go with my 'naked' suggestion, but that is pretty damn fine." A short, deep burgundy cape swung from his shoulders, the black-inked designs on his bulging right bicep stark against the white fabric of his toga. "Lucky it's warm, huh?"

My nipples didn't seem to think it warm at all. I moved to cross an arm over my chest, but Nate caught my hand. "That's kind of a go-to move for you, isn't it?"

"What? Oh." He was right. I'd become accustomed to disguising my figure in the clothes Damien chose for me and felt exposed without his guidance. "So, what exactly happens at a toga party?"

Nate guided me toward the heavy wooden door that opened into the bar. "Can't say I've ever been to one, but I suspect it's like any other party. The theme will soon be forgotten, and we drink. Speaking of which, Mai Tai still your poison?"

"Given the theme, shouldn't that be red wine? But I'll take water or juice." I wanted to remember every detail of the night. What I did or didn't do would be my decision, not clouded or excused by alcohol. Nate was perfect for a vacation fling if I could only work up the courage.

Nate rubbed the back of his neck, surveying me for a long moment. Then he nodded. "Good call. I'll join you."

He yanked on the door, pointing at the high, raised lip, to warn me to step up over it.

The music blasted from the bar with an almost physical force, enough to make me hesitate. Nate grinned, and my heart tilted.

No, it was an adrenalin burst; I had to stick to the science. But I returned his smile and pushed my way into the crowded room.

Nate's prediction proved right. Other than the togas, the theme failed to carry any further than a few papier mâché columns adorned with bunches of plastic grapes. The tight area undulated with people drinking, grind-ing, and flirting their way to a holiday high, some of them already only a couple of drinks short of procreating.

As we made our way through the crush, Nate bent closer. "Dance? Conversation is not going to be a thing, in here." He touched his ear and winced comically.

I nodded. On a floor this packed, no one would be able to check out my non-moves. And dancing meant contact, right? I glanced around, trying to find a designated dance floor.

Nate also scanned the room, then shrugged. "I guess we get down to it right here."

My stomach fluttered. Had to be nerves at the thought of dancing, not excitement at the innuendo.

Yeah, sure. Those darn butterflies had a hang glider rental service operating in my belly.

Nate's hands moved to my waist, the heat from them shooting to my core and creating thermals for the soaring butterflies. His eyes heavy-lidded, smoldering, he gazed down as he gradually drew me closer, not rushing the moment, apparently savoring the anticipation as I did.

A millisecond before our bodies touched, he glanced over my head. A scowl flashed across his face. His eyes narrowed, the green darkening, and he took an abrupt half step back, his sheer size forcing the crowd to part like the Red Sea, creating an oasis of space around us.

Exactly what I didn't want.

From my fingertips to my knees, every part of me ached to be closer to him. My nerve endings tingled, my skin throbbed. I craved his touch, the press of his body against mine, with an animalistic hunger I'd never experienced.

Yet his hands remained chaste on my hips, and he made no move to pull me closer. Rather, his arms were now steel rods, keeping me at a distance.

What the hell was going on? Two minutes ago, he'd been undressing me with his eyes. Now he was suddenly distant and stern, his jaw squared, lips pressed together in an angry, firm line. He wasn't even pretending to move with the beat.

The music changed, blaring something techno, and the lights flashed in discordant strobes. I stood on tiptoes to yell, "I'm cool if you want to sit this out, wait for them to queue up the good stuff."

Nate seemed to snap out of his mood, relief softening the hard set of his face. "Sure. Can't say this is really doing it for me."

My stomach lurched. Did he mean me, or the music? Frantically I replayed each word I'd said, every minute move I'd made. How had there even been time for him to change his mind?

Nate jerked his chin across the room. "I, uh, actually, I might grab a real drink. I'll get you water?"

I shook my head. The butterflies sank to the bottom of

my stomach like they'd been sprayed with DDT. "Mai Tai." Forget the no alcohol—clear head deal. Maybe I wouldn't want to remember tonight, after all. And we needed to drown the sudden awkwardness that iced the space between us.

As Nate headed toward the bar, a guy whose toga bore an unmistakable resemblance to its original incarnation as a bedsheet closed in on me. Unlike Nate, he didn't leave any air between his hot, sweaty body and my chilled one, grinding his hips against my thigh. His thrusting groin lifted the hem of my toga, and I clutched at the fabric, staggering backward, barely able to move against the press of bodies.

Bed Sheet leered at me, licking thick lips. "Hey babe, I wanna do some Roman with you." More octopus than human, his hands slid up my thighs faster than I could slap them off. "Roman-roamin, get it?" He labored the joke, his hands working overtime to make his intention completely clear.

I turned away, searching for a gap in the crowd, and he shimmied up against my back like I'd wiggled my ass in invitation.

Shit. I had no idea how to handle him. I most definitely didn't want to *handle* him. When I was with Suzee, all attention was on her. And this kind of thing never happened when I went out with Damien. Of course, sitting safely in the familiarity of the Lady Boyz audience was nothing like being thrust into the center of this party, where inhibitions had apparently been thrown overboard, the revelers growing more Bacchanalian by the second. Or by the sip. My throat closed as the press of bodies obscured my view of Nate's disappearing back. I spotted a safe space between two women and dived into it.

Not so safe. My breath snagged as one woman groped

my butt. The other slid her hand up the side of my face and pressed a wet, open-mouthed kiss full on my lips.

I made another lunge deeper into the crowd, trying to put space between me and Octoman and simultaneously limit body contact with anyone else. Seemed that I was the only person intent on doing so; short dresses were riding higher by the second, and more than one boob peeked from a barely-there toga. I'd seen this kind of stuff on my laptop, but being in the midst of it, surrounded by the sexual hunger, the air thick with pheromones and lust, had a totally different vibe than being a voyeur.

Dangerous, yet I had to admit, kind of exciting. And the fact that it excited me increased the risk factor; physiological arousal obfuscated critical decision making. I had to remember my purpose here, my boundaries and parameters.

I crossed my arms over my chest, scanning desperately for Nate.

No Nate, but my eyes lit on Travis, only a few meters away, an island in the surge of bodies. He raised an arm and hollered across the crowd. "Hey, Lissa. Come prop up the bar with me."

Screw the limited-contact plan. Elbows stuck out like chicken wings, I forced my way across to him. "Hey, Travis, how's it going?"

He looked at me blearily, grinning hugely. "This party is sick, huh? I ended up signing on for the unlimited drinks package." His face fell and he tapped a finger against his lips. "But that might not have been my best idea."

I tucked myself in next to him as a couple of guys crowded me from behind. The unaccustomed shortness of the toga left me feeling exposed, and I twitched at the hem.

It'd be easy to get knocked up in here without even noticing. "Self-inflicted pain? No sympathy "

"I'll remember that." Travis's gaze followed the movement of my hands and stalled on my short hem for a long moment. He shook his head slowly, as though it cost him great effort. "Nope, actually, I probably won't. Drink?"

"Nate's grabbing them. Thanks."

"Nate? Yeah, I saw him before." He shoved his glass onto the bar, almost missing the edge. "How come you're with him?" His tone came across petulant. Great, was he an obnoxious drunk? That had been yet another of Damien's less-than-stellar qualities.

"Uh. Well, we met here." Why did I feel guilty? Because Travis sounded angry? No, wait...he sounded *jealous*.

I had to hide my grin of delight. That was nothing short of freaking awesome. My ego needed the boost after Nate had pretty much fended me off on the dance floor. And he'd been lost a long time in the sea of female flesh and flashing breasts while supposedly hunting down our drinks.

A plastic cup appeared on the counter at my elbow. "Thought I'd lost you." Nate's deep voice trickled like treacle down my spine, instantly soothing my flare of neglect. Not that I had any right to feel anything other than horny. Boundaries.

Travis swapped his scowl from me to Nate. "She's with me, bro. You gotta go get yourself a hookup sorted, you're letting down the team."

I tensed. I wasn't *with* either of them, even though I instinctively willowed toward Nate. I *was* the hookup. Nothing more. That was my plan, Nate's invitation to the party wasn't like a real date. It was precisely what I wanted. We'd been thrown together by circumstance and the close confines of the ship—or maybe by a very bored deity, finding amusement in my see-sawing emotions and insecurity. But, whatever, this fling had rules.

"Trav...Trav!" The high-pitched voice caught both Nate and my attention, though Travis seemed deaf.

Nate lifted his chin toward a group of women making a giggling advance on the bar. "Seems like you've been spreading yourself around enough to cover for us both, bro."

Travis glanced over his shoulder at the girls, and then swiveled back, winking at Nate. "*Dude*. Two each."

Nate's hand closed over mine, where I still clutched at the hem of my toga. His knuckles brushed my thigh. "Later. I need some fresh air. Clear my head."

"Lissa's got no sympathy for alcohol-induced misery, bro," Travis intoned mournfully. "She's a hard woman."

Nate's thumb rubbed across the back of my hand, his words pitched low for only me to hear. "I'd say maybe she needs a hard man, then."

13

I snatched my hand back. What was with Nate's hot and cold routine? Did he think it turned women on? In which case, *shit,* was I that fallible, despite my supposed-smarts? Did a double degree count for nothing? Because I was sure as heck turned on.

But that had more to do with his toga than his attitude.

A sudden thought stopped me from drawing away from him; was it possible the contradictions in his behavior were because Nate was as conflicted about the boundaries as me? Because there was no point pretending otherwise; when Travis had suggested the guys split the incoming booby bounty, I'd been ready to scratch out the other women's eyes the second they honed in on Nate.

Like he was mine.

I pinched at the bridge of my nose, blowing out a tense breath. *No, no, no.* This was all wrong. I wasn't supposed to feel a damn thing except for horny.

"You okay, Freckles?"

I was being ridiculous. No matter how screwed up my head was—and I didn't even have alcohol to blame—Nate didn't have the same issue. Guys always got to make the call on relationship parameters. Whether they wanted it to be exclusive or a hookup, the choice was always theirs.

Unless, like Damien, they didn't grasp the concept of making a *choice*.

"Yeah, sure. You're right. Fresh air." Something had to clear my head.

"Grab your drink." Nate waited while I snatched up the foam cup. Then he tugged me toward a very unRoman mirror ball in the center of the room, where a couple of girls twerked hard enough to make me hope there was a chiropractor aboard.

"I decided to stick with water," Nate said. "Hope that's okay. Clear heads, no regrets." He glanced back toward the bar. "I'm pretty sure Trav's not going to remember anything by tomorrow."

Regrets? Did he plan on doing something we could regret? I sure hoped so because, despite my lack of experience, that sounded like fling-speak to me. At least one of us had an eye on the boundaries.

The noise of the crowd swelled as the music changed, and I squinted up at him. "Sorry, what?"

His chest swelled as he took a deep breath and pitched above the music. "I think we have to dance at least once. Tick it off the vacation bucket list."

Vacation list? For a traumatized second, I thought he knew about *The Vagina's Vacation* file, supposedly safe on my hard drive.

But then his arm slipped around my waist, pulling me in close, and I yelped, jerking aside my cup of water to avoid pouring it down his chest. And to keep my arm out of the way because, my nipples pressed hard against his abs, I didn't want anything between us. Not even the thin cotton of our togas.

Which wouldn't be an issue for long, as any moment now the fabric would self-combust.

Nate grinned, then pressed his lips to my ear. "It's okay, I don't mind if you get me all wet."

I so wasn't the one making anyone wet.

He tossed his drink back, nodded for me to do the same, and then took my cup, lobbing them both in the direction of an overflowing bin. "Better. I want two hands for this."

Those two hands sat on my waist, then slid down to my hips, tugging me against him.

The music changed from the thumping bass of dubstep to *Just Give Me A Reason,* and I swayed with the beat.

Entirely not my fault that rhythm insisted on pressing my groin to Nate's.

He didn't pull away. "Pink fan?"

"Diehard. She's one awesome woman." Kickass, like I so desperately wanted to be. "But I particularly love this song."

Nate's fingers splayed wider, shifting to rest on my butt cheeks. "Some things are hard not to like."

My pulse pounding, I leaned into him, closing my eyes to lose myself in the music. We weren't really dancing, but moving slowly together, the heat of Nate's body flooding through mine, his biceps crushing my shoulders. He smelled so good, and I felt safe, dwarfed by his presence, with his arms wrapped around me.

Safe. What the hell was I thinking? *Safe* wasn't what I'd find here, wasn't even what I wanted to find. I needed a disposable lover. I was allowing my brain to get far too involved. It was time to step things up a bit, tick some of those boxes before I reported to Suzee.

Taking a deep breath, I steeled myself, then angled my hip into Nate's groin, slowly increasing the pressure.

Nate jerked back, but I'd already felt his surge of interest. Heck, more like a tidal wave, than a surge. He could play hot-cold all he liked, but physical evidence couldn't be faked or denied.

My face hidden against his chest, I ground into him, making it clear I'd noticed his erection.

Not that I could miss it.

His length pulsed through our skimpy clothes, probing the softness of my belly. I'd not felt anything like it since... ever. With my knees about to give, in a second it wouldn't be my stomach he butted at.

And that'd be totally fine, too.

God, I wanted him so bad, with such a desperate, carnal craving. Now. I no longer had any doubts, just hot, urgent need.

Nate was the perfect holiday fuck.

As the song ended, his hand wound into the back of my hair, holding me still so he could speak close to my ear. "Now I *really* need to go outside. Do me a favor? Walk very close in front of me. It seems that Romans may have had steel-plated underwear. Or perhaps their maidens weren't hellishly sexy."

Walk in front of him? I could barely stand. But, lost in the heat of the moment, I had forgotten we were on a crowded dance floor. It seemed a little privacy could be an excellent idea.

Nate wrapped an arm around my waist, holding me close in front of him, like a shield. Lucky he was tall, so his erection rode in the small of my back rather than between my legs, or walking would've been impossible. Not that I was doing a great job of it anyway, moving like a drunken sailor as I rolled my hips to counteract the lust-filled swell of my labia.

I glanced at the floor, kind of surprised to find I wasn't *literally* dripping with desire.

It took forever to navigate the dance floor and, even if enough blood flowed back into my brain for me to find the way to my cabin, it was too darn far. I needed release. Now.

The cooler air as we stepped outside the noisy bar did nothing to quench my desire. Or dry my overly damp bits. Unsteadily, I led the way to the bow rail of the ship, Nate's penis pressed into my back like a pistol. Or a cannon.

A salt-laden breeze toyed with the skirt of my toga, the velvet dark wrapping me in a soft embrace. Face tipped up to the star-frosted sky, I tried to pick out familiar constellations, calm my fevered mind with science. But I couldn't focus my mind, couldn't think beyond the urgent need to get to my room or his room. God, even a lifeboat, whatever lay closest.

Still caged within his arms, I turned to face Nate, the steel railing against my back less hard than he'd been. The maneuver brought our faces close.

Nate stared down at me, his jaw tense, forehead furrowed. He dropped his hands from my waist and took a half step back. "Lissa, this isn't a good idea."

Oh, no, not a repeat of last night, when he'd kissed and run. What was his problem? Was he scared I'd angle for more than a one-night stand, try to trap him into a relationship? Given my truth, that would be kind of hilarious, if only it wasn't so frustrating. Surely he was smart enough to realize that the five thousand miles between our respective homes made me a safe bet?

And, more importantly, he'd be a safe bet. I should assure him that, on the list of things I most desired in my life, a relationship fell somewhere below un-anesthetized root canal surgery. "But why—" I glanced down as I spoke, and my gaze caught the tented front of Nate's toga. I smacked a hand over my mouth to stifle a slightly hysterical giggle.

He scowled and I panicked. Grabbed at him. My left breast, sans over-the-shoulder-boulder-holders, swung against his arm.

He sucked in a breath, audible over the rhythmic wash of the waves breaking on the hull, and his eyes narrowed. He seized my waist, pulling me hard against him, his rigid penis jabbing unrelentingly into my stomach. "Seriously? Can't say I've ever had a woman laugh at it before."

My hair billowed in the breeze, and I brushed it back behind my ear, willing my voice not to tremble. "Not funny. Actually, hot as hell." So much for not trembling. But I'd never had a guy have such an obvious response to me before. At least, not a positive one.

His hands moving up to grip my upper arms, a muscle in Nate's jaw worked. He took a deep breath. "Lissa, we have to talk."

Nothing good ever came after those words. And, in any case, conversational skills were the last thing I needed him for. I placed my finger over his lips. "I don't want to hear."

"But I need to tell you—"

"Stop. Really." He was the perfect vacation fling. No talking, no sharing, no bonding. No risk. "Unless you're warning me that you're with someone else, I don't want to hear what you have to say."

"No, that's not it—"

"Excellent." I dropped my hand, trailing my fingers over the bulge of his thigh muscle, teasing the hem of his toga.

Desire flared in his eyes and his reply was more caveman

than distinct words, a grunt as though he'd given up a fight. "Ah, hell." His hand worked into the back of my hair, tugging me close as his firm lips sought mine. But he wasted no time on the sweet kiss of the previous night. His tongue flickered, urgently demanding, across the closed seam of my mouth.

As I parted my lips, darting my tongue out to meet his, he groaned; hot, wet, and hungry, like he couldn't bear to move away.

His free hand wrapped my waist, supporting me as his knee angled between my naked thighs. I snaked my hands around the strong column of his neck, grinding myself against the hard ridge his leg offered. Shit, I was humping his leg. But I couldn't stop, the throbbing heat inside me building like a volcano working up to an eruption.

Nate's hand slipped from my head, gently encircling my throat, his thumb caressing my neck as he drove me back against the rail, his tongue chasing and tasting and tangling like he'd devour me.

I moaned as he palmed my breast. His fingers unerringly found my engorged nipple, rolling it through the thin fabric. The sensation shot straight to my groin, and the words shuddered from me. "Oh, fuck."

Nate drew back. His chest heaved raggedly, but he didn't release my nipple, teasing and pinching, his eyes intent on mine. "Is that a request?"

Yes. I wanted my clothes off, wanted the roughness of his hands against my naked flesh.

Nate waited, as though he needed my permission. When I didn't answer—couldn't answer—he pressed his lips to my throat, kissing across to the trembling pulse in my neck, then trailed his tongue up to my ear, nibbling on the lobe and murmuring something.

The blood pounding in my head, I couldn't distinguish his words. Couldn't coherently respond, in any case. I could only instinctively react to his touch, his heat. To the awareness that, unbelievably, someone wanted me as badly as I wanted him.

Nate shifted his leg from between mine, and I gasped, cold and bereft. Swayed my hips toward him, desperately seeking the friction.

His hand slid down my thigh, finding the hem of my toga and inching it up. "Lissa, do you want this?"

Yes! I blew out short, sharp breaths, trying to control the wanting, the need that welled up within me.

"Yes?" His fingers stroked across the flimsy fabric of my underwear, the slight friction sparking electric currents of desire through me.

I nodded frantically. Yes, whatever he was offering, yes!

The heel of his hand pressed firmly against my pulsing mound, but he shook his head. Moved his mouth back to mine, his tongue flickering, seeking and retreating. "You have to say it, Lissa. You have to say you want it." He stroked at my underwear again, tracing the cleft between my swollen lips.

I lifted my heel onto the rail, spreading my thighs wider, the toga bunching around my hips. "Yes," I moaned into his mouth. "Oh, yes."

His fingers instantly slipped past the fabric, gliding down my slit, and his breath expelled in a rush. "Oh, man. Brazilian? You've got to be kidding me."

Suzee's bon voyage gift evidently met with Nate's approval.

His breath panted against my neck, as though he fought for self-control as his fingertips slid up and down, and I undulated toward him desperately. "More?" he said, his green eyes glittering in the muted lighting.

I nodded, and he pressed me against the rail, kissing me deeply. His finger stroked, one more long, slow movement— then slid deep into my wetness.

"Oh, fuck..." Though I swore like a trooper in my head, I'd never uttered the word before tonight. Now it seemed the only thing I could come out with. That, and moaning as Nate slipped another finger inside me, hooking them forward to find my G-spot. He pulled back a little, watching my face as his thumb searched my folds, discovering my clit. Not that it'd be hard to locate, I was about to explode.

Suddenly, he withdrew his hand. Lifted his fingers to his mouth and licked at them. Tasting me. His eyes narrowed, and he grunted in surprise. "Fuck. You taste amazing." He snaked his hand down again, teasing at my clit, tiny flicking motions that instantly had me on the edge. "Like this? Or deeper? Tell me what you like, Lissa."

How the hell would I know? *Everything.* I liked everything he was doing. I whimpered, pumping against his hand. I needed to come. But I couldn't. Not in front of him. I had to get back to my room. Yet I couldn't leave this, it felt so damn good.

Nate brought his fingers to his mouth again, sucking hungrily, his breath a sharp exhalation of lust. "Do you have any idea how good you taste?"

I shook my head, frantic to have his fingers sliding up and down my slit again.

Lips pressed against my ear, he growled "No, I mean it. Do you *know* how good you taste?"

"No," I whispered, my voice cracking.

"No?" The crease in his cheek deepened, and he slid two fingers into me again, stroking until I shuddered, then brought them to his mouth. Eyes locked to mine, he sucked on one glistening finger. Then pressed the other to my lips.

They parted without my permission. My tongue swirled around his finger, drinking in my own musk.

"Oh, yeah," he groaned. "Oh fuck, yeah." Never breaking eye contact, he pulled his finger from my mouth and sucked on it. Licked at his lips, and then slid his hand back between my legs. His middle finger found my clit and he rubbed the hard nub with quick circular motions. Left hand cradling the back of my head, he pulled me close and thrust his tongue in my mouth, chasing the last trace of my juice.

The action brought me to the edge, and his plunging fingers sent me over. I exploded into a knee-trembling orgasm, bucking and shivering against his hand.

Nate slowed his fingers as I moaned. His iron-hard cock probed my stomach, and he moved his hand back to his mouth, tasting me again. He shook his head as I tried to hide my face against his chest, embarrassment suddenly flooding me. "Oh, no you don't, Lissa. I'm so not done with you. I need more of that." He slid his fingers back into my slick wetness, grinning wickedly as I trembled and shuddered with over-sensitivity.

Yet I dug my nails into his hard biceps, arching my hips toward his touch.

"You want more, too, huh?" he murmured.

"Bro, where you get to?"

Nate's eyes widened at Travis's bellow. "Shit!"

Whipping his fingers out of me, he squared his shoulders, shielding me from view as I tugged at my clothes, trying to steady my breathing.

My surrounds suddenly came into sharp focus. Public surrounds. Holy shit, I'd not only orgasmed in front of a man, but in public.

Nate's own chest heaved as he flashed me an almost-embarrassed grin. "That made for one hell of a cold shower."

Travis huffed toward us across the pitching deck. "Bro, you hurling or something?" He reached the rail, clutching it as though he'd fall. Clearly, the unlimited-drinks ticket had won. He staggered, grabbing at Nate's shoulder as a wave plunged the ship into a trough, then his eyes focused on me, recognition slowly dawning. He groaned in disgust. "Jesus. C'mon, Nate. The party's inside. You said you weren't going *there*." He jerked his chin at me. "She's a waste of time, said so yourself."

I froze, staring from one man to the other. Words of denial tried to form on my lips, but my heart clenched. Because I'd been here before, I knew what it was to be deemed worthless unless my income was factored into the equation.

Nate whirled to face his drunken friend. "That's not what I said."

"Yes, it is," Travis sing-songed, hanging over the bow rail to watch the foaming wake. "Thass exactly what you said. Right after I said she'd be up for it no matter what."

"That's not how I meant it," Nate ground between his teeth. His hand snaked toward me. "You've got to know, that's not what I meant."

My knees found their usual position. Locked together. Cold anger seethed where seconds ago I'd been warm and liquid. I'd been so stupid, thinking I could simply hook up with a guy, have a bit of fun. Nate had proved me right; men were bastards. If I'd been prepared to tolerate sly insults, Damien had been more than happy to continue our relationship. Which meant I'd been right all along; better the devil I knew.

I sidestepped Nate's grasp. "It's fine. I got *exactly* what I wanted." A predator couldn't be humiliated.

"Lissa—"

"Night, Travis. Hope you pick up. Goodbye, Nate." I ignored his outstretched hand and picked my way across the lurching deck. My head held high, my tread firm.

Meltdown could come later.

14

The day couldn't get any worse. Only a few hours till Mom and Mitch boarded, presumably accompanied by the evil step-sibs, and I looked like crap. Or how crap would look on a bad day, after crying all night instead of sleeping.

I threw my bag across the chair and took the aisle seat on the coach, so Nate couldn't sit alongside me. Just in case he boarded. Which he obviously wouldn't.

He'd had what he wanted.

Well, maybe not so much. I'd had what I wanted.

But nowhere near enough of it. Even though I was furious with him, my body quickened at the memory of his firm, assured touch.

Well, of course it was assured. No doubt he did this kind of thing all the time. *Bastard.*

The fact that I'd been more than willing to have sex with him didn't lessen my anger. Travis's slip made it clear that Nate not only didn't respect me but didn't even like me. Yet he'd generously decided, against his better judgment, to *go there*, after all. A pity fuck. Not the empowerment I sought.

"Where's your lover, hon?" Tex's less-than-soft query stilled the entire coach, breathless anticipation echoing in the hollow tomb.

I dropped my chin to my chest. Maybe I could disappear, like a self-consuming black hole. "He's not my—" Well, technically, he sort-of had been. And another tick off my spreadsheet. "He's not coming. We—"

"Here he is," Tex boomed approvingly. "Morning, gorgeous. I was worried there was trouble in paradise for a moment there, but I see you're both looking tired. When you're young, that's always a good sign, huh?" She stopped short of verbalizing the *nudge, nudge, wink, wink* bit.

Tex was right. Nate did look tired. More than that, he looked bloody miserable.

Good.

He paused alongside me, the column of his throat working, as though he searched for words. Finally, he gestured at the empty window seat. "May I?"

His voice cracked.

What the hell did that mean?

Regardless, he sure wasn't getting the seat with a view. It wasn't like I wanted to look anywhere but outside. I dragged myself across the seat, slamming down the armrest to create a barrier.

Silence crackled between us like dangerous static electricity waiting to spark a fire.

The coach pulled out to the driver's cheerful "Aloooooooha." Neither of us joined in the enthusiastically chorused response.

My gaze fixed to the window as the coach tunneled through narrow roads in the lush, tropical rainforest, I refused to focus on Nate's reflection in the glass. Or notice his arm brush mine. Or smell the spice of his cologne. Or feel the tension radiating from his balled fist on the armrest. What was he even doing here?

"Lissa." His voice low, my body quivered in instant response. "I'm sorry. You didn't deserve to be treated like that."

Deserve? Since when did what I *deserved* factor into my love life? I stoically continued facing the window.

The chair shifted as he leaned closer. "Lissa, I don't even know where to start explaining. There are things I should have said, things I should have told you. But now, all I can do is search for the words to make it right."

"To make *what* right?" I snarled, rounding on him, waving a hand between my chest and his. "There's nothing here. Nothing to make right."

"But I want there to be."

His simple words shook my foundation. Tears of confusion sprang to my eyes. Dammit, no, I didn't want anything between us. Not like that.

Except, except... *No!* Except nothing. I'd made my decision. Relationships led to pain, and Nate had already proved he was Potential Bastard Number Two. "Not happening," I told the window.

"Travis was off his face and being a dick. If it's any consolation, he's feeling pretty sorry for himself today." Nate folded the armrest up cautiously, watching to see if I'd slam it down again.

I didn't, because I wanted him closer. I wanted him to be able to come up with a reasonable explanation for what he'd said. Even though I knew it was impossible.

"Lissa, there's stuff we need to talk about."

I shook my head adamantly, watching his reflection. "No. No talking." I knew that lead-in. It had always ended with

Damien enumerating my shortcomings. I didn't need to hear that from Nate.

His roughened palm covered my hand where it lay clenched on my knee. "I want to straighten this out. We can't leave it like this."

I tugged my fist away. "Really? Then why didn't you come after me, last night?" Why was I even asking? I hadn't wanted him to follow me. Had I?

He blew out a short breath. "I couldn't. Travis was there..." His voice trailed off as I whirled to face him incredulously.

"Travis? You've got to be kidding me. You didn't want Travis to *know* we were getting it on, but you're here, now? Snuck out, did you?" Tex stirred in the seat behind us, and, though my voice was a furious whisper, I dropped it even lower. "You've got to know how piss-weak that sounds."

The muscle in the side of Nate's jaw jumped, and he grunted as though I'd struck him. "Jesus, it's not like that. I'm trying to explain, Lissa. Give me a damn chance." The side of his fist smacked the seat in front, but he ignored the startled expression of the occupant who jerked to face us. "Travis talks shit when he's wrecked. You had to know that I was totally into you last night. And the night before. Why can't you trust me on that?"

"Because you're all the same," I ripped back at him. The proof of what I'd long suspected caused a sharp pain, and I bunched my knuckles against my chest.

Nate stiffened, his tone harsh. "You'd shove me in the same category as that two-timing bastard ex of yours? Not even give me the chance to explain?"

Shit. I'd hoped Tex's blurted revelation yesterday had slipped by him. But maybe he did have a point. I prided myself on my analytical mind, yet did I verge on irrational in assuming all men shared Damien's traits? Was it possible I'd given Travis's drunken word-vomit greater weight than it deserved? Though his words had stung, it wasn't like I hadn't previously totally and humiliatingly misconstrued what he said.

I chewed at my lip, trying to remember the precise phrases he'd used, not allow my analysis to be clouded by inference and interpretation.

I'd planned to use Nate, so was it reasonable to be angry with him?

I blew out a long breath and scowled at the passenger in front of us until he turned back to the view from his window.

I'd given Damien seven years' worth of second chances; surely, I could give Nate a couple of days?

Take what I wanted. And then run away.

I uncurled the fist bunched on my knee and swallowed hard, making sure my voice wouldn't quaver. "You're right. There's nothing to sort out. No blame, no shame, in a holiday fling. Isn't that the way it works?"

Electricity arced through me as Nate tentatively threaded his fingers through mine, his callused thumb rubbing along my index finger. "But what if it's—?"

If I was going to make this work, Nate had to shut up. I leaned quickly across the space between us, my lips seeking his.

His fingers wound into the back of my hair, his mouth hungry on mine even as he tried to protest. "We have to talk."

No. I plunged my tongue into his mouth, stealing the warm coffee taste. Slid a hand up his thigh. The muscle tensed beneath my touch, and I thrilled at the realization of my new power; *he'd* begged me to come back.

I kissed him with everything I had, every subverted desire, every subjugated longing. He met my embrace, raised it a level higher with his fingers trailing my naked arms and legs, his tongue teasing and tasting and tangling.

I kissed him until my neck ached and my pounding heart hurt.

Eventually, gasping for breath, I pulled back. Hampered by the angle of the seats, I'd rested one hand on Nate's chest. Now I lay my head against it, pleased by the hammering of his heart. I pretended not to notice as he pressed tiny kisses against my hair, unbelievably sweet.

Shit. Did sweet even belong in *The Vagina's Vacation?* Doubtful.

My finger circling his nipple, I pinched him, bringing his focus back to the matter at hand. Or, judging by the swell in his tight cargo pants, the matter I'd like to have in hand.

Nate shifted his long legs and moved restlessly in the seat. I grinned. He wasn't intent on being all gingerbread sweet, then.

And I wasn't the only one aroused by our kisses.

"So, Iao Needle, right?" As we disembarked the bus, Nate squinted up through the misty drizzle at the towering monolith.

"I'm impressed by your knowledge."

"I'm more impressed—or maybe kind of intimidated—by the phallic stone of Kanaloa." He grinned at my expression. "Seriously. I read up on this one. Kanaloa, the god of the ocean. Apparently, you need to look from the base to get the full, ah, effect, though."

I shook my head, tapping a forefinger on the pamphlet the tour operator had provided. "No time to look from the base. We only have thirty minutes to sprint to the top of the lookout. One hundred steps. I'll race you."

As I made to follow the trail of tourists headed to the placarded starting point, Nate took my hand, holding me back. "Do you really want to go and stand in the crowd?"

"No choice. There's only one trail up."

He indicated the thick forest pressing in against us on every side, the car park the only cleared space. "There's about four thousand acres of jungle out here. I reckon maybe we could discover something pretty awesome off the beaten track."

My heart lurched in a manner that couldn't be healthy. "We're supposed to stick to the trails."

"I like breaking the rules." Walking backward, he coaxed me toward the banyan trees fringing the car park.

I didn't resist.

He glanced over my head, toward the coach. "No one's looking. Quick." Lunging into a narrow opening between the trees, he drew me along a barely visible trail bordered by dripping foliage.

After only a few meters he turned and tugged me against him like he couldn't wait any longer. His hands on either side of my face, his lips explored me, each lash of his tongue tantalizing and erotic, filled with tease and promise, as though we'd not spent a torrid twenty minutes making out on the bus.

God, I couldn't get enough of the taste of him, coffee, cinnamon, and hot, hard man. Kisses with Damien had been chaste, courteous necessities of greeting and farewell, the last couple of years merely a brush of air near my cheek. This...this was...primitive. I wanted to devour him.

We broke apart, and he shook his head, his chest heaving. "You had me worried I'd never get to do that again." His fingers threaded through mine, he turned to guide me deeper into the forest. "I should be able to make it a little farther, now."

My skin shivered with ripples of unbearable anticipation, though Nate had yet to slip so much as a finger beneath my clothing. But perhaps that wasn't what he planned? Though he'd led us from the main tourist route, the fact that a faint trail ran underfoot meant there remained a danger of others coming this way. Maybe Nate intended to play it safe, and we'd only make out?

That wasn't good enough. Though I could just about get off on his kisses, with only two nights of the cruise remaining I *needed* more. I needed the roughness of his hands on my naked skin, the strength of his body pressed against the hunger of my own. I wanted to explore everything last night's interruption had denied me. And, more than anything, I longed for him to explore me.

I wanted to be with a man who *wanted* me.

With each step deeper into the wild, tangled jungle my desire ramped up, an exquisite, aching, throbbing torment. Probably made worse by me focusing only on his tight backside. I didn't know where Nate was leading me, only that it was away. Away from the coach, away from the other tourists, away from the beaten path.

And, possibly, away from my careful plan.

The forest held only silence, our footsteps muted by the dense leaf cover on the damp ground, the warm, rich smell of rotting vegetation filling my nostrils. Trees bordered the path and stretched to entwine their branches overhead, creating a green tunnel for us to follow.

Partly hidden beneath the canopy, a boulder, three meters across and almost twice as tall as me, stood sentinel on the side of the track.

Nate drew me closer then settled his hands on the curve of my hips. Gently guided me backward, until I leaned against the moss-covered rock. He glanced around as if to make certain we were alone. "I'm hungry."

"Oh." I blinked in surprise, kind of annoyed he'd think of food right now. I mean, I loved the stuff, but priorities... I lifted a hand to point back down the path, toward the coach. "I pilfered fruit from the breakfast buffet. It's in my back-pack, but I left it on the bus."

Despite the thousand different shades of green in our woodland grotto, none matched the continually changing color of Nate's eyes. He shook his head, a smile playing around the corner of his mouth. "You're very literal, aren't you? That's not the kind of hunger I meant. In fact, it's worse than hunger. I'm ravenous. I tasted something so good, I can't get it out of my mind. I need more. Now."

"Oh." God, I hoped he wasn't into me for scintillating conversation.

He released my hips and shifted his hands to place his palms either side of my head, flat against the boulder. Without touching me, he leaned in close, his lips only a whisper from mine. Sandalwood, spicy and fresh against the decay of the jungle, enveloped me. I inhaled deeply, imagining hidden undertones, some lurking danger.

Nate's lips touched mine, and even though it wasn't our first kiss, my heart almost stopped. That this man *wanted* me seemed surreal. My holiday fantasy.

His caress different this time, Nate's lips explored my face gently. Seeking, but not insistent, as though he mapped my features. Tiny presses and pulses on my cheeks, my eyelids, the tip of my nose. Then back to my lips.

He kissed me softly until I moaned with pleasure, desperate to have more of him. My hands slid from the small of his back up to his shoulders, trying to pull him closer, though he was as solid and unmovable as the rock behind me.

He teased my lips with the tip of his tongue, grinning devilishly and shifting away a fraction when I tried to chase his mouth. Then he swooped back in, grasping my pouted lower lip between his teeth.

His shirt bunched in my fists as I tried to capture him. Hold him. Keep him. The way he kissed was everything. Promise, tease, and temptation. Maybe kissing *was* enough. For now.

He released my lip, kissing along my jaw, then down to the hollow of my throat. I arched back, offering the vulnerable flesh. It wasn't scientifically possible that the pressure of his lips on my skin could bring such intense pleasure. But, for once, I didn't give two test tubes about the science. Only the sensations mattered.

Nate captured my wrists, waiting until I managed to coordinate my muscles enough to relax my fingers and release his shirt, then pinned my hands against the moss-covered rock, above my head. "Do you trust me?"

Pinioned like a specimen, exposed and helpless, the words should have terrified me. Instead, they sent a thrill coursing down to my groin. I narrowed my eyes. "No." I'd never trust any man. "But I do want you."

He considered me for a long moment, then slowly pressed his lips to mine. Hands trapped, I writhed, trying to get closer, desperate to taste him. God, I knew what he could do with that tongue, and I needed him to do it again.

A chaste kiss only, and he withdrew, still holding my wrists. Smiled. Moved his attention to the side of my neck, tracing the leaping pulse with his tongue. His teeth found my earlobe, grazing the stud of my earring, then his tongue swooped around the rim of my ear. Flicked inside, his breath hot and wet.

Holding me captive, not touching anything but my hands and ear, his tongue teased in erotic rhythm. Tremors of delight quaked through my body. God, I'd come on the spot if he kept it up. My knees sagged involuntarily, and he tightened his grip on my wrists, the black ink of his tattooed sleeve glistening in the soft drizzle.

His mouth worked back to mine, his words a murmur. "So, you won't trust me, but you do want me?"

"Uh huh."

"We'll have to work on that."

No, we wouldn't. But I couldn't spare a thought for that right now. The blood pounded so hard in my head that it blanked out the rest of the world, making it seem that the small clearing we stood in encapsulated everything important in the entire universe.

Nate moved in to kiss me again, and I darted my tongue out, flickering it across his top lip, straining against his grip, arching to press myself against him.

He groaned, and I knew his control wasn't as perfect as he pretended. "Hell, Lissa." His tongue traced the seam of my lips, probed, then slipped into my mouth, urgent and searching.

Finally! I craned forward, giving every bit as good as I got, our tongues exploring and wrestling until we were forced to break apart, desperate for air.

Nate's eyes locked to mine. "I want you to *know* you've been kissed," he panted.

His words made complete sense. And I *knew*.

He released my wrists, stroking one hand down my cheek as he gradually pressed his body against mine. There was no mistaking the hard bulge in his pants, and I moaned, tilting my pelvis up to cushion him.

"Yes," he murmured, and I was unsure whether he asked or exulted. His hand followed the indent of my waist, traced the outline of my hips, glided across the fabric of my shorts, searching for the hem. Damn, why hadn't I gone with shorter shorts?

I shifted, trying to allow his questing fingers.

Laughter vibrated his chest, and he tugged the cotton. "I guess a toga would've looked kind of funny out here, but it would sure make for easier access."

Screw acting coy—not that I'd been doing so well in that department. But the new version of me had a mandate to get precisely what she needed, and that included a heck of a lot more skin-on-skin contact than was currently happening. I flipped the button on my shorts; I needed his fingers in me again.

Nate's hand slid into my shorts before I'd finished with the zip. Leaving my panties in place, he stroked the fabric along my cleft, teasing but never penetrating.

I shuddered, eyes flickering closed as I surrendered to the sensations. God, he made me feel so good. But I wanted more. I knew what he could do. What no other man had ever done.

And I didn't want it to be any other man.

The cold shock of the thought flicked my eyes open.

His gaze intent on me, Nate's absolute attention was so damn sexy. I angled my hips higher, moaning with frustration as his fingers continued to caress instead of plunging in to bring the release I needed.

Nate's breath came short, though his fingers never changed the smooth rhythm that had me soaking wet and pulsing with desire. "More?"

I jerked my head up and down.

He inched aside my underwear and stroked roughened fingers along my slick channel, increasing the pressure with each pass. "More?"

"Yes," I gasped, bucking my hips toward him.

He pressed his mouth to mine, his tongue thrusting as his fingers slid deep inside my swollen, slippery folds, and my self-control evaporated as my senses spun.

"More?" he asked again.

What more could there be? I was ready to come, and Nate's breath panted short and sharp as his fingers caressed me. His pupils huge with lust, his desire was as obvious as my own.

Yet, greedy for everything I'd never had, I managed to nod.

He hooked two fingers deep inside me, probing and pulsing, and I gasped in instant response, grinding down against the pressure. His mouth against my cheek, he murmured hoarsely "You know I need to taste you."

Good. The sight of his fingers in his mouth yesterday, after he'd finger fucked me, drove me wild. Now it would send me over the edge again, and I was more than ready to fall.

But Nate dropped to his knees in the leafy debris, and I instantly tensed. *God. No.* Not here, not now. It'd take me a hell of a lot more time to work up the courage to allow—never mind potentially enjoy—something I'd seen only in porn.

I should clamp my thighs together, and insist he back things off to a more appropriate level.

Appropriate? Who was I kidding? It wasn't like being fingered in the midst of a tropical paradise would feature in New Scientist magazine any time soon.

In any case, my body refused to respond to my rational dictate, operating purely on lust and longing, beyond my control.

As Nate eased my shorts and underwear to my ankles, my hands fluttered to hide my stomach. He cupped my naked buttocks in his warm palms. Guided me toward his mouth. Kissed the top of my mound, just once. His eyes glittered in the snatches of fractured light sneaking through the trees. "Lissa, do you want me to stop?"

15

I had to halt him. Protest, show a little decorum, practice some self-control. I was half-naked in a jungle —which was probably filled with all manner of leeches and creepy-crawlies—with a man on his knees between my thighs. It was a sure-fire way to pick up some kind of nasty tropical disease.

But Nate's breath caressed my swollen clit, and I shuddered in ecstasy.

Anyway, penicillin could fix just about everything, right?

He breathed on me again. "Do you want this?"

My hands shifted to his head to push him away, but instead, my fingers clawed into his short hair, pulling him closer, urging him on. "Yes! Yes, now, yes."

His tongue flicked against my clit, and my hips jerked violently, bucking against his mouth. He blew softly, the warmth brushing like velvet moth wings across the intimate folds of my exposed flesh. I moaned, trying to spread my legs farther apart, hampered by my clothes...which were, God, around my ankles.

"Lift your foot." Voice muffled, he tapped my shin.

I shifted my hands, flattening my palms on the rock behind my hips, seeking balance, grounding from the stone. Which, despite millennia in this place, had surely never witnessed anything like this. Nate drew my shorts and underwear over my left foot, and then hooked my calf over his shoulder. I glanced down, then, embarrassed by his intent scrutiny between my legs, darted my gaze back up to the leafy canopy.

His fingers traced my labia, gentle but commanding. He knew what he was doing. "You're so beautiful."

I trembled, trying to hold still as anticipation shredded me, every nerve ending raw and awake. I couldn't believe he was going to do this...that I was going to *allow* him to do this.

Nor could I fathom how desperately I wanted him to do it.

When the touch of his tongue came, it was so brief I thought it existed only in my fevered imagination. But there it was again, tracing my swollen lips. My breath caught in my throat, and my calf pressed more heavily into Nate's shoulder as my right leg almost gave way. Why did we never practice this pose in yoga?

Nate's voice rang with urgency. "Lissa, I need your permission. I want more. Tell me you want more."

I nodded, though he couldn't see me. "More."

He groaned, his fingers digging into my bottom as he buried his head between my thighs and plunged his tongue into my slit.

My reaction totally primal, I grabbed the back of his head, grinding against his mouth. His tongue darted in and out, the rough stubble of his chin layering exquisite sensation upon sensation. The orgasm seized me instantly, and I convulsed and shivered as I cried out, my eyes screwed shut and teeth clenched as waves of indescribable pleasure centered on the man kneeling between my thighs.

As the surges of ecstasy receded, leaving me snatching for breath, Nate slowed his movements. As I half-sobbed, half-moaned with the pleasure of absolute release, he pinched the smooth lips of my labia together and planted a kiss, like he sealed a deal. Then he stood, his chin glistening with my juices. "I can't believe you taste even better when you come. Though you've ruined salted caramel for me."

"What—? Why?" I gasped.

He grinned. "Because every time I taste it, I'll be instantly hard, thinking of you." Breath musky, his mouth covered mine as he toyed with my nipples. His erection pressed hard into the side of my stomach, his voice honey-thick with desire. "Do you always come like that?"

"I don't...I haven't..." What could I say that didn't make me sound totally pathetic? I tugged my shirt down, trying to hide my nakedness.

He stilled my hands, caressing my stomach with a callused palm. His eyes narrowed, clearly his processing go-to. "You haven't...what?"

I let my gaze slide past his. We should move before someone found us.

Or before I was found out, exposed as a fraud. Melissa, not Lissa.

Nate's finger and thumb captured my chin, tipping my head so he could watch my expression. "You mean you haven't had an orgasm before?"

I shrugged, looking over his shoulder, now wishing other tourists would materialize. "Of course I have. Just not...with someone. And I've never done...no one's ever..." Okay, there were no words for where I was trying to go. That tee printed with pictures of cats I didn't yet own was going to be a necessity in my near future. Then he'd get the message.

Nate's intaken breath was a hiss of surprise. "Fuck me. No one's ever gone down on you? Is that what you mean?"

Humiliation hardened my tone. "Yeah, well, it wasn't high on the list of things Damien liked to do. Apparently, my parts are all wrong." I couldn't resist the snide taunt. Bloody Damien. Not only had he stolen years, but he'd made me some kind of freak.

Nate ducked his head, forcing me to meet his gaze. "Oh, believe me, sweetheart, there's nothing wrong with your parts." His fingers slid along my swollen slit, and I mewled.

Like a kitten.

Shit. Those damn cats.

I pushed him away, my face burning. I had to remember he was only a holiday screw. I didn't owe him any explanations. I just needed him to stick around long enough to provide what I wanted. And, even though I was weak-kneed and panting, I knew I wanted more of him. "Turn around. I have to...I don't know...I can't go back like this."

He only turned part way, watching the path we'd come in on, but I could swear he was laughing.

One hand on the boulder, I kicked the panties from around my ankle up to my hand. Patted at the welling moisture between my legs. "Damn!" Stupid thong. Uncomfortable *and* useless.

Concern furrowing his brow, Nate swung around. "What's wrong?"

I scrunched the underwear in my hand. "Nothing."

His glance traveled to my fist, partly hidden behind my back. "Here, give them to me." I shook my head, but his hand remained outstretched, and I reluctantly relinquished the sodden scrap. His eyes widened. "Not enough, huh?" He shoved the panties into his pocket, and grasped the neck of his Vans tee, pulling it over his head. "Here, use this."

God. He was so perfect, he could have been airbrushed. His broad shoulders and sculpted chest tapered to a narrow waist. A deep V defined his hard, flat stomach, dragging my inspection lower.

My desire flared again.

Surely that shouldn't even be possible, the phenomenon existed only in the ridiculous realms of porn and male fantasies? I'd have to do more research. "No, I can't." I put a hand out to refuse the tee. Happened to rest my palm on his pecs, the nipple hard beneath the heel of my hand.

He pressed closer as my fingers explored the ridges of his abs, before sweeping across the plain of his stomach. "Sure, you can. Our fellow travelers will think I worked up a sweat climbing to the lookout, trying to match your athletic prowess. Ahh!"

My searching hand had trespassed inside the band of his low-slung cargos, sliding over the jut of his hip bone. I grinned. Boxers. Predictably American, according to my television viewing.

Eyes slit, Nate tipped his head back as I fumbled with the buttons, seeking the bulge that had tented his pants since we left the coach. Except I didn't need to search, because he was...huge. Even compared to the men of my vast experience—ninety-nine-point-nine percent of them on porn dotcoms—he was...well endowed.

Wriggling my hand through the fly of his tight boxers, I palmed his silky-hard shaft. He throbbed at my touch, and I leaned forward, my tongue teasing his erect nipples.

Nate groaned and thrust into my hand, his penis pulsing against my palm. His nostrils flared, jaw taut as his fingers wound into the back of my hair, jerking my head back so he could kiss me.

Gripping the rigid shaft, I slid my fingers to the head of his dick, my thumb gliding through the pre-cum, circling and pressing. "Oh, fuck." I could barely breathe, the words choking against Nate's mouth as his hard-on swelled in my hand. "Fuck, I'm going to come again."

His bare knee found my wet cleft, and I ground myself against the hard warmth, my stomach coiling tighter and tighter as I fisted his throbbing muscle. My breath came in short, sharp pants and my back arched. The tension built, writhing and churning and whirling within me, swooping with roller-coaster swiftness, then climbing up, up, up, before exploding into a shattering orgasm.

Nate's lips moved against mine. "Are you kidding me? Did you just get off on touching *me*?" He looked down as if checking for evidence.

And there it was, smoothed across the tanned skin of his leg, in all its shimmering glory. The flush mounted my cheeks, and I bit at my lip, releasing my death-grip on his flesh. God, what would he think?

"You're fucking awesome. I've never known a woman like you." Nate's fingers traced my hot, swollen folds. "And I'm really sorry to do this. I know you're sensitive right now, but I *need* one more taste." He plunged his fingers deep within me again, the heel of his hand pressed against my engorged clitoris, and I shuddered in exquisite agony, my muscles gripping him tighter than I'd have believed possible. He brought his fingers back to his mouth, sucking at them as though determined not to waste a drop.

If two orgasms were possible, mathematically, the potential had to be infinite. I was so far from done. "I want you inside me."

Nate's eyes narrowed, sudden confusion etching his face. He swayed toward me, the hard length of his cock pressed against my naked belly. "I want you. So bad, you wouldn't believe. But not yet. I have to—"

The coach horn sounded.

"Shit." Nate grabbed the back of my neck, kissing me hard, as though it was the last time. "Here, use my shirt."

I shook my head, pulling my own shirt back down. Located my shorts and tugged them on. Commando. Not comfortable. Definitely not hygienic. "I noticed a restroom in the car park. Uh, you probably need to pay a visit, too." I avoided looking at his leg, the edge of the fabric and the golden hairs darkened by my dampness.

"Or not." Nate took my hand, guiding me back toward the distant noise of the parking lot. "This may be my favorite vacation souvenir. We won't be able to do this in Kauai, tomorrow, though."

Disappointment cut through my post-coital lethargy. "Why not?"

Nate slowed to look at me "Kauai. Wettest place on Earth. This is only the second wettest, and I damn near drowned."

I winced. "Sorry."

He halted, pulling me into his arms. "Oh, hell, no. Don't misunderstand me. You're fucking amazing. I love how wet you get for me."

I didn't know how to accept the unfamiliarity of a compliment and tried to deflect instead. "My mom boards this afternoon. We have a mother-daughter pre-wedding dinner tonight, then the reaffirmation of vows thing tomorrow, anyway."

"Yeah, I know." His tone heavy, a shadow crossed Nate's face.

Obviously, I talked more than I realized. I didn't recall giving a day or time for the wedding circus.

And now, more than ever, I didn't want to attend. Not only was it an unwanted family gathering of an unwanted family, but it would steal precious hours I could have spent with Nate. We only had one day left.

16

I held still as Mom air-kissed near my cheek, and then
pushed me to arm's length, her lips tightened into a
cat's bum of disapproval. "Melissa, you've put on
weight, haven't you?"

I hid my sigh. There'd be no point interrupting this
particular train of thought, I may as well let Mom roll on
down the line with it. Pray for a derailing in the near future.

Mom got in her own long-suffering sigh. "We'll have to
hope the dress still fits. There is a tailoring service onboard,
isn't there? I don't know that there'll be enough in the seams
to let out, though. Elle's fits perfectly."

A whole ten seconds until the first mention of a step-sib.
Mom was evidently making an effort. "I go by Lissa, now,
Mom. Anyway, how have you been? Where's Mitch?"

"He's having a boys' night." Mom giggled girlishly as I
took my seat at the restaurant table, and I gritted my teeth.
"We'll have to stay away from the bars, it'd be bad luck to
run into him."

I forced a smile. Luckily, it worked well with my teeth

still clenched. "Maybe he should have had his show onshore. I doubt strippers are permitted aboard."

The bottom of the menu rapped the table sharply, one of Mom's '*Not amused*' signals. "I hardly think that's an issue. Anyway, we'll have a quiet night, just the two of us, and catch up, don't you think?"

My surprise hard to hide, I deliberately schooled my features. "Really, Mom? Just us?"

Mom fluttered her fingers, displaying sparkly polished nails. She probably wouldn't appreciate if I shared the toxicity rating of that particular combination of acrylic and aluminum. "Elle and I had our special time together already. A full spa day. Manis and pedis, a hot rock massage, and a facial. The poor girl needed a bit of mommy-makeover time, you know how it is? Well, I don't suppose you do. But Elle, Justin, and the baby won't board until tomorrow morning. Of course, it's very difficult for the poor darling to stay anywhere with Justin Jr. Babies require so much time and paraphernalia, don't they? Well, you wouldn't know, would you? Such a sweet baby, though." Mom signaled the waiter. "We're ready to order. What would you like to drink, Melissa?"

"Mai Tai, please." It was the first thing that popped into my head. Well, right after 'Kill me now' and 'I haven't even seen the menu yet'.

Mom pursed her lips. "That's a cocktail, isn't it? Do you realize how many empty calories there are in that?" She handed the menu to the waiter. "We'll have two glasses of chardonnay. And two chef's salads."

I'd originally planned to learn from my cab-ride mistake and hit the minibar before facing Mom, but on a wave of euphoria from my hardcore makeout session, I'd felt invincible. Briefly. But, even with Mom unintentionally trying to prick my bubble, the ecstasy still tingled through me, the mere thought of Nate enough to quicken my heartbeat.

"What are you smiling at?" Mom's sharp tone questioned my right to smile. Or perhaps it was just that the expression sat particularly alien on me. Not that Mom saw me often enough to know.

"Nothing. Just happy to see you, Mom. You know, making the most of every moment." And longing, every moment, to get back to Nate. Our time limited, there remained more to tick off Suzee's list.

Fingers tightening around the napkin, my forehead creased in thought. Nate had another week of leave, said he'd spend it in Honolulu, surfing and other manly-type stuff that instantly had me picturing him half naked. I sucked in an uneven breath, forcing my mind from the image.

Other than Tuesday, my week in Honolulu was wide open. There was no reason for the cruise to end my time with Nate; in Waikiki, he'd said he was open to us catching up after the ship docked. Sure, he'd played it cautious in case things didn't work out aboard, but today had proved him wrong.

The rules for holiday hookups were my own creation. Well, mine and Suzee's. In any case, I could...not break them, exactly, but maybe bend them a little. Nowhere in *The Vagina's Vacation* spreadsheet did it specify that said vagina required more than one lover, only that each of the goals Suzee listed should be checked off. And if Nate was prepared to assist my mission, I wouldn't need to waste time looking for another candidate.

Not that I had any interest in another lover.

No. That wasn't right. That mindset belonged to Melissa, insecure as always, afraid of a challenge. *Lissa* had plenty of interest in further conquests, that was half the point of the vacation. Conquer and crush. But right now, it simply made more sense to capitalize on what was already available.

And I was all about logic.

Over the course of dinner—no refills of wine—I heard more about Elle and the simply divine Justin Jr. than I'd have believed possible, given the kid's eight months of life. Fortunately, rabbit-food made for a quick meal.

Mom folded her napkin and placed it on her plate. "Now, let's see if we can get you into that dress."

It sounded like she expected to place a call to room service for a shoehorn and a tub of goose fat. I reflexively sucked in, hands pressed against the slight rounding of my belly.

The habitual gesture changed to a caress, memory stilling the anxiety Mom always invoked; Nate had kissed my stomach, his tongue exploring my navel. He'd run his hands over my curves, cupped my buttocks, and groaned with pleasure as he lapped between my thighs.

I missed him. Already.

He'd said that he and Trav had a quiet night planned—but how quiet could a night with Travis really be? The younger soldier had his unlimited drinks package to use, so they'd be sure to hit a bar or two—and Trav would no doubt hit on a girl or two.

I frowned, trying not to think of Nate with other girls. An unfamiliar spear of jealousy plucked at my core.

It was a pointless, weak emotion. Nate had made it clear I had no reason for insecurity, yet I was allowing a fear that Travis would lead him astray to unsettle me. I guess it was because their friendship struck me as odd, given their distinctly different personalities. And Travis's drunken rant hadn't helped.

Knife and fork neatly aligned on my plate, I stood to leave the table. When I'd finished with Mom, I'd track Nate down. Corner him in a dark bar, somewhere. Head for one of the lifeboats. My stomach somersaulted at the thought. So much I wanted to do with him and, even with an extra week, so little time. Unless, Tuesday, if things went well...

"Melissa, are you listening?" Mom snapped her fingers and the waiter jerked to attention. Clearly, he'd already had a run in with her. I caught his eye and shook my head slightly, and he deflated with relief. At least one of us was off the hook.

Mom reached for her handbag, swinging from an enamel clasp on the edge of the table. God forbid her leather should touch the same patch of floor as a common vinyl bag. "We need to have an early night. Lots to do tomorrow. Come on, we'll go to my cabin and try on the dress, and I'll collect my bags."

Something was off about that sentence. More off than the rest of the dinner. "Collect your bags?"

Mom huffed. "I'm staying with you tonight, remember? I can hardly stay with Mitch the night before our wedding."

Remember? Pretty darn hard to remember something that came as a blindside. And, again, it wasn't exactly a wedding. More importantly, there went any chance of seeing Nate tonight. Unless I told Mom about him?

One glance at Mom's business-like expression squelched that idea. Still, the ceremony was scheduled for mid-afternoon tomorrow. Allowing time for the photos and 'light celebratory meal', I'd still have the night with Nate. A thrill tingled through me. *The night.* I knew exactly what I intended to do. Well, sort of. But I was pretty sure Nate could be relied on to come up with some good ideas.

Mom led the way through the maze of corridors, swiped her room key, and thrust open the door.

Spread across the bed in all its 1980's pink-marshmallow glory, lay *The Dress*. Taunting me.

I closed my eyes.

Opened them again.

Still there.

I approached the bed cautiously, as though the dress of my nightmares would rise up and try to smother me in a swirl of dry-cleaning fluid.

One finger extended, I poked the monstrosity. Twitched at the fabric.

Taffeta rustled, nylon lace crackled.

"Lucky I kept it, isn't it?" Mom practically beamed. "Go on, pop into the bathroom and put it on."

I couldn't argue. Not that I ever argued with Mom, anyway. But it wasn't my formal, my date, my anything. It was Mom's day.

Wrinkling my nose against the odor of mothballs—as though any insect would have wanted to come near it—I held the dress against me, smoothing the skirt down. Maybe it wouldn't fit. "I don't think I can even get this into the bathroom, Mom." Five layers of tulle underskirt enabled the dress to stand by itself. With a bit of luck, it'd waltz off.

Mom patted at her perfect hair. "Oh, yes, of course. I'll just pop out onto the balcony. Call me to zip it."

Predictably, the dress fit perfectly. I looked like a bag of Pascall's pink-and-white marshmallows. Well, like a white marshmallow being dog-piled by the pink ones, anyway. God, what if Nate saw me in it? "Mom?" Panicked, I called louder, "Mom?"

Warm air gusted in as Mom slid the door open. "Hush, Melissa, I could hear you on the balcony. Oh, isn't that just lovely? Aren't we lucky it still fits?" She twirled her finger, and I turned obediently, the wind-up ballerina on a music box.

Mom plucked at the skirts. Because they needed to sit just that little bit farther out.

"Mom, the reaffirmation's in a private venue, right?" One where there was no risk of Nate seeing me.

Mom looked appalled. "Absolutely. The ceremony will take place on the main staircase. I'm sure I told you this, Melissa. You really weren't paying attention, were you? Mitch's nephew, Todd, will play us in on the grand piano in the foyer." She pronounced it *'foy-air'* as though that lent exclusivity to the main entrance of a cruise ship.

The main entrance that everyone used, passed through, wandered around, took photos in. Shit. I stared at mom, dumbstruck. If Nate passed through the *foy-air*, I'd be displayed in all my confectionary glory.

Mom's hands continued the description. "Todd has composed a special piece for my entrance. Of course, we'll descend the first two floors in the glass lift, so even those at the back of the crowd will have a view." Her index finger twitched like an admonishing schoolmarm's. "I admit, it is a little tricky. I need to face the spectators, obviously, but then I'll have to turn to exit the lift. Still, I expect the audience will want to view my dress from every angle."

She spun, holding imaginary skirts in one hand, the other extended above her head. "It's obviously too late for this year's ceremony, but I really should speak with the captain. I don't think it unreasonable to expect a better design on a vessel this size, do you? Maybe they could install a rotating floor in the elevator, or have a hologram of confetti that shades the glass as the bride turns, so there are no awkward moments?"

Like the inexcusable non-turning lift floor, my brain had stuck. On the word *audience,* the three syllables inferring the embarrassing affair was a show to be benevolently shared with the undeserving masses. "But...private? On the staircase?"

Botox precluded Mom's eyebrows from rising. "Melissa, would you please *engage*? The ceremony is open for all to enjoy. Why would I be selfish about sharing such a joyous occasion? The reception, of course, will be a private affair."

God. Please let Nate be onshore, checking out the sights of Kauai. Getting wet without me. There had to be a way to prevent him from seeing me in this monstrosity. Slash and burn? Hook my heel in the skirt that hung to my calves, and rip it beyond repair?

Mom stroked the fabric I bunched in my fists. "I've always loved that dress."

I grimaced guiltily. Mom's day. I had to remember that.

The fabric creaked under Mom's caress. "But there's something not quite right. It doesn't sit well on you, does it? I don't know if it's the color or the cut, but it really doesn't do a thing for you."

Way to make me feel even worse about tomorrow.

Mom's immaculately manicured finger commanded attention. "I do have an idea."

Please let it involve scissors.

She crossed the three steps to the robe and threw it open. Reaching in, she removed a hanger covered by a garment bag. Held it toward me.

I eyed the bag dubiously. What fresh hell lurked within? I squinted at Mom, who regally lifted her chin toward the offering. "Go ahead, Melissa."

"Lissa," I corrected without any hope. The zip snagged as I drew it down and pulled the nylon aside to reveal an elegant trumpet-shaped dress in my favorite shade of deep rusted-red. The underdress fell from a wide, ruffle-edged V-neck to mid-thigh, and was overlaid with a floating layer of sheer, floor-length gauze in the same shade. "Mom..." I breathed.

Mom waved away my words. "Take it out. We still have to hope it fits. I did buy some Hollywood tape because you've always been busty. Of course, I didn't realize you'd allowed that matter to get quite so out of hand. That neckline is cut low, so we'll have to hope we can tuck all of you into it, won't we?" She clicked her tongue against her teeth, patting her own neat bosom. "You do realize, it would only have taken a simple phone call to let me know you'd put on weight? Elle's dress fits perfectly, of course, but the color isn't her at all. Still, she was more than willing to agree to it, when I explained how well it suits you."

"Mom, it's beautiful." Despite the couple of jabs at my figure, I couldn't hide my delight at the fact that Mom actually remembered my favorite color.

Lips pursed, Mom nodded at the dress. "It's a shame you've let your hair go, but at least this shade will bring out the highlights, make it appear less mousy. Really, Melissa, why didn't you think to mention you were in such a mess? Elle and I have appointments with the stylist in the morning, but I'd assumed you'd still have that lovely, neat bob. Why would you change it after all these years? It'll be so much work to get your hair back to blonde. Not that we'll be able to get you in for a color now, in any case. But we'll have to see if the poor man can tame that wild frizz." Mom lifted one of the ringlets that hung over my shoulder. "I assume the humidity and sea air make it look worse than usual? It can't possibly always be such a mane. Elle's very clever with hair. I'm sure she'll have some ideas."

I swallowed the inundation of negative messages without comment. Practice made me perfect, at this, at least. "It is a really lovely dress, Mom. I appreciate the thought."

"Well, I wanted something that would be special for you. Elle was very understanding about it. Of course, she already has a husband."

Yep, there it was, Mom's old one-two punch. Maybe I should just flat-out invite Nate tomorrow, prove to her that I was capable of getting a man. Not of keeping one, clearly, but at least of attracting one.

Except I wasn't crazy enough to allow my family anywhere near Nate. I could last twenty-four hours without him, then I'd spend every remaining minute with my holiday fling. My stomach dipped unpleasantly. The end of the vacation suddenly loomed horribly near.

Mum indicated a stack of suitcases. "We need to call a porter to move these to your room."

"It's okay, Mom. I've got them." I needed the distraction.

IN THE MORNING, Mom claimed the shower first, which suited me fine. I was happy to hide in bed for as long as possible, trying to put off the inevitable. I needed to find my Zen and dig deep to dredge up some goodwill toward the evil step-sibs.

Mom's constant prattling about Elle and the baby the previous evening hadn't helped, but at least she'd barely mentioned the boys. Maybe they'd moved farther afield, smart enough to stay out of the confidence-sucking toxic black hole of Mom's immediate environs.

I rolled over, looking out of the full-length balcony window at an almost indistinguishable horizon of blue ocean meeting blue sky, on another perfect Hawaiian day.

Perfect, because in a few hours, day would give way to the night. The night that belonged to Nate.

Mom emerged from the tiny bathroom looking like she'd already been to a beauty parlor. Having slavishly followed Damien's strictures and guidelines as to how I should look over the last seven years, I would be overjoyed never to step foot inside any type of beauty establishment again.

Except for the waxing Nate had appreciated. My lips curved.

Mom slapped at my leg through the bed linen. "Come on, darling, it's time you were up. Champagne breakfast in thirty minutes. How on earth are you going to make yourself presentable in that time?"

I rocketed upright in the bed. Breakfast? "Mom, you didn't tell me that. I thought we were being casual, just saying hi to everyone, and then all the wedding stuff was later?"

Mom sighed. "I told you, Melissa. Honestly, maybe you should get your ears checked. Or is this you not listening to me *again*? I thought we'd outgrown all that palaver."

Selective hearing had served me well in my youth. Now, I tended to block Mom from my conscious thought process, paying lip service to her conversations. "Okay, Mom, chill. I'll be there. Just get out of my way, so I can get ready. Uh, how formal is it?"

"Cruise casuals, darling. You've something nice, haven't you? Not those scruffy outdoor clothes you were wearing when I boarded yesterday?"

They *were* my nice vacation clothes. 'Sure, Mom. Go on, scoot. I'll be there." Scrunched in a laundry bag, those *nice* clothes smelled like sex anyway. I'd not been able to rinse them out and hang them in the bathroom to dry while Mom flitted about the cabin, her presence filling the small space more completely than a football team could.

Mom picked up her handbag and checked the contents. "Very well, then. I must go early, anyway, so I can stop by the hairdresser. I'll have to warn him he's going to need to cancel everyone else, this morning, won't I? It'll take all his time to sort you out."

I nodded stiffly at Mom's retreating back. Prison orange really would not be my shade, so murder probably wasn't a great option.

Showering briefly, I clambered out, dried off, and then tousled my hair, leaving it to curl and do its thing. Mom would have it straightened and rolled and pinned to a thin nothingness later on, anyway. Denim shorts and a loose peasant blouse were the best I could find in my case. The dress I'd worn out with Nate in Waikiki may have worked, but it was creased beyond redemption. Roman sandals laced to my knees, a flick of mascara, and a dusting of nude powder. Pointless, as it didn't really hide my freckles.

Freckles. The thought warmed me, and I smiled at my reflection. Screw them all. I looked okay. Because Nate thought I was more than okay.

A slight frown creased my brow. At some stage, he'd stopped calling me Freckles, changing to Lissa, but I'd not noticed when it had happened.

I flicked over my cell, checking the screen. *Not* because I missed him. I couldn't because it was a vacation romance, no ties. But because I *wanted* him. Yes, that was acceptable.

The only message was from Suzee. *'UPDATE?????? The countdown is ticking, and spreadsheet waiting to be filled in...I hope that's the only thing still needing to be filled? Besides, this guy sounds hot AF, and I want to hear MORE!'*

Before I'd met up with Mom yesterday, I'd sent Suzee

lurid texts—followed by a moment of buttock-clenching panic when I feared I'd hit the wrong contact name—detailing my Maui make-out session.

The time at the top of the screen caught my eye. *Shit.* More ammunition for Mom, because Elle sure as heck wouldn't be late. I snatched up my room card and slammed the door shut behind me. Dozens of identical doors flashed past as I pounded along the corridors. Not waiting for the bank of elevators, which always filled too slowly with tourists on each of the eleven decks, I sprinted up the stairs and shouldered through the external doors that led to the outdoor swimming pool. A gust of salt-laden air, heavy with the dense vegetation of the mountains that draped the shoreline, beat me back a step. I paused for a second to regain my breath, then pelted across the deck, through another set of doors and into the restaurant, busy with travelers surrounding the lavish buffets, fueling themselves in preparation for a day of onshore sight-seeing. No sign of Nate, though. I wound swiftly through the crowd, making my way to the sun-splashed rear deck, where cane lounges surrounded glass-topped tables.

A cream-colored, gold-tasseled cordon halted me.

The uniformed steward standing guard glanced at me, and then apologetically indicated an embossed sign resting on an easel in front of the barrier.

O'Connell

Wedding Breakfast Function.

Invited guests only

YEAH, that would be Mom's degree of casual. I tossed back my hair, flashed the steward a smile, and stepped over the low rope. "It's okay. I'm a bridesmaid."

Half expecting to be tackled from behind, I hunched my shoulders as I made my way toward the bow. Mom probably hired bouncers to keep out the riffraff.

I wasn't late, because Mom had pulled her old trick of fudging the time. How had I forgotten that one? Mom had always been chronically late for my school functions and even my graduation, but there was hell to pay if anyone dared make her wait for anything. She'd perfected the habit of rigidly specifying a meeting time, but timing her own arrival fifteen minutes later.

Apparently, Elle hadn't been trusted with the real time, either. Seated on one of the comfortable chairs surrounding a flower-bedecked table, it was immediately evident that providing the latest O'Connell prodigy unfortunately had not rendered my stepsister frumpy or bedraggled. No flabby baby belly protruded above her impeccably cut linen shorts, no miasma of baby vomit clouded her. A flaxen-haired cherub lay awake, but predictably smiling, against her Kardashian-clad shoulder.

Elle looked up and probably caught the scowl on my face. "Melissa! How awesome to see you again. It's been so long, y'know?"

I pasted on a smile. "It's Lissa, now. And, yes, ages, when was it last?" Summer vacation, twelve years ago. Seduced by the apparent camaraderie of our darkened bedroom one night, I'd had shared my six-month crush on Ben Wilder. Elle had suggested we double-date with Ben and his mate… and then she'd made out with Ben, dumping me with his pimply friend.

But, hey, old history, right?

Elle indicated the baby with a nudge of her chin. "This is Justin Jr. Oh, that's right; you've not met my husband, Justin, have you? You did know I married, though?"

Seemed Mom's rhetorical questioning was contagious. "I think Mom mentioned it."

Elle patted at the uncomplaining baby's back. "Justin's gone to round up the boys. Carole will be mad if they're late, but I'm sure they'll get here any second. I haven't seen them for ages, y'know? Can't wait."

I, on the other hand, would be totally cool with waiting another decade.

Her focus moving beyond me, Elle's face brightened—if it were possible for a flawless complexion to do so. "Oh, speak of the devil! About time you showed up. You're cutting it awful fine with Carole. I sent out a search party. Guess you're hungover, huh?"

The deep voice behind me rang familiar. Way too familiar. "You know me, Elle. No deployment, no training; no early rising."

17

I spun around, finding myself inches from Nate's chest. The chest I'd licked yesterday. "You two know—" I halted as Nate's eyes slid past me, and he stepped forward, bending to kiss Elle's cheek. One massive hand cradling the infant's head, his thumb softly brushed the baby's silken hair.

Elle stage-whispered to the baby. "Do you remember Uncle Nate? He's the awfully naughty one."

Uncle? Nate was Justin's brother? My mind whirled, putting it together. If I'd scored an invitation to Elle's wedding, I'd have met Nate a year ago. In fact, he'd probably been best man, and I could have been a bridesmaid, and everyone knew how that particular movie played out.

Weird that he hadn't mentioned he was also here for a vow renewal. Though, with more than one function on the ship's itinerary, there was no reason for him to make a connection between Elle's involvement in a wedding, and mine. Still, it seemed odd he'd not said anything.

Inexplicable unease churned my stomach. Why was he

ignoring me, his attention entirely focused on Elle and the baby?

"Don't you listen to your mommy," Nate growled to the infant.

Elle grinned at him, then gave a little leap of excitement, pretending to shield the baby's eyes. "Uh-oh, here comes Uncle Trav, and he's definitely hungover," she cooed. "You'd better not even look at him."

Uncle *Travis*.

No.

As Travis strolled up with another shorter, darker man, who had to be Elle's husband, Justin, my gaze darted from Elle to Travis to Nate.

All so alike.

How had I not seen it before?

But Elle, Travis, and...Nate?

No, MJ. My eldest stepbrother's name was MJ.

"Melissa!" The voice boomed from behind me as my stepfather joined the group, snaking an arm around my waist. "You look gorgeous. I take it your mom kept you on the straight and narrow last night, unlike my lads?" He pounded Nate's shoulder. "Wasn't even sure you'd make it today, Junior."

Junior?

"Seemed like you had worries enough to drown a fleet." Mitch's friendly thump turned into an embrace as he flung an arm around Nate's shoulder, determined to make clear what I needed to deny.

Junior. Mitch Junior. MJ.

Fear and dread were a cement lump in my stomach. "But...Nate?" I implored him with a glance, begging the green eyes to meet mine.

Mitch waved a dismissive hand. "Oh, I always forget. Lad

hates to be called Junior, changed to his middle name years ago. But you can't teach an old dog new tricks, huh? He'll always be Junior to me. Guess your nephew will suffer the same fate."

Elle, Travis, and MJ. The O'Connell siblings. My evil-steps.

The deck tipped beneath my feet, despite the calm ocean, and I grabbed dizzily at the back of a chair. I'd made out with—*almost screwed*—my own brother.

Well, stepbrother, if I wanted to justify it.

Which I did. Desperately. Except...there was no way to make this okay. How had Nate not realized? He knew my name, why I was here. He should have known—

Oh, God. He did.

Mitch Senior boomed "Sit down, kids, sit down. Carole will be here in a moment. I think she fancies the idea of making an entrance."

I sat in an untidy rush, dismay and revulsion clawing slowly up my throat in an unstoppable wave. Nate—Mitch Jr.—took the chair alongside, still not looking at me. I jerked away as his leg brushed mine.

Fuck. That wasn't all that he'd touched.

The oxygen wasn't reaching my lungs.

Travis sat opposite us. Nodded to Elle, and then to me. "Morning, sis...and sis."

Christ. He knew, too. He'd always known. That's why he'd been so disgusted when he found me and Nate together at the party.

Because it *was* disgusting.

My *brother.*

Elle leaned forward as Travis lifted his sunglasses. "What did you do to your face? Carole's going to kill you."

One eye swollen shut, Travis gingerly touched the bruise on his jaw. "Ran into Nate's fist. Two of them, actually. Bastard has a habit of waving those things around when he takes exception to my opinions. No matter how valid they may be."

I clutched at the edge of the table. Nate had said yesterday that Travis was feeling sorry for himself after upsetting me—clearly, he'd made sure of it.

Elle reached across the table, grasping Travis's chin to twist his face from one side to the other. "Oh my God, Trav, you're going to ruin the photos."

Shit. Photos. Me and my brother-lover digitally captured forever. I swallowed rapidly as bile filled my mouth. Glanced across to measure the distance to the side of the ship. Never mind the contents of my stomach, maybe I could hurl myself over. My skin turned hot, then clammy. Dark spots danced before my eyes, the low murmur of my siblings' conversation pounding my ears.

Jesus. My *brother*. How could I ever move beyond that vile reality?

Mitch pushed back his chair, his sons following suit, Travis quickly pulling his sunglasses back down and ducking his chin. "Here's the beautiful bride. Time to get this party started."

Mom breezed in, managing to look surprised to see everyone waiting for her. Well, she'd be a hell of a lot more surprised, soon.

Except, I would never say anything. I realized that instantly. Nate had trapped me. What we'd done was disgusting, taboo, and— Sandalwood wafted past as Nate took his seat again, and I curled my fists closed, nails digging into my palms as I tried not to cry. *No.* My longing for him was a remnant physical need. Nothing more. Once my brain had time to fully comprehend our disgusting relationship, the desire would instantly evaporate.

And that couldn't happen a moment too soon. Because, God, my *brother*.

Predictably, Mom dictated that the chairs be rearranged, so she wouldn't have to squint into the morning sunlight. Nate bent close as he grasped the cane arms of my seat. "I have to talk to you."

I shot him a venomous glare. "Really? A little late, don't you think?"

He shook his head, the green eyes locked to mine, begging. What did he have to beg for? He'd had his fun. It was only a matter of time till he spilled, made me the butt of the family jokes. *Poor Melissa, so hard up she has to make out with her own brother.*

Except, didn't that make Nate every bit as bad as me?

Obviously not, because he'd done it willingly. It was probably some sort of bet he'd cooked up with Travis.

But Travis's mashed face?

None of it made any sense.

I wanted so desperately to run away. But we were on a damn ship, where could I go? How had I fled from the mess with Damien, only to run straight into this?

Mom beamed around the group. "So, family catch up time? Though, *we* all know each other's news, don't we?" Her smile specified the O'Connell clan. "I guess Melissa can bring us up to date on the happenings on the other side of the world."

The flush mounted my cheeks as all eyes swiveled to me. All except Nate's. Head bowed, he stared at the floor. "Nothing new my side," I mumbled.

"Oh, nonsense," Mom trilled. "You've yet to explain why Damien couldn't make it at the last minute."

"Three months' notice is hardly last minute, Mom." And she could have asked in private, last night.

"I'd say it's very last-minute when you're passing up the chance for an all-expenses-paid cruise, wouldn't you? I think Mitch and I are entitled to an explanation. You know we had to pay the single supplement for your cabin?"

"I'll fix you up—"

Mitch waved me off. "Don't worry about it, sweetheart. Your mom's just teasing."

Justin coughed and turned to Travis, starting a rambling and loud conversation about football, or baseball, or something else that I couldn't follow. I liked him.

"Melissa?" Mom wasn't going to let it go.

I had to shut her up, get the attention off me so my brain had space to work. As though there was a way to logic my way out of this mess. "Damien and I broke up, so it would've been kind of weird to have him along, don't you think?"

Mom's lips pursed. "No need to be snippy, Melissa. Obviously, I'm aware of that much. But I want to know why? You've been together so long, why throw it all away now? I've been saving my Frequent Flyers to come back to Australia for a wedding. At the very least, I expected my first grand-baby to come from you. Justin and Elle only knew each other a year before they married. You and Damien have been together for, what, five years?"

"Seven." Not that it made any difference.

Elle bounced Justin Junior on her knee, cooing in baby talk as though she could distract Mom. She'd have more luck pulling a guided missile off course.

Mom sighed, folding her hands in her lap. "Seven years. What happened, Melissa? It's because you stopped making an effort, isn't it? I can see you've let yourself go. Poor Damien."

Clearing his throat, my stepfather tried to subvert the interrogation. "Leave the girl alone, Carole. She doesn't need to explain. It makes no difference, now."

Mom quelled him with a tiny lift of a tattooed eyebrow. "Hush, Mitch. Of course it does. If I can't tell my daughter where she's gone wrong, who is going to help her?"

Where *I'd* gone wrong? "For God's sake, Mom, Damien was into wearing my clothes. Okay? Is that what you want to hear?" The words burst from me and the entire table fell silent, their attention riveted to the spectacle I provided. How pathetic was I? Sitting alongside a stepbrother I'd made out with, while confessing that my fiancé had been using me for free bed and board for years, interested in me only as a mannequin to dress up, a living doll for him to groom.

18

Mom's eyes, as blue as the surrounding ocean, showed no understanding. "Well, there's nothing wrong with that. Mitch likes one of my sweaters. Of course, it's far too large for me, I'd never wear it. But that's hardly an excuse for throwing away years, is it?'

Travis grunted, trying to hide his amusement behind a coffee cup. Justin looked from me to Mom. Elle's hand froze on the baby's back. Nate stared at the floor.

I sighed tiredly. Damien's choices were far from the biggest problem in my life, right now. "My *underwear*, Mom. And my makeup."

Travis spluttered, and Mitch clapped him on the back. Elle suddenly didn't look so perfect, her mouth hanging open in astonishment.

Mom shook her head sadly. "Oh, Melissa. I did try to tell you that the way you acted would cause problems."

I could barely breathe, my hand spread across my chest to ease my lungs. "The...way...I...?"

Mom reached over to pat at my forearm. "Melissa, you

put so much into your job. It was all about you. Studying for years, then working all the time. You weren't even home to cook the poor man his dinner, were you? You simply didn't pay him enough attention. Oh, I could see this coming, years ago."

"See what, Mom? That my fiancé would be into wearing my lingerie? Or that he'd be trying to hook up with some random on a dating site?" Despite my anger, I toned down the revelation, the ultimate betrayal I'd discovered when I clicked the emailed link to find intimate pictures of Damien tagged *'male seeking male for fun times and/or relationship'*. Though I'd known about his cross-dressing for almost two years, Damien had assured me that it was nothing more than a hobby. So, I chose to do nothing. Accepted it because, in my own way, I loved Damien.

Or at least, I loved the security of having him around, the only constant in my life.

But that email had been the game-changer. I'd thrown Damien out, preferring being alone to being used.

I scowled at Mom. "Given your omniscience, an early heads-up might have been handy. It would have been nice not to waste so many years."

Mom's *tut* was loud enough to move a stable full of horses. "Don't be ridiculous, darling. Damien wasn't like *that* to start with. It's clearly a phase he's going through. You've emasculated him. Turned the poor boy gay."

"Jesus, Mom, you can't *turn* someone gay. It's not a phase, not something he chose. I'm pretty sure this has to be a damn sight harder for him than it is for me. I might be bloody mad with him, but even I know he didn't do it for kicks."

Nate's knee pressed against mine. I should pull away. Couldn't. He drew out his words lazily. "Lissa's right, Carole.

If sexuality was a choice, you'd find every girl on the ship panting at her cabin door. Not just the guys."

Oh my God! He thought I needed his half-assed defense? Or the pathetic hidden compliment? Unlike Damien, Nate's attention to me had purely been for kicks. He didn't need to pretend otherwise, now.

Mom projected her special '*for the O'Connell's*' smile at Nate. "Do you really think so? That's so sweet of you, Nate. But, you see, Melissa made an effort today." She scrutinized me through narrowed eyes. "And that's precisely the kind of thing I'm talking about, Melissa. You flatter a man by caring whether you look good enough to be seen with him."

I sucked in a ragged breath. Could I stand without falling? My head felt like it'd been whacked with a sledgehammer, and my heart thumped so hard it caused a physical pain.

Mom turned back to Nate. "You wouldn't remember Lissa when she was younger. Studious, didn't care about her clothes or hair. I really thought I'd managed to guide her through that stage. Lord knows, I tried. But I guess poor Damien found the apple rolled back to the bushel, didn't he?"

Nate's arm draped along the back of my chair and I flinched away from him. "Actually, I remember plenty, Carole. Lissa was shy, barely spoke the few times we visited. Her hair was a lot shorter, and she usually had a pencil stuck through it, because, you're right, she was always studying. It didn't take me long to discover that there was no point trying to talk to her. Anything I wanted to know, I had to ask Elle. Or, I should say, pay Elle to divulge." He flashed a grin at his sister. "Cost me a month's allowance to discover Lissa always wore rockers instead of runners, because she figured they made her look taller. And another two months' worth to persuade Elle to double-date with her."

Elle's laughter pealed across the ocean. "I should have charged you twice as much for that one, you cheapskate. That kid had the worst breath."

"I would have been good for it." Nate's voice had dropped octaves, the warmth insinuating itself into the shriveled recesses of my heart. I clenched my thighs. *No.* I couldn't react.

Yet I held my breath, let the cadence of his words caress me, as though they had actual meaning.

How did Nate remember such detail, when I couldn't even connect this rugged soldier with the nineteen-year-old adolescent I'd barely met? I'd have had more chance of recognizing his shoes than his face because I'd spent any enforced contact time staring at the ground. But no way in hell had he been this tall, this broad, this...manly.

I refused to allow the word *sexy.* Because that would be sick.

Travis leaned in. "Was that date the guy you said you were going to punch out?"

Nate shook his head. "No. The date was when only Elle went over to Sydney with Dad. Remember that huge international phone bill, Dad? That was me, scheming with Elle."

Mitch snorted "Didn't you tell me that was an accident? Phone left off the hook after you'd called me, or something? You could have just said you were watching out for your stepsister."

God. There it was. The relationship.

"As I recall, she wasn't my stepsister, then. But, yeah, I'm sure we cooked up some kind of story."

"So, who was it you were jonesing to punch, then?"

Travis seemed eager to hear someone else had copped a share of his brother's fists.

Nate crossed one foot over his knee. "The last time we went over, Lissa had senior formal. The asshole she went with tried to put the hard word on her when he brought her home. But something spooked him, and he drove off with his pants around his knees. Hopefully never to be heard from again." Nate raised an eyebrow at me, trying to confirm the fact.

The smashing bottles in the back-alley Matthew had parked in, the thumping on the steamed-up car windows that scared him into releasing the death-grip he had on my neck as he tried to... encourage... me to blow him.

Nate had been watching out for me, even then.

Self-appointed protector of an endangered species.

My fist lay on the table, white-knuckling the napkin. Nate dropped his hand over mine. Where everyone could see it.

No reason why he shouldn't; he was my brother, after all.

His thumb caressed the side of my hand. "Anyway, enough of that trip down memory lane. Lissa, I don't think you've been introduced to our brother-in-law, Justin. Though I'll put odds on that you've heard all about him."

I withdrew my hand from Nate's, shooting a fake grin at Justin, then quickly dropping my gaze so he wouldn't see my mortification. "Do you have a crazy combined family, Justin? Or a *normal* one?"

Justin held up both hands in surrender. "I'd have to say my family rates as pretty boring. But I think I've been absorbed into the O'Connell's."

"And we're so happy to have you," Mom slid in neatly. "Isn't this the most beautiful addition to the family?" She took the placid infant from Elle's arms, and Justin Jr. immediately started crying. I could have kissed him. Mom jiggled the baby up and down, switching her gaze from Nate to Travis. "You boys will be settling down next, I guess? More grandbabies for Mitch and me?"

Travis snorted in his coffee. "Don't look at me." He side-eyed his brother. "And I'd say Nate's got some serious shit going down before he gets anywhere near there. We'll see how silver his tongue really is."

Crap. His tongue. I didn't need to be thinking about that. Not now.

Not ever.

And Travis clearly intended to stir shit. How long until the rest of the family—*our* family—found out about me and Nate?

I was definitely going to chuck. "I, uh, I have to go. I have some calls to make for work."

Mom sighed, a gust long enough to match the rising wind. "Doesn't that just prove my point? You're supposed to be here for a family function, Melissa, not to work. It's very unfeminine to be tied to your desk all the time. You'll never attract a man if you keep this up."

Travis practically hooted. "I wouldn't say she has any problem with that last bit, Carole. Quite the opposite."

Fuck. He was going to out me. I shoved back from the table, my empty water glass rolling to the edge.

"Don't go," Nate muttered so quietly I wasn't certain I hadn't imagined it. But it didn't matter, anyway.

I smiled sweetly at the group, not focusing on anyone. "Actually, I have to go confirm a job interview, Mom, as I have a plan to get out of that office. Your entire morning's taken up with getting your hair done anyway, right? So, you won't miss me while I do the boring stuff that I happen to find somewhat necessary, given that I pay my own way in the world."

I strode from the table, expecting some cataclysmic retribution for my outspokenness. At least on the scale of a tidal wave.

Drowning would have been okay.

Elle intercepted me as I reached the cordon, well away from the table. Coffee cup in hand, as though she'd been headed toward the machine situated in the dining room, she dropped the other hand to my arm, her voice an urgent mutter. "Lissa, I don't know what's going on. You're weird. Nate's weird. Travis is...well, Travis is a dick, nothing new there." She grinned. "But, nice move with your mom. I was cheering for you so freaking hard, y'know? Only on the inside, of course."

She paused as we reached the silver behemoth of a coffee machine. "I wish I had the guts to stand up to Carole, sometimes. Tell you what, I'll come by later and help with your hair. But, in exchange, you have to lie and pretend that the bridesmaid's dress doesn't look as hideous on me as I know it does. Your Mom was adamant about the color, said it's your favorite."

I'd been tricked by Elle's pretended friendship years ago. But apparently, Nate had a hand in that deception, too.

And it had been *years* ago. People changed. Some people. But did they change enough?

No matter what, I had to somehow get through the day. Better that Elle was on my side, for a while, at least. "Sure, that'd be great. Mom's got my number." *So does your brother.* "Text me when you want to swing by."

I practically sprinted to my cabin. Seated on my bed, I made the call, confirming my interview time. Not that there seemed any point right now, but it'd been part of my plan coming over here. That, and magically changing my past and my future by getting laid in Hawaii. Yeah, well that'd worked wonderfully. I was so not a loser anymore.

I flicked open Suzee's number, but then closed it down again. What could I tell her? Damien had made me look pitiful enough, but I'd done an even better number on myself.

I heaved myself up and traipsed across the room.

Showered again. Basically, because I didn't know what else to do with myself. And because I felt dirty.

But not so dirty that my fingers didn't wander down my body as I thought of Nate.

God, what was wrong with me? I had to think of him as my *brother*.

Not as the man who'd wanted me, who'd touched and teased me. Who had protected me.

Except, he'd failed to protect me from the greatest danger of all; Nate, the man who lied to me.

I dragged my clothes on. Slumped on the end of the bed and stared at the blank TV screen. Wished the closed-circuit movie channel offered Red Dog. I needed an excuse to wallow, sob rather than have to think about my actions— both yesterday and today. Mom and Mitch's big day—again —and I'd acted like a spoiled teenager, storming off and making it all about me.

Though Mom and I weren't close, hadn't been since Dad died, I owed it to her to get my shit together. I had to make sure Nate didn't let on about what we'd done. Mom would never be able to cope with the scandal.

Then I'd get the hell off this ship, and out of the O'Connell's golden lives.

My legs like lead, I took the stairs up a couple of decks

slowly, hoping an excuse to avoid the necessary confrontation would appear.

But maybe that was part of my problem. I didn't stand up for myself. I didn't confront anyone, because I didn't want to hurt their feelings. I'd never told Mom how her constant criticism ate at my self-esteem, or how deserted I'd felt when she chose the O'Connells over me.

I'd never explained to Damien how much he'd hurt me, how he'd destroyed my trust in everything I thought I understood about life and love. How I felt used and useless, still a child searching for approbation.

Telling him wouldn't have changed anything, but perhaps I'd owed it to myself. Maybe that would have given me closure.

It was time for me to grow up.

Travis was exiting the cabin as I turned into the corridor. My feet tangled and I hesitated. I hadn't given a moment's thought to him being there. Dumb, as he'd specifically said he and Nate were sharing.

It would have been great if he'd been so clear about certain other things.

Arms crossed, he blocked the doorway. "Ah, Freckles. Reckon we may have to change that nickname to Feisty, hey sis?"

I winced.

Travis grinned. "Too soon?"

It would always be too soon. "Is N-Nate in there?" Damn. That would have sounded a ton better if I didn't stutter.

Travis narrowed his eyes. Uncrossing his arms, he let his shoulders drop, along with his attitude. "Yeah, he is. You want in?"

I nodded.

"Okay. Just..." He scrubbed a hand through his short

hair. "Just don't break his balls, okay? I know I was giving him shit, but he's kind of not doing too good."

Why did my heart twist at his words?

Travis swiped his key card and shoved the door open, closing it behind me as I stepped inside.

19

The cabin was identical to mine, except for the boy-mess strewn around and the smell of cologne.

Nate's cologne.

It took a second for me to realize that I was alone, the shower running in the small bathroom, then I grimaced. Nice move, Trav. If I fled now, he'd no doubt be waiting in the corridor to tease me. With every minute, I remembered exactly how it had felt to so intensely dislike the O'Connells that the bitterness was almost physical. So much for the passage of years. It was hard to believe I'd been stupid enough to actually like Travis over the last few days, until his drunken blurt at the party the other night. Which had still failed to provide the information I deserved.

I dropped to the end of one of the beds. No way was I leaving without sorting this. For once, I was going to force closure on something in my life. I'd tell Nate precisely what I thought of his behavior, and lay out exactly how he needed to act to get us through the next few hours.

I hadn't even moved on to thinking about how I was

going to force Travis to follow my edicts, though. Maybe Nate could take care of that. This was his damn mess.

A *mess*. That's how I had to think of this situation. Something to be cleaned up, sanitized, disinfected. Controlled waste to be incinerated.

Not fixed. This could never be fixed. I daren't even let my mind go there, toying with the idea like it was a possibility, like there was some way out of this nightmare. Some way Nate could persuade me that his actions hadn't been a deliberate, calculated, cruel joke.

The noise of running water ceased and I tensed, gathering my feet under me; I still had seconds. I could change my mind, bolt for freedom. If I pretended the thing with Nate had never happened, never mentioned it, maybe he'd do the same?

Except, his behavior at breakfast had been a long way from circumspect, almost like he didn't even care if Travis wasn't the only one to know of our dirty secret.

With Elle already suspicious, it wouldn't be long before Mom got her nose in. We needed to hash this out and bury it. Come up with some sort of united front.

No, united was the wrong word. I daren't even think that. We were only united by our need to hide what we'd done.

A pain jabbed and flared behind my eye. My stomach lurched. God, no, I couldn't do this. Couldn't face him. Because, for some reason, Nate's betrayal hurt worse than Damien's lies had. Worse than my mother's desertion had.

Which made no sense at all. I'd only just met him. At least, I'd only just met this adult version of him. I had no right to hurt, only to anger.

I shoved a frantic hand through my hair, my mind spinning. Later, this could be sorted later. When I'd untangled my thoughts, my...*feelings*. I had to get out of here.

I lurched up from the bed.

Too late.

The bathroom door banged open and Nate appeared in a billow of steam, a Viking striding through the mist. Fresh-inked by the shower, the tribal tattoos covering his arm glistened dangerously as he pulled up short, staring down at me. A towel slung low, water droplets ran down his ridged abs, leading my eyes straight to the V formed by his narrow hips. The *Iliac Furrow. Orion's Belt.* I had to keep my mind on the technical terms. Not let the fine trail of damp, golden hair draw my eyes lower.

"Lissa."

I didn't stand. Probably couldn't. And the area wasn't big enough for us to go toe to toe, anyway. The two steps he'd taken from the bathroom had Nate's shins pressing against my knees, his heels hitting the bar fridge.

I tipped my chin up defiantly, resolutely keeping my eyes on his face, not letting them travel down again. His hair darkened by water, he smelled of soap and toothpaste. And I quivered, instantly slick and throbbing with memory.

My physical need demanded I forget why I'd come here, but I refused to surrender. "Why didn't you tell me, Nate?" Good. My voice was harsh and didn't tremble. "Did you think it was funny? You and Travis, playing the ultimate prank on your stupid stepsister?"

Nate closed his eyes, but I didn't want him too. He had no right to hide from me.

And, even furious with him, I didn't want to be robbed of the last few moments of looking into the changing shades of sea-green.

"Lissa." His biceps bulged as he scrubbed one hand through his hair. His knuckles were scraped and raw, and now I knew why. Travis's face. Nate had been defending my feelings. Protecting me.

No. Nate cared nothing for my feelings. Why did I keep allowing that ridiculous notion to sneak into my head? His actions had been as calculated and premeditated as any careful experiment.

He reached toward me but stopped before he made contact. His eyes asked questions I couldn't read.

Didn't dare try to read, because I was going to twist them to what I wanted.

Because I wanted everything he'd said to me to be the truth. I wanted him to prove that he'd not known my identity, that it'd been an accident, not a cruel joke, that he was as much of a victim as I was. I wanted him to tell me that we were going to find a way to work this out. Because I ached for his touch. Desperate to lean into his embrace, the longing sobbed in my throat.

But I had to remember: he'd hurt me. And I was done with giving that power to anyone.

His words came reluctantly. "I've been trying to work out how to explain. To make what I did seem reasonable. But I've got nothing."

My heart plummeted.

He took a deep, uneven breath, forefinger and thumb pinching at the bridge of his nose. "I thought you looked familiar at the airport, then realized why when we were at the hotel in Waikiki. Figured it'd be funny to string you along for a bit. Guess I was kind of trying to get payback for you never noticing me when I had a crush on you a decade ago." He rubbed a hand around the back of his neck, his bicep bulging. "I figured you'd soon catch on if I kept tossing out hints. In any case, Trav was sure to open his mouth."

Despite the cramped space, Nate dropped to his

haunches, warily putting his hands on my knees. "But then I fucked up."

God, his hands. I tightened every muscle in my body and held my breath, willing the pounding of my heart not to betray me. *Brother, my brother.* When was my brain going to link my body with that immutable fact?

Nate's jaw tensed, his lips firming into a hard line, rimmed with white. "I fucked up big time, because I realized that I was falling for you. That you were funny and shy and crazy sweet. And so many other things that I hadn't been looking for, so many things I didn't think I needed in my life."

I pressed a hand against my ribs, keeping my heart in place. What the hell was he saying? And why now? I'd thought I wanted him to come up with a plausible excuse for his behavior, but the truth was that it was just too late. I didn't want to see the torment on his handsome face, didn't want to hear the words that tumbled from his beautiful lips. Because my pain was all his fault.

He rubbed a hand across his eyes, eventually releasing a ragged breath. Then he stood quickly, using distance to hide the evidence of his weakness. But his eyes glittered. "I knew I'd pushed it too far, I'd left it too damned late to tell you who I was. You'd made it clear what you thought of me, of my family. So, I came up with this crazy idea; if I could get you to fall for me, you wouldn't care about our family connection, even when you eventually found out. I mean, it's no big deal, right? It's not like we're blood relatives. Hell, we didn't even grow up together." He paused for a heartbeat, staring down at me. Then his voice dropped, edged with desperation. "Lissa, if you want me even half as much as I want you, we'll be able to work around it."

My gaze locked to the whorls and trails of his black-inked arm, as though the patterns could lead me out of this maze of pain and confusion,

Exactly the emotions Damien had awoken in me. I swallowed the surge of desire his nearness brought. That physical reaction was exactly what he'd exploited. "What sort of bullshit fantasy is that? You did things to me, Nate. Things that I wouldn't have allowed if I'd known who you were." I ignored the voice inside me that shouted liar. Maybe I would have allowed him to touch me, even if I had known.

Nate shoved both hands through his hair, his voice low and urgent. "That's the only reason I didn't go all the way, Lissa. It *had* to be your choice. That's why I asked for your permission every single god-damned move I made."

My mirthless laugh barked across the small room. "Asked my permission? You have to be kidding me. It was hardly an informed choice, was it? You get me wet and panting, then ask if I want it, but don't mention *who* you are? Jesus, you let me think we had something special going on, and all along you knew how wrong it was, that it could never be." My own words slammed my gut. *Something special.* What was I talking about? I'd only ever intended a holiday fling, anyway, I'd never wanted more than that.

Had I?

Nate shook his head. "It can *be*. Hell, Lissa, we're adults, we can do whatever we want. And I want you."

"You're my fucking *brother*, Nate."

"No!" His hands fisted at his sides. "Only in name. We're not blood."

"Are you messing with me? Do you want to argue over semantics? Or do you want to go out there and tell our parents what we did? God, do you have any idea how I feel?" *Manipulated.* Again.

Of course he had no freaking idea how I felt.

But he bloody well should.

My fingers curled in the bed cover.

And he damn well would.

I rocked back on the low mattress, my gaze fixed to his. Took a deep breath to mentally change gears. Then I ran my tongue over my lips. Purred the words, low and sexy. "Do you want to know how you made me feel, Nate?" *Used.* "How about I show you?" *Dirty.*

Still seated on the bed, I leaned into him, planting a soft kiss on the flat, hard plane of his stomach.

His breath caught as I trailed my lips slowly to his hip bone, then traced my tongue down one side of the deep V that led diagonally to where the towel was slung low and loose.

Nate responded instantly, the green of his eyes deepening in arousal, his nostrils flaring as his hips swayed toward my face.

I slipped my hands under the towel, caressing the taut muscles in the back of his thighs. The white towel tented, and I snatched the fabric away, dropping it across my lap. His penis sprang free, fully erect.

Like every other part of him, it was perfect. Honey gold, rather than sun-bronzed. Hard and thick, the length gave it a slight bend that I was pretty sure would increase my pleasure. Not that I'd ever find out. "Do you want me to show you how I feel, Nate?" *Degraded.*

"Lissa..." His throat worked as he swallowed, and I could read his confusion. Good. That was the first emotion he'd made me feel.

My hands slid to his butt. Longing trembled through me.

No. I had to teach him a lesson. I leaned closer and breathed softly against his cock. It twitched in instant response, pre-cum glistening on the tip.

I wanted it.

Wanted him.

But this was about vengeance, not desire.

Tongue extended, but not quite touching him, I gazed teasingly up at Nate through my eyelashes.

A muscle in his jaw bunched and jumped, but he shook his head. "Lissa. We have to talk this through."

Too late. I wrapped one hand around his shaft and swirled my tongue over the head of his dick. Salty and sweet.

His abs tensed as he tried to pull away. Or maybe tried to find the resolve to pull away, because if he'd wanted to, he sure could have. Instead, his hand moved to my face, stroking my cheek.

No. I didn't want him to do that. This had to be hot and hard. Pure sex, no feeling. Swirling my tongue again, I sucked him deep, fisting the base of his shaft to prevent his length from choking me.

Releasing the vacuum, I slid him out of my mouth like a lollipop, balancing the weight of his cock on the tip of my tongue. Then I sucked him deep again. Faster and faster. Every fifth suck, I withdrew completely, and lapped at the quivering head of his penis, my tongue driving him closer to the edge as I squeezed his balls.

Leaning back on the bed, I pulled away. "Do you want me to stop?"

Shock flashed across Nate's face as he recognized his own words, realized what he'd done to me. His expression betrayed him; abject despair and desperate hope overpowered by lust and desire.

Perfect.

Sweat beaded his face, the blond stubble glinting under

the downlight. His chest heaved as he fought for breath. "Jesus, Liss."

His words little more than a groan, I knew I had him.

I bent forward again, licking and sucking. The heels of my hands slid into the perfect indents in each of Nate's butt cheeks, urging him on, increasing the tempo. I skimmed my hands up, into the small of his back, and then raked my nails viciously down his tanned skin. I'd mark him, as he'd scarred my heart.

Nate grunted in sharp pain and surprise, arching closer to me, his hips still thrusting. His hands wound into my hair, trying to direct me, but I ripped them away. I was in control of this, not him.

One hand massaging his balls, I angled my head so I could take more of him. My jaw ached with the punishing rhythm. My free hand gripped his butt, forcing him deeper, harder, faster. His cock spasmed and he tried to pull back, his voice hoarse. "Stop now, Liss. I m gonna—"

His balls in my palm, my index finger stroked the sensitive skin of his perineum, his groin bucking against me in uncontrollable reaction.

"Jesus!" His entire body tensed, the muscles bulging beneath taut, sweat-slicked skin. His cock impossibly grew harder, pulsing in my mouth. His balls tightened and I squeezed, working my finger in a tiny circular motion on the sensitive spot. I might be sexually inexperienced overall, but this was the one thing I was damn good at.

Nate groaned, sliding one hand to cradle the back of my head, his hips thrusting as he tried to get in deeper. As his eyes half-closed, his teeth gritted and head thrown back, I relaxed my jaw, allowing him to take control as his orgasm peaked. "Ah, fuck!" His cock jerked and twitched, and he exploded in hot, thick waves in my mouth.

"God." His entire body shuddered and he staggered back to lean heavily against the fridge, chest heaving as though he'd run a marathon. "Jesus, Lissa."

Silently daring him to look away, I opened my mouth, winding my tongue through the creamy contents, smearing his cum across my lips. With one finger I chased a dribble of semen from my chin and tongued it clean.

Swallowed deliberately.

Licked my lips, then displayed my empty mouth.

Those nights of internet study had taught me the finishing touches.

Nate groaned again, a deep, knee-trembling sound of partially-sated desire. "You're amazing. So, we can work this out, Lissa? We're good now, yeah?"

I stood, tossing the towel from my lap to the far side of the room, where it hit the door to the tiny balcony. "No, we're not good. We're *even*. I used you like you used me. Goodbye, Nate."

He lunged for me, but I slipped from the room.

The grand parting had been every bit as powerful as I intended.

Nate now shared my shame, the proof of his guilt sweet in my mouth.

Yet I'd been robbed. There was no closure. Instead, I felt empty of all hope, filled instead with yearning and desire.

Because I still wanted him.

20

E lle stood behind my low chair, looping my dark hair into an intricate configuration. I tried not to watch her in the mirror; she had the same golden skin and glowing streaked-blonde looks as her older brother, though her eyes were like Travis's rather than Nate's; blue, not green. Maybe I should have gone to the hairdresser, not refused the appointment in a childish effort to spite Mom.

Elle caught my perusal and pulled a face, scrunching up her nose. "You know, I could have finished this in half the time."

I lifted an eyebrow. While I didn't want to make conversation with the evil-step—*any* of the evil-steps—close quarters made refusal kind of impossible. Though I'd done a good job of avoiding talking to Nate. Pretty easy with my mouth full.

Elle lowered her voice conspiratorially. "I *could* have done the job quickly, but it's nice to escape from Justin sometimes, you know? Little Justin, that is. The big version is okay—well, as far as men go—but the little ones are so much work, y'know?"

One more '*you know*', and I'd point out that no, I bloody didn't know. "He, um, he seems to be a pretty perfect baby. Really cute." Genetically blessed.

Bobby pins muffled Elle's words. "Oh, he probably is a good baby. What would I know?" She shrugged. "Because he was so unexpected, I think I kind of have it in my mind that everything's hard, you know? I had no time to mentally prepare for how different my life would suddenly be."

"Unexpected?" It sounded like Elle was inviting questions. Great, because prying into this revelation might keep my mind off the delicious, illicit images that kept forming. The memories and desires that refused my conscious control.

Elle held the brush above my head. "Didn't Carole fill you in? I thought for sure she'd spread that juicy bit around." Laughter sounded in the corridor outside the cabin, and Elle glanced at the door before continuing. "Justin and I had to get married so quickly, I couldn't even invite you to the wedding. Not that it was really a *wedding,* anyway. Quick in and out at the registry office." She sniggered. "Kind of fitting, seeing as a quick in and out's what led to the wedding in the first place."

She caught my shocked reflection in the mirror and waggled the brush at me. "Oh, no, it's not like that. I would have married Justin anyway, one day, y'know? He's super sweet. It's just that JJ kind of hurried things along."

"Oh, I didn't realize." Was I expected to commiserate or congratulate? "Still, it must be kind of awesome, knowing you created something so adorable."

Elle nodded, chewing on her bottom lip. "Yeah, thanks. I

guess it is. Thing is, we'll be buying a people mover before you know it." She slid her free hand down to her belly. "Promise not to tell Carole, but I'm pregnant again." She made her eyes huge with horror but patted contentedly at her flat stomach. "I swear Justin's freaking sperm jumps across to my side of the bed while I'm asleep, because I do not recall having any fun with this one."

She went back to pinning coils of my hair. "Anyway, enough about my boring mom stuff. Your life's far more exciting. You have to let me live vicariously, remember what it's like to be young and free."

Exciting? My life? "Well, we're the same age. And, as for the joys of being free, I'm sure you heard enough details at breakfast."

Elle rolled her eyes. "Pfft. The loser boyfriend? You kicked him to the curb, good job. Move on, who's next on the menu?"

Menu. I pressed my lips tight together, rather than give in to the desire to lick them. Nate couldn't be on my menu ever again. I *had* to hate him. Because what else could there be?

"Ah, you've clammed up on me, huh?" Elle grabbed a handful of hair and gently jerked my head back, squinting in mock interrogation. "Don't you remember how this works? I tell you that I let Scott Tamby finger me, and you tell me that you're hot for Ben Whatshisname. A secret for a secret. So, you got my secret. Now you owe me. And what I want to know is, what's going down with you and my brother?"

Shit. The blood sped into my cheeks.

Elle laughed, massaging my scalp where she'd tugged at my hair. "Hot damn. I knew there was something. I've never seen Nate get up in Carole's face like that. You know we're all scared of her, right?" She put down the brush and swapped it for a tail comb. "I cornered Travis after breakfast but he wouldn't spill, even though I just *know* his punch up with Nate had something to do with you. And there's no point me trying to get anything out of Nate, he never talks, y'know? Strong, silent type." Elle pouted. Gorgeously. "So, the only way I'm not getting left out of this family drama is if you come clean. Pleeeeeese. I'm always excluded."

Elle thought *she* was excluded?

Some pathetic, needy part of me longed to share my misery with this new version of my stepsister, a bubbly, friendly woman who maybe could have been my ally. If it hadn't been her brother—*my* brother—we were talking about.

Or not talking about. Because if I even tried to explain that the thought of leaving tomorrow, of never seeing Nate again, sliced my heart like a thousand paper cuts, shredded my soul, and exposed emotions I'd never realized I was capable of, Elle would know our dirty little secret.

I met Elle's concerned gaze in the mirror. "I...Nate and me, it's..." I needed to say 'gross'. But that wasn't the word that trembled on my lips. *Thrilling. Undeniable. Illicit.* "It's nothing."

A tear worked free.

Elle grabbed for a tissue, dropped to the bed, and snatched at my hand. "Oh no. Lissa, what the hell's going on?" All the teasing laughter had left her voice, and she threw an arm around my shoulders. "Nate's down at the bar drinking himself blind and refusing to speak to Dad or Trav, and you're up here, crying. What's the go?"

Jesus, so much for keeping it private. I had to get a grip. Biting the inside of my cheek until I tasted the warm tang of blood, I blew my nose and forced a smile. "It's nothing. Really. Just a misunderstanding. You know, sibling style." Yeah, if *Flowers in the Attic* were my family memoir.

Elle pursed her lips. "Well, I don't like seeing two out of three of my siblings looking so freakin' sad. We've waited forever to all get back together, and this is supposed to be a party. What can I do?"

I shook my head. "Don't worry about it. Anyway, if you're going to make the most of your few minutes of freedom, shouldn't we be having a glass of champagne while we get ready? Oh, crap, sorry. I guess you can't?"

Elle patted her breasts. "Double whammy; I'm still feeding Justin. Mind, looking at these flat puppies, you'd swear there was nothing in them, right? I tell you, I'd kill for your double Ds. I have to wear a padded bra under my padded bra." She tugged at the elastic of her bra through her shirt, releasing it with a loud snap. "As your mom made clear to the entire boutique when I tried on that god-awful bridesmaid's dress. Hey, that reminds me. When you shut down Carole with that stuff about the job interview, was that for real, or were you blowing her off?"

I'd planned to keep the interview a secret, see how it panned out before telling anyone about it—and probably never tell my family, anyway. But any topic was safer than where this conversation had been headed. "Like I'd dare lie to Mom?"

Elle clapped her manicured hands. "Oh, I hear you, sister! I'm so scared I'll accidentally let on about this pregnancy, then Carole will find out I told you first, and—" she drew a finger across her neck. "It'll be freakin' curtains for me. Anyway, the job?"

"An eco-tourism company."

"Still working in marine biology, though?"

Elle knew my profession? "Yeah. More hands-on stuff than lab work." Because I'd stupidly thought that maybe I could escape the inner librarian and save the sea turtles at the same time.

Elle heaved an over-staged sigh. "Just as well. Your mom would go nuts if you threw your career away, you know. She doesn't miss an opportunity to point out that her child is university educated and has letters after her name. Guess the rest of us all fell short."

Wait, what? "But you heard Mom riding me about how I study and work too much. Pay too much attention to my job and not enough to-to other things."

More like a sixteen-year-old than a pregnant mom, Elle jumped onto the bed knees-first. "Hey, she's *your* mom. You got to know that's just her style. So, is the interview an internet hookup? That'll cost a fortune from the ship."

"No, regular interview. In person."

"Oh, when you get back to Sydney?"

"No. The job is here."

"Here?" Elle jabbed a forefinger into the plush mattress. "Here, as in Hawaii?" She grabbed hold of my hand. "You're kidding, that'd be freakin' amazing! But don't you need a work permit, or visa, or something to work in the US?"

"Apparently not. Mom's one of you lot, so I get a free pass. Just a matter of getting the job." That, and deciding if I even wanted it, anymore. With both Hawaii and Australia romantically tainted, maybe I needed to set my sights on a new country. One that encouraged ownership of multiple cats. And banned men.

Elle tapped rapidly on her chin, looking out of the cabin window at the lush mountains of Kauai. "If you're staying, and Nate's transferred back to the same base in Oahu that Trav's stationed at, it looks like I'll have to get on Justin's case about relocating here. Keep the family together, y'know? Not that anyone in their right mind would argue about moving to Hawaii. Justin is in IT, he can work from anywhere. And it'd save Carole and Dad a fortune in trips to visit little Justin." She tapped a finger on her chin, a slight crease marking her brows as though she seriously considered the prospect of us all living close to one another. "Hey, how cool would it be for JJ to have his only aunt close by? This is going to be so awesome. Melissa—I mean, Lissa—you *have* to get that job."

I faked a smile, my fingers so tightly intertwined, they ached. I'd blow off the job interview. The Hawaiian Islands might have been large enough for me to avoid the boys, but not if Elle planned for us all to play happy families. I couldn't bear to regularly see Nate and pretend I felt nothing.

And no way could I admit what it was that maybe I felt for him.

Because, if seven years had taught me anything, it was that my emotions couldn't be trusted.

MY HEART SQUEEZED as I descended in the glass lift with Mom and Elle. Alongside his father on the broad landing of the sweeping staircase, Nate locked terrible.

Well, handsome as hell in a dark suit, but still, terrible.

Guilt twisted my stomach. We were supposed to be square now; I'd used Nate as he'd used me. But the truth was, his attention had never left me as devastated as he now appeared. Maybe because that had never been *his* intention.

Elle huffed, leaning toward me as the elevator halted a floor above the landing. "Sibling spat, you say? That's my favorite brother down there, looking about as happy as a turkey at Thanksgiving. And you're my favorite sister. One of you is going to tell me what's going on."

Mom snapped to face us, and I froze like a teenager caught climbing out of a bedroom window. Mom would never understand. Hell, what was there to understand? Every family wanted to boast near-incest, right?

"Girls. Stop chattering. Everyone's waiting for my entrance, and we're bunched in the lift like a group of schoolgirls in the bathroom."

"Sorry." We unintentionally chorused the apology, drawing out the syllables, and Elle sniggered as we bent to pick up the meters of white train, dutifully following Mom from the elevator.

It seemed that plenty of tourists shared Travis's views on not wasting cruise time on shore excursions; dozens of people were grouped in the foyer at the base of the white staircase.

Yet it didn't matter how many strangers stared up at us. Only Nate mattered.

Clutching at the hibiscus-wreathed balustrade, I couldn't bring myself to look at him again. It wasn't only shame that tortured me. It was a sense of...loss.

Elle settled the cloud behind Mom and reached across to give my hand a quick squeeze. "Okay. Don't tell me. Not yet, anyway. But I'm not completely stupid and, even though he's my brother, Nate's one of the most decent guys I've ever known. You two have to sort this."

Maybe I should ask Elle if Justin had ever lied to her, ripped out her heart on the pretext of caring? Apparently, it was a male go-to move. And a long way from decent.

"Girls," Mom murmured warningly, her lips not moving from the artificial smile she'd purchased.

Cousin whatever-his-name-was struck the chords on the piano, something like a cross between the Star Wars theme and God Save the Queen, and Mom started her regal descent down the plush red-carpet centerpiece.

Each step brought me closer to Nate. His eyes a stormy green ocean, his clenched jaw gave a hard thrust to his chin. And, while every fiber of my being screamed that I should run to him, the one rational portion of my brain held me back. Men couldn't be trusted. I'd given Nate the chance he'd begged for, the chance to prove he wasn't like Damien. And my *brother* used the opportunity to lie to me, to manipulate me to get what he wanted. Just like Damien.

As I moved toward Nate, I could feel the tension emanating from his rigid body, his legs planted like tree trunks, hands fisted at his sides. But was it fury that left his lips pressed together in a hard, uncompromising line, his eyes glittering as he stared at me across the few feet separating us?

How could I tell? I didn't understand my own emotions. I needed to hate him, but it wasn't hate that left me bereft and hollow; it wasn't hate that made me lean toward him, a moth to a flame; it wasn't hate that had me replaying every second we'd shared, recapturing his smell, his touch, his taste.

But I had to hate him because he'd betrayed me, and allowing any other emotion was far too dangerous.

As the celebrant concluded the service, Nate silently offered me his arm so we could descend the remaining stairs and sign the witness register.

I took it hesitantly, futilely biting back the sob that struggled for escape. This would be the last time that I'd ever touch him.

His arm tensed, bicep flexing to capture my hand, and I felt the ragged intake of his breath before he spoke, low and deep, gravel washing across a beach. "Are you okay?" There was no anger, only concern in the tone that caressed me.

I swiped at more tears, refusing to look at him. Couldn't look. It hurt too much. "Yeah. Weddings, you know."

"Sure. That must be it." His voice broke and I wanted to throw myself into his arms. How the hell could this hurt so bad? I'd come here intent on a vacation romance, and that's what I'd found. I'd planned to love him and leave him, anyway, so why did Nate's deceit bother me? I could walk away from them all, never look back, never think of our affair again.

Couldn't I?

I released Nate's arm as my feet touched the level deck, quickly distancing myself from him. Travis handed me a glass of champagne and jerked his chin toward his brother. "Jeez, Freckles, how about you throw the dude a lifeline? He looks about ready to jump overboard."

"I'm sure he knows how to swim." Despite my snippy response, I chewed my lip, sneaking glances toward Nate. Neither Travis nor Elle evidenced any reservations about me and Nate being together. And, if I was being logical, why should they? Nate was right; we weren't related by blood, hadn't even grown up in the same household. He was such a stranger, I'd not recognized him.

But, if the family connection wasn't truly the issue, why did I feel compelled to reject him, even though doing so was tearing me apart?

For once, science couldn't supply an answer.

At the reception, served at the Captain's table in the

formal dining room, I was seated close enough to Nate to smell his aftershave, imagine his embrace, hear his voice — if he'd spoken. Instead, he maintained a tortured silence. Hopefully, Mom and Mitch only had to pay for what was consumed, as neither of us were eating. I drained my glass, and both Nate and Captain Ahab rushed to refill it. Nate's hand brushed mine, and I jerked away, covering the reaction by reaching for a bread roll and shredding it onto my plate as I pretended interest in Ahab's crusty old flirting.

If I emptied my glass again—which I could quite easily do, as drinking seemed to provide the only anesthetic for the raw feelings I didn't want to ponder—would Nate refill it? Could I accidentally touch him one more time? But if I touched him, where would it end? I'd have no self-control.

Because, brother or not, I still *wanted* him.

The need grew within me, a craving that went beyond the physical. I had to get out of there, away from the sweet risk of his narcotic presence.

I shoved my chair back. "Mom, I'm calling it quits. I have a bit of a headache, and I still need to pack."

Mom narrowed her eyes, and I braced myself for the barrage of accusations detailing my lack of gratitude. The faded blue gaze turned toward Nate, then back to me. "Sure, darling. You go and sort out what you need to. Elle said that you have that interview after we dock tomorrow, right? You need to be bright-eyed and bushy-tailed for that, so don't stay up too late."

It would have been better if Mom had been her usual acerbic self. The unfamiliar words of caring brought tears to my eyes yet again. For God's sake, what had happened to tears for Red Dog only?

The carpeting in the warren of long hallways muffled

my slow footsteps, but not the voice that hailed me as I reached the corridor that led to the sanctuary of my cabin.

"Lissa. Wait up, hon. I can't walk that fast, and Bill is even slower than me." Tex puffed alongside, a battleship at full steam. "Gracious me, there's a lot of exercise involved with these cruises. Darned if I don't forget, every single year. Next year, I think we'll get a couple of mobility scooters, what do you say, Bill?"

As usual, Bill said very little.

Tex fanned herself with one hand. "The weather's coming up bad, isn't it? The forecast says there's a tropical cyclone blowing in. Your dress is just gosh-darned gorgeous, honey. We watched your momma and poppa get hitched again, but we couldn't take our eyes off you and your young man. Such a striking pair. Y'all should think about having your wedding on here. Tell you what, I'll give you our details, y'all stay in touch. If you have a cruise wedding, we'll see if we can't make those our dates, too."

I shook my head. "There'll be no dates, Tex."

Tex's earrings jangled in consternation. "Honey, you look sadder than the ass end of a wet week. Y'all got the end-of-vacation-blues?"

We'd reached my room, I had my key card in the slot. Maybe, having got her momentum up, Tex would keep waddling by if I remained silent.

Nope.

She wheezed to a halt. "Honey, what is it? Oh no, not you and Nate?"

"Ah, trouble in paradise?" Bill's input startled me. "Don't worry, darlin'. There's nothing that can't be mended if you have the will and a breath of life left in you."

The jewels on Tex's fingers sparkled as she applauded. "He's so right, honey. I'll let you in on a secret." Apparently, there was no necessity to lower her voice and keep it secret. "Bill and me went through a rough patch a while back. We were headed for Splitsville. But then I ended up in hospital —Serious Women's Troubles, you know."

Yup, and now so did the entire cruise. I twitched the door handle longingly.

"Anyway, the doctors operated on me, and they messed it up. I darned near bled to death on that table. And when I came round, my Bill was sitting there holding my hand as if he'd never let it go, tears pouring down his face harder than the Niagara Falls. Right, sugar?"

Bill had gone back to nodding.

Tex snuggled up to his arm. "And, right then, I understood that all I wanted in the whole world was my Bill. I didn't care no more about the no-good whore he'd been hooking up with."

Whoa. I so did not see that one coming. I tried not to let my eyebrows creep into my hairline.

"And I didn't care about her, neither," Bill affirmed. "Because when I thought I might lose Tex, I realized that life is worth nothing unless you have something worth losing. It didn't matter what either of us had done in the past, it mattered what we *could* do for each other in the future."

The girlish giggle from Tex had me checking the corridor for a fourth participant in the bizarre conversation.

She squeezed Bill's arm like a tourniquet. "And I sure make an effort to be *doing stuff* for him now, right Bill?"

"Any more of that kind of effort, and you'll see me off with a heart attack, darlin'."

Ugh. I needed to get out of here.

Jowls juddering, Tex patted at my hand. "Anyway, honey, the point is, it don't matter what your guy's gone and done to you. If you love him and you're truly meant to be together, you'll find a way forward."

Love? My entire experience of love was encapsulated by seven wasted years with a man who'd only loved my financial support, who'd manipulated me sexually and emotionally, who'd stolen my right to make choices for myself.

How the hell would I even recognize love?

21

Once I'd escaped into my cabin, after promising Tex I'd do everything I could to fix my 'relationship' with Nate, I threw all my belongings into my suitcase and backpack. Undressed and crawled into the double bed, pulling the covers high despite the tropical warmth. Trying to hide.

I took my phone with me. Somehow, I had to explain to Suzee what had happened. I stared at the illuminated screen. If I dialed Suzee's number, my texts from the previous day would flash up. Messages where I'd giggled and swooned about what I'd done with Nate. How fine he was. How hot. What an awesome lover. How I'd mark off all the squares on Suzee's chart, couldn't wait to tick the final box before the end of the cruise, by getting Nate into bed.

Nate. My *brother*.

Except, he wasn't really.

But, if that wasn't truly the issue here, I still couldn't fathom what was.

Even though I'd half expected it, the knock at the door

startled me. Nate's deep voice almost blended with the throb of the ship's motors as we churned through the waves, made mountainous by the increasingly foul weather, back to Oahu. "Lissa. We need to talk."

I burrowed further under the blankets, praying he'd leave. But terrified he would. Holding my breath so I didn't miss a word.

"Lissa? We can't leave it like this. Let me in."

Other voices sounded loud in the hall, coming closer, calling good nights and farewells and promises to meet again. I imagined Nate dipping his chin in acknowledgment, his perfect lips curving into the slightly asymmetrical smile that creased his cheek. I wanted him to be smiling at me.

The voices faded, and the door handle rattled. "Lissa. I'll stay here all night if I have to. Talk to me."

My heart beat faster, and I flung my legs free of the covers. God, I wanted to go to him. I wanted to throw open the door and tumble into his arms, held safe against his broad chest. Desire trembled through me, but the emotion was much more than lust. So much more, that I couldn't risk thinking about it, daren't put a name to it, despite Tex's advice.

He knocked again. "Lissa, at least let me know you're all right."

I pulled the covers back up. He knocked again and again, his voice increasingly hoarse as he pleaded with me. Begged. Tried to explain.

Tears streamed down my face as I stared at the ceiling, moving my gaze inch by inch over the white surface, counting the perforated squares of soundproofing foam. Trying to focus on the task. Tex made a good case for ignoring the past; but if I allowed Nate in the cabin door, I'd allow him in my heart. And that would hurt too much. I couldn't risk becoming vulnerable again.

A new voice punctured my counting. Travis. "Dude, you've got to let it go. She's just not into you. Move on, man."

Nate's voice sounded broken, thick with tears, and the door vibrated as though he slumped heavily against it. "Fuck off, Travis."

I turned off my light, lying in the darkness, still staring at the ceiling as the ship churned and plowed through a raging ocean in the growing storm.

Tapping on my door. "Lissa? Come on, sis. It's me. Elle. Talk to me, at least. Tell me what's going on."

I pretended not to hear my stepsister.

Time passed, but I could still feel Nate's presence, separated from me by the inch-thick panel.

Hours later, another female voice, an answering mumble from Nate. Then silence again.

My stepdad's deep tone sliced through the gloom that shrouded my room. "Nate. Come on, son. You can't sit out here all night. Someone's sure to call security. She can't go anywhere, we'll sort it out in the morning."

Nate's reply was muffled, as though his head was in his hands. "I don't know how to fix this, Dad."

"Is it that important?"

"More than I could ever have imagined."

Mitch Senior sighed heavily. "Then go to bed, get a couple of hours' sleep. We'll have a family meeting at breakfast."

A family meeting? Seriously, they'd discuss our incestuous behavior over coffee and croissants? Mom would actually have good reason to lecture me on my faults. She'd get to drag up all my past inadequacies, yet again. Fury darted through me and I jerked upright in the bed.

No way in hell was I letting that happen. I was taking control.

I waited a few minutes, then rose quietly and scratched at the door, listening for a response. Nothing. I slipped the chain and peered into the deserted corridor. Swallowed the hard lump of disappointment that warred with my relief, and quickly bolted the door again.

The ship made dock at four a.m. and I sat on my bed with the balcony door open, listening to the shouts of deck-hands, the splash of ropes hitting the water, the trundling of wheels as disembarkation ramps were placed. By five a.m. I'd hauled my suitcase down to the reception lounge. The steward at the night desk blinked at me in bleary-eyed confusion. "Miss, disembarkation doesn't commence until seven. You've another two hours, and you're entitled to breakfast before you leave."

I laid on my most winning smile. Not that I'd ever won much with it. "I know, but the ship is docked, and I have a meeting I must get to." I'd stick with the truth, as close as possible. At least my neat gray suit, heels, and pressed white blouse lent my story some credibility. Hardly tropical island holiday gear, though God only knew how creased I'd look in six hours, when I finally made the interview.

If I made the interview.

Why was I so incapable of making a decision on even something as simple as whether to go for the job or not? Why was my brain refusing to cooperate on the most basic of issues? Was it because I'd allowed Damien to mold and guide me for so long, I now needed someone to tell me what to do, tell me what was right, what was permissible?

Had coming to Hawaii, the whole *Vagina's Vacation* plan, really been my disguised attempt at grabbing control of my life?

Of course it had. I didn't need to be a shrink to figure that one out.

What I did need was some space to figure out my own head. Make my plans and decisions, without having my hand forced.

I squared my shoulders and speared the steward with a level gaze. "If it's a problem, my luggage can be unloaded later. My f-family is still aboard, I'll arrange for them to collect." Despite my surge of determination, tears pricked at my eyes. "I really have to get off, right now." In my imagination, a huge figure vaulted over the balustrade, barring my exit. Or maybe he snatched me up, threw me over one broad shoulder, and carried me off into the sunset. Sunrise.

In reality, the steward picked up the desk phone, spoke quietly, and then waved me forward. "That'll be fine, ma'am. We'll scan your ID so you're registered as departing. I hope you enjoyed your voyage with *The Spirit of Ohana* cruises. We consider you part of our ohana, and we'd love to see you again. Please be aware that unattended baggage remaining in the dock area by three p.m. will be destroyed. Security measure." He ran through the housekeeping by rote, barely taking a breath, but then focused on me. "Are you sure you wouldn't like a coffee before you leave? I could probably have the kitchens bring up a bagel."

"No, that'll be fine. Thank you so much for your help." I flashed him another smile that tore at my insides, and moved quickly to the scanner and the gangway. To escape.

No cabs were waiting on the damp, near-empty dock, only a limousine on the far side of the park. I shouldered my backpack and legged it through the misty rain toward downtown Honolulu, finally finding a cab rank and a sleepy driver to take me to Outrigger Waikiki.

Back to the start.

Head against the car window, I watched the teardrops trickle down the outside of the glass. Like the rain that had fallen on me and Nate in Maui.

The thought stabbed sadness through me, and I closed my eyes, trying to shut out the memories, the pain, the longing.

"Outrigger Waikiki Beach, ma'am." The driver woke me, and it took a moment to gather my thoughts. I'd been dreaming of Nate. Dreaming of his arms, his lips...other bits. God, had I talked in my sleep? The driver's gaze gave away nothing. I tipped him extra, anyway.

There was no point making my way to reception to check into Outrigger, my room wouldn't be ready this early. I should change hotels, in any case. Nate knew I had a room here. But Mom and Mitch had prepaid the booking, so it'd be ungrateful not to stay...and maybe nowhere else would have a vacancy...and I couldn't really afford the expense... and I was making excuses because, though I was hiding from Nate, hiding from decision-making and commitment, still I didn't want to run too fast.

I crossed Kalakaua Avenue and ducked up Dukes Lane, where Nate had promised to take me to find souvenirs. Trawling a couple more streets, I found a diner serving all-day breakfast. A pot of black coffee tempted me from the counter.

Any normal person would lose their appetite when faced with the decision I wrestled; I ordered the full break-fast with pancakes and coffee. Portfolio spread open on the table, I stared blankly at my notes, trying to force my brain to work mode, not allow other thoughts to intrude. I'd attend the interview because I'd committed to it: and that's what I was all about. Commitments and security. Besides, I needed to keep my options open—even though, right now, I couldn't get a logical grasp on what those options were. My brain was filled with longing instead of my usual analytical processes. Where there should be regimented columns of pros and cons, there were only wistful memories of the hours spent with Nate and a hazy idea of what the future could have been.

Which was ridiculous, because the future was *never* going to extend beyond this week.

At nine, I slung my bag over my shoulder, tossed a handful of notes on the table, and waved to the waitress behind the counter.

"Aloha. I hope you have a nice day," the waitress called.

I paused. I'd planned my route, retentive as always, but had to second guess myself, make certain that I was taking the right course. "Where do I catch a bus to Hanauma Bay?"

The woman pointed through the window, though not much was visible past the thick paint advertising the breakfast which now sat heavy in my gut. "Directly across the road. Do you have snorkeling gear?"

Did I look dressed for snorkeling?

The waitress waved aside my unspoken question. "You can hire there. It'd be a shame to miss out on something you can remember your entire life, right? Only in Hawaii."

Though the bus took the scenic coastal route, winding past a panorama of black cliffs, the lapis lazuli seas below alternately foaming against jagged rocks or forming languid pools, depending on the bay, I paid little attention. Worrying at my fingernail, I stared blankly out of the window, the waitress's words ringing in my ears. Something to remember for the rest of my life. *Only in Hawaii.*

But did I want to remember? I could flee back to the

safety of my laboratory and my imagined cats, right now. I hadn't told Suzee the rest of the story, so I could act like Nate had never been anything more than the momentary conquest I'd intended.

And then I could spend the rest of my life wondering what would have happened if I'd been a bit braver, if I'd stayed another week. If I'd given Nate another chance.

Maybe I should allow the interview to decide the course my life took. If I got the job I'd stay, and see if Nate came back. If I didn't, I'd go home immediately.

Relinquishing my fate to something beyond my control seemed far less terrifying than making a decision and owning the consequences.

I scowled at my reflection in the salt-bloomed glass. There it was again; exactly what I'd spent seven years doing. Allowing Damien to control and manipulate me, rather than taking control myself. I'd stayed with him, rather than take a risk and face the world on my own. Always, I'd taken the coward's route.

I jerked upright at the realization, the portfolio sliding from my lap to the dusty bus floor.

Melissa was the coward, not Lissa.

Damn it, I could do so much better than this. I'd left my life on the other side of the world, prepared to make a new start, yet now I made excuses not to take a risk with Nate? No one in the family had raised so much as an eyebrow—well, Botox had stolen that choice from Mom—but both Elle and, in his own way, Travis, seemed to be open to the relationship. My mother's opinion was...unimportant. *Yes!* That was it. Excitement curled through me: no one else's judgment mattered. Why had I never understood that? I didn't break any law by being with Nate, it wasn't illegal, or wrong, or even immoral.

No matter how hard I tried to hide from it, I knew what Nate made me feel. And that emotion wasn't anything I could quantify in a laboratory test or validate in an experiment. So, was I rejecting him because of the block in my own head, rooted in my determination not to become vulnerable again?

Only I could decide if the potential gain was worth the risk of pain.

But first, I was going snorkeling. Because it'd be a shame to miss out on something I could remember my entire life.

Only in Hawaii.

DISEMBARKING the bus amid a crowd of beachwear-clad tourists an hour later, I'd arrived at the research facility far too early for my interview. I made my way with the throng down the steep, cemented path to the beautiful white sands of the lagoon.

Sea wrack from the previous night's storm formed treasure troves begging to be explored. A small hut hired out wetsuits and snorkeling gear, and I checked my portfolio and clothes into a locker.

The familiarity of donning the thin neoprene suit comforted me, taking me back to my roots in marine biology, the student days I'd spent diving the pristine coast of South Australia, researching the intricate world of Leafy Sea Dragons.

The warm, salty water wrapped me in a crystal embrace as I waded in, slid beneath the lapping waves, and pulled on my flippers. I blew the snorkel mouthpiece clear, relaxed into the ebb and flow of the tide, and cruised over the deep volcanic trenches and reefs with lazy kicks of my legs.

The physical action cleared my mind and the underwater beauty washed away my tension. Brilliantly-colored fish nosed up to me, flipping fins to move out of my way as my flippers eddied the water. Bright urchins and anemones starred the rocks, and a dark shadow moved across the brilliant white sand on my left. I twisted sideways, then held my breath as a majestic sea turtle glided toward me, huge, dark eyes round with curiosity. If I stretched a hand, I could wave away the geometrically patterned yellow, black, and silver humuhumunukunukuapua'a that schooled around her, and stroke a finger across the turtle's shell. But I had no need to touch.

Like fragrant oil, the water soothed my temples, easing my mind as it stirred my almost-forgotten passion for the marine environment. A passion for so much more than sitting at a desk, bringing home a good paycheck.

The turtle circled me unhurriedly, dipping one long flipper to make the turn, then slowly cruised from sight.

I took a deep breath, the noise echoing like Darth Vader shared my snorkel. Salt stung my eyes from leaks around the edge of the poor-fitting mask. It was time to get out, rinse off and wriggle back into my interview clothes. Because now I knew that I *had* to land this job.

I was more, so much more, than a hollow desire, a need to be loved. I had qualities, and abilities, and a right to demand more, both from life and from myself. To hell with caution. This was where I was needed. Where I was meant to be.

I surfaced, shucked my flippers and peeled the mask over my hair as I picked a path through the volcanic rock to the beach.

"Finished already, Miss?" the attendant at the snorkel hire booth asked as he took my gear.

"Only for now. I'll come back with my own equipment another day and spend longer. Can I hire a towel, please?"

I collected my clothes from the locker and showered. Twisted my wet hair into a braid and tugged on my gray suit, struggling to get the sleeves over damp skin.

High heels in one hand, I hiked barefoot back up the long, steep path.

Then I sat, puffing slightly, on a wooden bench on the cliffs overlooking the endless blue promise of Hanauma Bay.

Fringed by a palm-studded green lawn and white beach, the almost fully-enclosed circle of the bay was highlighted by patches of sand peppered with darker areas of deep water and rocks. Unpredictable. Mysterious. And endlessly beautiful.

Like my life had the potential to be, if I embraced it.

Clarity had finally arrived on a caffeine-infused cloud.

Nate *had* tried to warn me, he'd tried to explain so many times. But, intent on fulfilling my dream of a holiday fling, I'd shut him down.

He'd done nothing wrong. He wasn't like Damien. I had to stop comparing him—anyone—to my ex-fiancé.

I'd set up the whole experiment incorrectly. I'd been working toward a defined outcome, determined to prove my theory right; I'd subconsciously set it up so every man would fail.

It was time to say goodbye to Damien. Forever. Time to move on.

I worked the engagement ring off of my right hand. Stared down at it for a moment. Then I stood, walked to the edge of the high cliff, and flung the jewelry toward the ocean.

It fell short—way short. My grand gestures tended to go

that way. But hopefully someone would find the tiny diamond in the sand, and it would bring them far more joy than it had me.

I didn't need it. I'd found the path that might lead to my own happiness. It might not. But whichever way it went, the totally uncontrolled experiment would definitely be worth the risk.

"Aloha, Miss."

"Aloha." I returned the porter's greeting as I strode across the tiled entrance to Outrigger Waikiki two hours later. I took the escalator up to reception. It was too slow, so I stretched my legs, climbing two stairs at a time, the sand from Hanauma Bay gritty in my shoes, my skin still tingling from the salt of the ocean.

I remained standing as I checked in to my pre-arranged room, so the receptionist would recognize my urgency and expedite the process. As soon as she handed my room key over with a bright smile, I strode to the elevator. Lips pursed, I blew out a tense breath, impatiently tapping the card against my chin in a flurry of nerves.

I had to get to my room, change out of my suit, and call Elle. My stepsister would tell me where to find Nate, probably even help me work out what to say to him, how to apologize. I had to at least try because maybe we did have something worth pursuing—though, logically, the chances were I'd already pushed him away too far, hurt him too much. He'd probably given up on me. And I'd have to accept that, despite the sudden, searing pain the thought caused in my chest.

Nate hadn't given up.

He waited outside my room.

One leg bent at the knee, foot against the wall, his massive shoulders were slumped. My steps silent on the luxurious carpet, he didn't look up until I was upon him.

My heart twisted. Where my newfound hope had buoyed me through the day, lending me purpose and determination, despair had ripped Nate apart. Dark shadows haunted his green eyes. He hadn't shaved, the golden stubble longer than I'd seen it before. Deep grooves etched his tanned cheeks.

He shoved himself from the wall. "Lissa." His voice cracked with disuse, as though he'd waited for hours. "Lissa, I know you don't want to hear this, but I have to say it before you leave. Please."

I brushed past him, not quite touching, and flicked my room key through the slot. "Come in."

Confusion clouded his eyes. "I...no. I need to say this, first."

I lifted an eyebrow. "Are you afraid to come in?"

A sad smile lifted the scar beneath his lip. "Yeah, well, there may be something in that." He straightened his shoulders. "Lissa, I screwed up. I totally own that. I made the wrong call. But I've been thinking all night, and I have to know. Is the issue honestly that we're sort-of, kind-of, but-not-really related? Or is it because of what that bastard Damien did to you? Is the problem really that you believe you can't trust anyone, and I'm such a dumb fuck, I proved you right?"

It kind of irritated me that he got there so quickly, after I'd spent hours working out exactly the same thing. When I didn't reply, didn't shoot him down or storm away, Nate approached me cautiously, sliding his hands up my arms. The electricity sparked between us, and I willowed toward him, the north to his south. I couldn't tear my gaze from his mouth, so close now, so close...

His voice dropped lower. "Because if it's a trust issue, if it's transparency you need, I'll be completely transparent with you. Lissa, I wasn't looking to fall in love, but I've fallen for you. And I know I've fucked it up, and I know you see me as your brother, and I know you live five thousand miles away. And I don't know how to fix any of that." His hands tightened on my arms. "I only know that I'm in love with you, and it hurts. I never expected it to hurt, but it hurts so fucking bad because I'm terrified you're going to turn around and walk out of my life."

I took a deep breath.

Steeled myself.

Turned away from him.

Walked.

Shoved open the door and entered my room.

Then I dropped my backpack and swiveled back to Nate. Thrust out my hand. "Hi. I'm Lissa Holbrook. Nice to meet you."

Nate froze for a heartbeat, then strode forward, kicking the door shut behind him. His hand engulfed mine. "Nate O'Connell. I suspect we may be somehow related."

"Not in any way that matters."

His grip tugged me closer. "I'd like it to be in a way that matters." His gaze locked to mine, his lips descended slowly.

The drought broke.

But it wasn't a drought caused by a lack of sex; it had never truly been that. My emotions dammed up since Dad's death and Mom's desertion, I'd not allowed myself to *feel* anything for years.

Now I kissed Nate with all of the anxiety, despair, hope, lust, and desire I'd repressed forever.

He groaned, crushing me to his chest. His hands scooped up over my shoulder blades and cradled my head, his tongue exploring my mouth.

My fingers found the hem of his shirt, tugging urgently at it, and he whipped it over his head, releasing me for barely a second. Relief shivered through me at the reality of his skin beneath my hands. My fingertips fluttered across his stomach, traced his ridged abs, and circled his nipples, greedily trying to cover every inch of him. His thumb stroked across my lower lip and I swirled my tongue around it, then took it in my mouth, sucked on it in a way I knew he'd remember.

A grunt exploded from him, the green eyes blazing with fire, but I stepped away. "We have to meet our family for dinner. I should change." I shrugged out of my jacket, flipping open the buttons on my prim blouse, one by one. "Problem is, I left my bags behind, so I don't have fresh clothes. Guess I'll have to take these off and press them."

"Let me help you," Nate murmured, closing the space between us. His rough hands grazed my shoulders as he slipped the blouse off, pressing a kiss against each collar bone. Snapped my bra open with a practiced move.

I caught at the lace, cupping my breasts to hide them, prolonging the moment.

Nate pulled back. "Sorry. Too far. I'll stop."

"No. I don't want you to stop. Not ever." I dropped my hands, inviting him to look his fill.

Nate groaned, spinning me around so he was pressed hard against my back, nuzzling my neck. He took the weight of each breast in his palms, thumbs gently brushing across my achingly erect nipples, his chin on my shoulder as he watched them respond to his fondling. "God. You are so beautiful."

Without moving away from him, I unzipped my suit pants and let them drop to the floor. Kicked them aside. Stood there in only my lacy thong.

Nate's breath escaped in a jagged rush. "Really? Are you sure?" He closed his eyes as though he could shut out the temptation, but clutched me against his chest, his erection pressing into my lower back.

I turned within the circle of his arms, reaching for his fly. "Yes, Nate. Yes. Yes, to everything you ask me."

His hand slid across my breast, and he kissed down the side of my neck, trailing molten lava. He bent lower, his lips tracing the full curve of my breast. Then he grunted in sudden amusement.

I squeezed the front of his pants, feeling him deliciously thick and hard. Hard for *me*. "Seriously? I have my hand on your dick, and you dare laugh at me?"

Nate's voice vibrated through me like the thunder of last night's storm. "I can't reach all the parts I want. I need to take you to bed, Lissa. I want you spread across that mattress, with not a god-damned thing between us. And then I'm going to touch and lick and taste every inch of you."

"Uh huh." Okay, so not the sexiest reply, but I'd just about come on the spot.

The cleft in Nate's cheek deepened, and he slid his hands to my barely-clad butt. "Perfect handful." His fingers traced the narrow thong, and I quivered in anticipation.

Cupping my cheeks, he lifted me easily. I wrapped my

legs around his waist and arched my back as he bent his head to my breasts.

At the first hot, wet contact, the warning tremors rippled through me. "No. Don't."

He pulled back, studying my face. "You want me to stop?"

"Yes. No. I mean, I don't want you to, but if you don't..." I shrugged, sliding my gaze from his. Damn, I couldn't come now. I had to wait for him. This had to be so right.

Nate breathed against my nipple, and I quivered, closing my eyes. His mouth moved against my breast. "You mean that wasn't a one-time thing? You're going to come if I do this?" He swirled his tongue around my nipple. "Or this?" He sucked the hard nub into his mouth, flicking with his tongue.

"Oh, God." I arched back farther. I couldn't wait for him. I needed to come now, right now.

Nate gripped my butt tighter, pulling me rhythmically against his abs. "Come on, Lissa. You know what I want. Give it to me."

I could barely breathe, the pressure building and surging within me as I focused on the heat between my legs. His mouth found my nipple again, and I abandoned myself to the sensation, grinding against him as the orgasm seized me. Both my self-control and fear dissolved as electricity arced within me, every nerve ending in my body vibrating as I thrust my hips toward him, rubbing my wetness against his golden skin as he held me safe and I cried out my need and longing.

"I need to taste you." The words were a sexy growl against my neck as Nate carried my limp form to the bed and lowered me to the soft mattress. He hooked his fingers through the lace strip on either side of my panties and drew them down and off. Dangled them above me. "I'll add these to my collection."

"Oh! You didn't keep...?"

His smoldering gaze raked my naked body. "Oh, hell, yeah, I sure did. You're going to have to take my credit card and hit Victoria's Secret, ma'am, because every time you cream your panties, I intend to keep them as a trophy. And I'm very big on trophies."

"Oh, I can see you're big."

Nate laughed and moved away from my searching hand. "Uh uh. Not yet."

"But I want it," I pouted.

Nate traced two fingers from my collarbone down the valley between my breasts, leaning to kiss first one nipple, then the other, watching as they doubled in size. "Oh, believe me, I want it too. But I told you I plan to taste every inch of you first. I want you to come on my tongue, Lissa. I want you to moan and beg and cry out my name. Will you do that?"

"Yes," I whispered, my fingers in his hair as he kissed the mound of my belly. "Oh, yes."

His hand closed over my stomach, tugging gently. "Christ, you're so soft and squeezable and perfect." He kissed lower. "And I did mean to remark on the fact that I was right, that first night."

"Right?" I could barely get the word out. His finger stroked down my wet cleft, and I almost screamed.

"Right. Brazilian. Beautiful."

He shifted onto one shoulder so he could see what he was doing, slowly caressing up and down my slit. "You're so swollen and wanting."

Wanting. Longing. He had no idea. I clutched at the sheets beneath me, trying to control the excitement that spiraled from the pit of my stomach, stealing my breath and my sanity.

His finger slipped inside me, and I arched up to him. "More?" he murmured.

"More," I panted.

He slipped another finger in, withdrew them, and then slowly re-entered. "Faster?"

"Faster."

His fingers angled toward my G-spot, and I trembled and moaned at his rhythm. He withdrew them again. "Can I taste you now?"

"Yes. Oh, God, yes."

Crouched on the floor, Nate seized my hips and pulled me closer to the edge of the mattress. Bending my knees, he placed my feet flat on the sheets. He moved between my thighs, pressing kisses on my ankles, up my calves, the inside of my knees, my thighs.

I shuddered with hypersensitivity, needing him, wanting him, but knowing I'd shatter at his touch.

His broad shoulders didn't fit easily between my legs. "Drop your knees out to the sides," he instructed. Then he breathed against my clit. "Now? Lissa, do you want it now?"

If he didn't do it now, I was going to come anyway, the sight of his blond head between my splayed thighs enough to tip me over the edge. "Yes!"

His tongue drove deep into my slit, one long, hot lick from back to front.

"Fuck!" I sobbed, tightening my grip on his hair. "Yes!"

With one hand he parted my labia, his tongue tracing the delicate folds, guiding him to the hard nub. As he found my clit, his fingers slid into me. Sucking and fucking me at the same time. I threw a leg over his shoulder, greedily forcing his tongue deeper as I exploded into orgasm, bucking from the bed as I shoved myself closer to his mouth, his tongue and fingers sending ripples of unbearable pleasure shuddering through me.

As I heaved for breath, my heartbeat slowing back to near normal, Nate moved up the bed, tugging a corner of the sheet loose to dry his face. He kissed me, his tongue slipping into my mouth like it had into my secret folds, and I nearly fainted from the heady musk, the instant desire that filled me when he was close.

And the lack of oxygen. Technically, that could have something to do with it.

As he caressed my breast, his erection pressed against my thigh. I slid a hand between us, trying to work it into his jeans. I remembered that beautiful length. I wanted to see it again, I wanted all of it.

Nate snatched a breath and rolled away from me. "I'm sorry; I'm not real good at restraint around you. Best you just leave that in there, or I'm not going to be able to control myself."

I pushed myself up on one elbow, my pussy wet, throbbing, and sensitive. But I wanted more. "I never asked you for restraint, Nate. I want you. Inside me, now. I want you to fuck me. Fuck me hard, so I never forget it." If our relationship was to be founded on honesty, this was a good place to start.

"Christ," Nate groaned as I clambered to my knees and knelt alongside him, tugging at his Levis. "Do you know how fucking sexy you are?" He reached for my pendulous breast, lifting his hips so I could drag down his jeans and boxers.

His cock sprang free, and I sighed with pleasure. "And you're beautiful." I wrapped a hand around the silky shaft and scooted down the bed further, so I could bend to kiss the head.

Nate half sat, reaching to stop me. "No. If you do that, I can't last. And, unlike you, I'm probably only good for one round. Well, maybe two. I want to make love to you, Lissa. But first, I have to go find a pharmacy."

"What? Oh." I tried to hide my giggle. Nate had been so unsure of himself, he hadn't brought any condoms. Somehow, that was so much hotter than if he'd flipped one out of his wallet.

His penis throbbed, and I ran a thumb through the pre-cum as the engorged head pulsed in my hand. "I don't think you're going to have much luck tucking this back in your boxers. Anyway, you don't have time to go downstairs."

Concern creased Nate's forehead. "No time? Why?"

"Because," I pressed a hand against his shoulder, pushing him down onto the bed. "You know what touching you does to me. And I'm *touching* you, Nate." I threw one leg across his thighs, straddling him. "Don't worry, I've got us covered." I tapped my shoulder. "Implant."

Nate's hands found my hips, lifting me up a little as he gazed at the pouted flesh between my legs. He groaned, a throaty sound of pure desire. "Fuck, Lissa."

"Command? Yes, sir." I gripped his cock, angling it into my wetness as he held my weight. I moaned as his mushroom head slowly spread my lips, probing me. Thighs quivering, I moved my hands to Nate's chest.

He vibrated with tension. "God, I want to be all the way inside you, Lissa. Are you okay?"

"Yeah." I kept my eyes closed for a moment, concentrating on the sensation between my legs. "Just, you're kind of...big." Damn, I'd thought this position would give me more control, but if I relaxed, he'd be painfully deep inside me. Online porn obviously wasn't that great a study tool.

"And you're kind of tiny." Nate's palm caressed the side of my face, his half-smile changing to a look of shock as I inched him further inside me. "And so fucking tight. And hot. Jesus." His jaw spasmed as he clenched his teeth, and I inched lower still.

I moved up and down experimentally, adoring the unadulterated lust that played across Nate's face. One hand cupping my breast, his eyes were almost closed, teeth clenched on his lower lip, nostrils flaring. But I could tell he was holding back, afraid of hurting me. "Nate, I can't take all of you this way. Not yet." And it was killing my thighs. I'd have to find a yoga class and work on strengthening them.

His eyes flashed open. "Will you let me show you how? Can I make love to you, Lissa?"

"Always yes."

Nate used his stomach muscles to easily pull himself partially up into a sitting position. Hands on my waist, he lifted me off his rigid penis and set me down astride his stomach.

I tried not to sigh with relief. Also tried not to wriggle my butt against the hard ridges of his muscles as his abdomen tensed with the effort of maintaining the position.

Nate slid his hands under my armpits, pulling me close as he caressed my shoulder blades, his lips trailing the side of my neck and nibbling at my ear. His mouth shifted to mine, his tongue seeking, moving in erotic rhythm.

I responded instantly, winding my arms around his head, crushing him to me as I inhaled his spice and salt and sweat.

I wanted to make love with him.

Cradling me so I was still wrapped around him, Nate

stood and turned to lay me back on the bed. Slowly, he lowered his body to cover mine, taking his time, allowing me to adjust to his weight. His penis lay like an iron bar between us, a hot length pressed into my thigh, the head jabbing the soft mound of my belly as he rocked against me.

Our kisses deepened, and Nate slipped a hand down into my wetness, stroking me unbearably close to orgasm.

"Now, do it now," I gasped against his mouth.

Nate shifted his weight and positioned his penis between my swollen lips. He rubbed the head up and down my slit, deeper with each pass. "Now?"

"Now," I panted, arching up to meet him. "Ohh." My moan was of pure ecstasy as he slid within me, filling me to the brim. I'd never felt anything like it. Such a sense of... completeness. As though we were made to fit together. Even though I knew that wasn't biologically possible, science didn't have a darn thing to add to the perfection of this moment.

He eased away from me, and I flashed my eyes open.

He was watching, waiting. "Again?"

"Yes, again!" I closed my eyes, feeling every inch of him as he impaled me, then slowly withdrew. "Again!" I lifted my legs, locking my ankles around his waist.

He pulled away, biceps bulging as they held his weight. Shook his head warningly. "Ah, don't do that. I can't hold back if you do that."

I tightened my legs, brushed my hands up through his soft underarm hair, and dug my nails into his back, pulling him down so I could lick and bite at his nipples, my words disjointed with lust. "I don't want you to hold back, Nate. You have to understand, I *need* you to not be able to control yourself around me. I need you to want me desperately."

"Lissa, I want you more than you'll ever realize." His

cock thickened and twitched within me, and I slammed my feet back onto the bed, lifting my hips to meet the powerful thrusts as he plunged into me.

"Yes, yes," I gasped. With Nate, it would always be yes.

The intensity built, rippling through my body, my internal muscles gripping him more tightly than I would have believed possible. I was panting for release, longing for it, yet denying it for as long as possible, clinging to the sweet moment.

Nate shoved back to his knees, seized my hips, and pulled me hard against his groin. His shoulders bunched, muscles knotted as he pumped into me, and I tumbled and somersaulted into orgasm, grinding against him with bruising force.

My abandon tipped Nate over the edge. The powerful column of his neck stretched back, eyes closed and jaw tense, he surged into me, filling me with his hot seed.

LATER, we lay curled together beneath the sheet, too exhausted to move, but not wanting to waste a moment in sleep. Nate's arm beneath me, his fingertips lazily stroking my shoulder, he occasionally pulled me close, nuzzling my ear or kissing my hair.

His phone buzzed. "I don't even know where it is," he grumbled, his pectoralis major tensing beneath my cheek as he made to push upright. "Some hussy tore off my clothes and flung them all over the place."

I leaned over the edge of the bed to search the floor and Nate slapped my naked bottom, then bit it. Voice muffled, he mumbled "God, I'm so stuffed, but I want you again. Stop tempting me with this." He grabbed my hips, burrowing his tongue up between my thighs.

One day, I'd have a word with him about his unhygienic practices. Maybe. But not today.

Giggling, I lurched back onto the bed, handing him the phone. My stepbrother's picture flashed on the screen. "It's Trav."

"Fuck Travis," Nate muttered.

"No thanks. I've already screwed the only brother I want."

I squealed as he rolled on top of me.

"Dirty talk is it?" he growled. "I think I can rise to that."

I wormed my hand between us and closed it around his length. "I see you already have."

The phone buzzed again and I sighed, though in truth it was partly relief at the interruption; I wouldn't be able to walk if we spent much longer fooling around in bed. "Saved by the bell. We're not late for the dinner, are we?"

Nate thumbed the screen. "Nope. Trav wants to know if I've killed myself yet. Suppose I could tell him I'm half dead?"

My palm smacked against his chest, though my fingers lingered in a caress, adoring the ridges and planes of his body, tracing the tiny scars I'd one day get him to tell me about. "No, you cannot. But I do hope you have some bright ideas about how we're going to explain this." I gestured at the bed.

"Got it covered. I'm going to say I was seduced by a wild Australian. Everyone knows your wildlife is dangerous. I'll totally get the sympathy vote."

"In your dreams. I'm going for a shower while you come up with something brilliant. The ball is totally in your court on this one."

Nate caught my wrist as I tried to get up. "Don't be long, Liss. We don't have much time."

"I thought you just said we're not running late?"

His handsome face suddenly etched with sadness, Nate shook his head. "I'm not talking about dinner. I mean until you leave." He tried for a grin, but it slid crooked. "Then Trav's fears may be well-founded."

"Aw, c'mon. A big, tough soldier like you can manage without me for a while." Kneeling on the bed, I leaned toward him until my breasts crushed against his chest, nipple to nipple. His pupils instantly dilated with lust, despite the melancholy that carved furrows in his cheeks.

"A while?" He seized on my words as his hands spread to span the small of my back, pressing me closer. "How long is a while? Can you get more leave? I've no more due for three months, but I can get off base easy enough, if you can get back here before then."

I smoothed my hands over his chest as I pretended to consider his suggestion. The muscle was ridged beneath my hand, his skin firm and warm. With that to pet, I'd never need cats. "Well, I guess I could come back..."

"When?" His entire body suddenly still and alert, Nate dropped all pretense of joking. "I need to know when, Lissa. Because I don't know how long I can last without you. I don't even want to think about you going, but I need to know when you'll be back."

Nate's words should terrify me. They encompassed everything I'd convinced myself I dreaded hearing. And yet, they were everything I suddenly needed to hear. This man had no intention of using me. He offered himself, openly and unselfishly, and he hid nothing.

I met his imploring green gaze. "How about if I could get here before Christmas? Maybe spend it with your—our —family?"

"Christmas? As in *this* year? In a couple of weeks? Listen, if you can wrangle the time off, I'll pay your fare, okay? Every time. Whenever."

I screwed up my nose. "Hmm. I can probably manage to fund it. A one-way ticket isn't that much."

"One way?" Nate shoved himself up on one elbow, his low tone urgent. "What do you mean?"

I couldn't tease him any longer. "That job I went for? I got it. And it's based here. I'm only ducking back to Australia to tie up a few loose ends." Put my house on the market and say goodbye to some things I should have let go long ago. Give my furniture to Suzee. Oh, and tick off *all* the boxes on *The Vagina's Vacation* list.

It was Nate's eyes that held me captive, not the gentle hand he slid behind my neck. "Lissa, you're not messing with me? You are coming back? To me?"

He didn't try to hide his need, and I no longer had to hide mine.

I lay on top of him, relishing the slightly-rough texture of his skin against mine, the hardness of his muscles, the heat kindling through me as his hands stroked to the small of my back and then swooped down to cup my butt.

"Yes, I'm coming back." I pressed my lips to his, sealing the promise.

Daring to love Nate was without question the most dangerous experiment I would ever conduct.

But, for the first time, I didn't care about the theories, the hypotheses, the variables, or the quantifiable results.

Because, at last, I'd finally learned to trust myself.

EPILOGUE

I couldn't contain my grin as the unmistakable sounds of Chris Isaak crooning Mele Kalikimaka —the Hawaiian Christmas song—swirled through the baggage claim area. Cheesy, bright, and a perfect welcome back to paradise.

My luggage was embarrassingly easy to identify on the carousel; Suzee had managed to find packing tape printed with the deep blue, red, and white Australian flag and had liberally bound each of my cases with the bright ribbon.

Despite being the hub of hours of travel for thousands of people, the airport pulsed with excitement and anticipation as Christmas cheer and vacation joy collided in an exuberant cacophony of sound and color.

I hauled my bags onto a large trolley, then hunched over the handle, putting some muscle into shoving the behemoth along a concourse edged by white pine trees, each hung from tip to trunk with sparkling crystals. A glittering white Christmas theme should look out of place in the tropics, yet it didn't. As I'd already learned, Hawaii was a magical land where the impossible became entirely possible.

Brandishing a passport with a photo that actually looked like me, I passed swiftly through Customs with practiced ease. Well, as it was only my second venture from Australian soil, *practiced ease* might be a bit of an exaggeration. Though at least I'd managed to brave the recycled-air germs of the plane's bathroom, this time—mainly because I didn't want to cause a single second's delay once I'd disembarked.

The electronic doors on the far side of the Customs area whooshed open, and I pushed the luggage cart out into the balmy caress of a Hawaiian winter.

And jerked to a halt, my heart suddenly expanding in a manner that was biologically impossible yet, at that moment, both entirely plausible and painfully tangible.

Directly outside the doors, blocking the view of the bank of potted hibiscus, stood a uniformed military man. His legs spread apart, balancing the width of his shoulders, his hands were behind his camo-clad back, his gaze fixed rigidly straight ahead.

My over-sized heart thumped double time, but I wasn't concerned.

I knew without a doubt that the sensation had nothing to do with biology.

And everything to do with pure chemistry.

"Soldier," I nodded at him.

"Ma'am." Though he fought to keep a neutral expression, his lips quirked, tugging the fine white scar on his chin. "Protective order, ma'am. I'm to accompany you to your lodgings."

"Accompany?" I cocked my head to one side. "I was rather hoping that you'd toss me over one shoulder and carry me off into the sunset."

In seconds, I'd be back in his arms. Three weeks apart had been almost unendurable—and more than long enough for me to realize that, although I didn't *need* Nate, I sure as heck wanted him.

Because I was madly, irreversibly, irrevocably in love with the man.

And that fact was more than okay.

Nate's grin broke through and he strode forward, quickly closing the space between us. "Yours to command, Ma'am. Always."

ACKNOWLEDGMENTS

My gratitude, as always, to numerous people:

Taylor, who listens to all of my moaning and does a fair job of pretending interest.
Sandie Docker, my rock and shoulder
Lindsay Landgraf Hess, whose critiquing is a novel in its own right
Anne Raven, who can always be trusted to do a fast, thorough critique
Elena Jagar, a staunch friend who can be relied on for invaluable feedback
Marty Mayberry, my writing partner, with whom I speak every day
Tina Kelsall, who finds time in her hectic schedule to give feedback
Josette Arthur, who generously shared her invaluable editing knowledge

HAWAIIAN TABOO

~ A BILLIONAIRE ROMANCE MELTING THE TROPICS~

EAT I have down pat, whether it's pot noodles in the Solomon Islands or Europe's Michelin star cuisine
PRAY - praying for your ex to fall off the Harbour Bridge counts, right?
LOVE? Well, love sucks.

Corporate lawyer Sara is all about the rules. Until, in a far-too-young-to-have-a-midlife-crisis moment she swaps practicing law for cleaning cabins aboard The Spirit of Ohana, five-star dining for onboard buffets, and love for....well, fantasies are a girl's best friend, right?

At least, they are until one dark and stormy night, when she drags an impossibly attractive, cocky Brit from the ocean...

Rick's had his fill of gorgeous women throwing themselves at him. Doing his damnedest to spit out the silver spoon that hampers his philanthropic ventures, the last thing he needs is to be rescued from a tropical cyclone only to find himself consumed by Hurricane Sara.

Yet the fiery cabin steward is undeniably intriguing--not to mention, hot as sin, all voluptuous curves and sassy innuendo. But she seems determined to keep him at arms' length and, for the first time, he's tempted to commit to the chase.

Unless Sara can overcome her distrust of wealthy, entitled men, and Rick is able to set aside his belief that women are only after his money, these two natural enemies can never become lovers, their affair doomed to be hotter than Kilauea and shorter than the brief cruise.

Turn the page for a sneak preview...

CHAPTER ONE

~RICK~

I ducked, as though that'd stop the wave breaking over me —not that another drenching would make a modicum of difference. My clothes, several hours past sodden, slopped against water-wrinkled flesh, and salt puckered my mouth with an ironically unquenchable thirst as the mountainous ocean churned around me.

The thundering fusillade of waves against the towering cliffs grew fainter as swirling currents forced my yacht out to sea, and I snatched a brine-laden breath. Drifting farther from land wasn't ideal, but the glimpses I caught of jagged rocks piercing the foaming waves proved it sure beat the alternative. The wind whipped my sopping shirt into a cat o' nine tails, and I blinked the stinging spray from my eyes, vainly peering through the twilight for a pinprick of light along the storm-lashed Hawaiian coast.

Legs spread, I wound a rope around my arm and gripped the tiller. The boat surged and plummeted. Balancing shouldn't be any more difficult than swinging the mallet while mounted on one of Mother's damn ponies, but this was uncomfortably reminiscent of a rollercoaster ride. I hadn't been on one of those since Vanessa Cottesloe-Meyer had declared her undying devotion. Possibly unrelated, but I'd promptly been sick all over her fancy red-soled shoes. No thirteen-year-old should even have access to Louboutins.

The following two decades had cemented my dislike of both rollercoasters and women with double-barreled surnames.

The boat plunged from a wave. Defying gravity, my body hung weightless for a nanosecond, then dropped in a stomach-swooping freefall, slamming to a halt as my bare feet smacked the slippery timber deck.

Damn! I shook my head, heaving for breath. Hindsight being twenty-twenty—and totally useless, right now—it might have been a good idea to flash the cash and charter a luxurious, fully-crewed, penis-extension yacht. Not that I needed the genital compensation but, thinking of wood, a bit more between me and the raging ocean wouldn't be intolerable.

Sucked up a sheer black wall of water, the yacht teetered on the curling crest, the twenty feet of timber and polished steel bobbing like a spent champagne cork. The wave exploded. The boat plummeted. Shuddered and jerked. The timbers screamed as she threatened to tear apart.

The gut-stealing impact shot the air from my lungs, along with a bellow of exultant laughter.

This close to death, I felt more alive than I had for years.

Except, it wasn't like I truly challenged death and threw caution to the wind. Much as I liked to pretend I diced with danger and flew under the radar, it was a load of cods. I had fail-safes in place. For starters, if I'd been truly intent on disappearing, I'd have paid cash for the boat. Hell, could have paid it a hundred times over. Instead, although I'd used a pseudonym to hire the yacht, I'd paid by card. A card Marty would have had a trace on the moment he realized he'd been given the slip. In fact, the lugubrious personal security guard had probably been on my tail before I'd even reached the south-eastern coast of Big Island.

I used a sodden sleeve to swipe at my face, succeeding only in grinding salt deeper into my eyes. Marty would no doubt have helicopters out at first light and the coast guard patrolling. All the usual malarkey. Still, the stolen hours of solitude, watching the red-orange lava trails of Kilauea sinuously ooze down purple dusk-shadowed cliffs and disappear into the ocean in hissing geysers, had been worth the imminent fuss.

Until Mother heard about it, anyway. I winced at the thought of her lemon-sucking disapproval. Really, though, as she was only happy when she was unhappy, my sojourn in Hawaii should have her verging on acidly ecstatic.

I lurched as the yacht climbed almost vertically through the darkness, her bow pointed to where the stars should have been. She leveled on the crest of the wave, clung to the pinnacle for eternity, then dropped from the curl.

We hit the trough with a smack that reverberated through the timbers, ringing in my ears even through the water that closed overhead. Only the fraying fibers of the coarse rope looped around my forearm connected me to the boat as the tiller ripped from my grasp.

The deck heaved and bucked as the craft struggled to right herself, forcing her way up from the deep, sloughing off water like a breaching whale. The bow shot into the air, then the keel slapped down as the boat found horizontal.

A sharp crack sounded for'ard, and the braided

remnants of the backstay cable fluttered in a tattered flag above my head. The sail pouched with air and billowed like a parachute, deceptively soft and elegant—and almost hiding the jagged pole of the mast that swung toward me on the amputated cable. With no time to move, I closed my eyes and braced for the inevitable impact.

CHAPTER TWO

~SARA~

The storm-driven waves foamed far below the side rail I hung over, the occasional whitecap rearing like a mountain, forcing me to retreat. Though the wind tugged at my ponytail and whipped escaped strands across my face, the pelting rain had eased some. My fifth stint on *The Spirit of Ohana* and we ran into a rare hurricane, proving the old sea-faring myth: a woman aboard brought bad luck. Not that I had sole claim to the jinx title; I'd willingly share it with about a third of the other crew members, and about half of the fifteen hundred passengers.

Instead of plowing through the massive swell of the next wave, the ship surged up and over. I clutched at the white-painted handrail, biting back a squeal as the vessel bottomed out with a thud that quivered through the reinforced steel hull. An adrenalin rush chased the flash of fear and I braced my legs to ride out the rock and roll. Eyes squinted against the salt spray, I gazed across the dark ocean, toward the invisible coast.

Kept busy in the cabins, making uncountable beds—well, not exactly uncountable, I knew precisely how many sheets I had to tuck and how much time to allocate to cleaning other people's toilets—I'd missed the highlight of the Big Island passage; an evening viewing of the Kilauea volcano bleeding lava down the black cliffs.

Which was fine. The red and orange ooze of demon vomit, hissing with evil anger as it reached the sea, was a little too end-of-the-worldish for my taste. I preferred when my free time coincided with the sun-drenched seventeen mile stretch of the Na Pali coast. With majestic emerald-green cliffs divided by cascading waterfalls and hidden valleys, the unreachable, untouched land stirred my soul, the rugged wilderness hinting at promises of freedom.

Not that I had any need of hidden promises. I tucked a strand of wind-tangled hair behind my ear, grinning as it immediately escaped. Truth was, I'd been sort-of-free for months now. Ever since Simon had suggested we meet in Honiara at the conclusion of my placement with the Public Solicitor's Office in the Solomon Islands.

To celebrate our wedding anniversary, he'd said — despite the fact we'd not celebrated in seven years.

Give us chance to reconnect, he'd said.

We could go and visit the orphanages, he'd said.

Maybe that'd stop me banging on about having a baby, he'd said.

Lied through his perfectly veneered teeth, he had.

I ground my own teeth together at the memory, my hands wringing the life from the rain-spangled guardrail. Better that, than Simon's neck. His non-arrival on the flight from Australia hadn't been even close to a surprise. He'd always said Third World countries were undeserving of either his time or his tourist dollar.

Though I'd known where he'd be, I'd phoned anyway. To check he was still alive —so I could kill him.

Not literally. That would definitely be against the rules.

In our luxurious Sydney apartment, Simon had pitched his voice to drown out the soft background music. Dire Straits' *Romeo and Juliet*. "Sorry, Sara. Last minute trial. Been run off my feet."

The narrow camp bed in my bare, two-meter-square room tipped as I jerked the phone from my head, staring at it: *Exhibit A of one philandering husband's deception, Your Honor.* Did Simon think me an idiot? Last minute trials in our shared profession were a logistical implausibility. I mashed the phone back to my ear like I could squeeze the truth from it.

The susurration of Simon's crew-cut gray hair brushed the mouthpiece as he turned away, murmuring something, his words muffled by a rustle of linen. *One-thousand-count Egyptian cotton bedsheets.* Then his voice boomed again. "I tried to call, but your cell was out of range."

The quickly stifled giggle in the background of the call proved his lie. Most likely his probably just-out-of-diapers PA, Emma. No forty-year-old man needed a vacuous blonde nineteen-year-old assistant. Not unless he could afford a Viagra addiction.

Of course, Simon could afford any drugs he fancied.

I hadn't felt angry. Not then, anyway. Just tired. So tired, I didn't think before I spoke. "Simon, maybe we need to talk about a divorce."

Silence for a moment, then Simon's measured, professional tone, betraying neither shock nor regret. His best court performance to date, or finally, some honesty? "Sure, we can take a break, if you think it best."

Best? Hell no, I didn't think it best. Best would be not having wasted eleven years of my life.

I hadn't replied. Staring at my hand, I'd willed each of

the fingers to slowly unclench, white flesh turning back to pink. Winced at the flash of gold from my wedding band.

"Let's stay friends, though," he said.

"Go fuck yourself," I said. Well, no, I didn't. But I should have. Thing was, he had nubile Emma doing all the fucking he required —which left me with no reason to rush back to Australia.

Screw my non-existent marriage.

Screw my supposedly perfect life.

Screw practicing law.

The local orphanage needed volunteers. I'd spend a couple more months in the Solomons, exploring another country, another culture. *Another life.*

Go all Eat, Pray, Love. Not exactly one of the life-goals teenaged Sara had aspired to in glittery purple pen in a heart-embossed, locked diary fifteen years earlier, but the break would give Simon and I time to think about what we really wanted from a relationship that'd long been foundering worse than the storm-driven ship.

I licked the tang of salt from my lips and turned my face full into the gusting wind. Eleven months ago, I would have huddled in the lush interior of the cruise ship —heck, I would've had the stateroom and room service, probably never even stepped out onto the deck. Most certainly not during a hurricane. But things had changed. I'd changed. My time in the Solomon Islands had instilled an appreciation of the simple things in life. Basic food, basic shelter. The thrill of opening my eyes to a new day with absolutely no idea what it would bring. No fail-safes, nothing was routine or pre-ordained.

When work on the Islands wound up, I'd looked for a new experience. Cleaning toilets on a cruise ship clearly the farthest I could get from the lifestyle that came with a lucrative law practice, the menial tasks allowed me the mental clarity to focus on improving my better self. Unfortunately, it seemed spiritual enlightenment still lay somewhat out of my reach, and the *Pray* part of my new philosophy tended toward entreating the flavor-of-the-week deity to shove Simon off the Sydney Harbour Bridge. Preferably while wrapped in the embrace of too-sweet-to-steal-your-husband Emma.

My stomach rumbled, and I swiped mist from the face of my watch and tilted it toward the muted yellow glow of a deck light. A little early yet to turn down the last of the beds before I took a dinner break. Whether dining in Michelin-starred restaurants in the United States, months of pot noodles in the Solomons, or the endless buffets aboard *The Spirit of Ohana, I* never had a problem with the *Eat* part of my mantra.

Love, however...I drummed my fingertips on the rail as I stared into the dark. Forget about love, I'd settle for sex. The sojourn in the Solomon Islands had been spent metaphorically licking my wounds —while my husband was no doubt happily engaged in licking something else. But shifting to Hawaii and working in close confines with the ship's entertainment director had, well, stirred my juices. Not that a cocktail of lust did me much good. Jay flirted outrageously —and I'd quickly learned my ten-day roster on the ship required packing twenty pairs of panties —but our employer had a strict *No Fraternization* policy.

And, despite my new life, I was all about the rules.

The ship shuddered through another wave, and I thrust my hands into the pockets of my windbreaker. My fingers brushed my cell. I could try my luck with the internet before the evening round of room-service calls started. Maybe this time the email I needed would be waiting.

Though I couldn't log in to our bank account from the unsecured onboard service, I'd directed—no, I had *requested,* one never directed Simon—to transfer several thousand dollars to the Solomon's orphanage. Much as the kids craved affection, only money had any real power to help them. Simon was right about that much; money was King. Just not the way he used it.

But, for the last two weeks, my texts and emails to Simon had gone unanswered. For some reason, after months of surprisingly civil conversations where he'd urged me to take the time I needed to sort out what I truly wanted from life, and I'd pretended to be unaware of his latest affair, he'd gone to ground. Or, more like, gone under the covers. Between Emma's taut, tanned thighs.

A gust of rain forced me from the rail, toward the scant shelter of the dripping metal walls of the ship. As I retreated, a flash of white against the murky, churning ocean caught my attention. Orca! I lunged back to the rail, eyes stinging as I squinted into the bluster. There it was again, a patch of light on the dark, though it surfed the waves, rather than swim through them. I frowned. A dead whale?

The ocean surged, bringing the carcass closer. No, not a whale. A boat? The rain hurled flurries in my direction, and I rubbed the disbelief from my eyes, one at a time so I didn't lose sight of the object. Definitely the remnants of some sort of vessel. Must have slipped its moorings in the storm.

Shit, what should I do? The debris posed a shipping hazard, I'd have to alert someone.

I half-turned toward the heavy storm doors that sectioned the rain-lashed deck from a plush, carpeted passage. By the time I'd dragged them open against the banshee howl of the wind and found my way to the bridge, the wrecked craft would be far in our wake. And I'd look like an idiot for causing a fuss.

The crippled vessel wallowed. It'd soon sink safely out of the way. I shoved a palm into my eye sockets, trying to stop the salt sting, then looked back to sea. The small boat crested another wave, the height bringing it more clearly into view.

What the hell—? My pulse spiked, shock turning my fingers to ice as the pounding of blood in my ears competed with the thunder rolling across the sky.

A person huddled in the bottom of the yacht.

No, it couldn't be a person.

Fishing nets. Or the sail, torn from its restraints. Or old clothes, rags. Anything but—

The bundle shifted as the yacht hit a trough. A white face gleamed stark against the night.

Oh shit. Shit, shit, and triple shit.

I scanned the deserted, rain-soaked deck frantically. Why wasn't there some sort of smash-and-sound-the-alarm device? Trains had them, and it wasn't like they risked running afoul of shipwrecks. I needed help. Now.

A hand raised feebly from the waterlogged hull of the yacht as *The Spirit of Ohana* pulled away from it.

Alive. Crap. That was bad. Well, good. But bad.

I raked my hands through my hair, tugging a decision from my brain. By the time I found help, the stricken yacht would have been swallowed by the vast ocean. Already it plunged and bucked on the wild seas fifty, maybe a hundred feet away.

I paused, staring. I could do that, easily. The pool at home was sixty feet and, until the last few months, I'd swum twenty-five laps. Morning and night.

Of course, the pool didn't have a wave machine churning

out sky-scraper sized breakers, or a population of the myriad stingy, bitey things that no doubt inhabited this part of Oceania.

Fuck.

The yacht had drifted beyond the stern and out of the bubble of security created by the lights of *The Spirit of Ohana.* I shucked my flat leather shoes and my jacket. Snatched up a life preserver, the lump of plastic refusing to part from its housing anywhere near as easy as it should. I clambered onto the slippery bottom rail. Damn movies; Kate Winslet had managed to make this look easy and graceful. In reality, it was like trying to mount an eel.

The storm door into the passage gusted open and slammed against the white metal wall with a dull clang. Thank God, the cavalry. Or Marines, or Coast Guard, or whoever.

I dropped one foot back to the relative safety of the pitching deck, trying to make my cowardly relief appear nonchalant.

The butter-yellow light framed my room-mate, Melanie. One-hundred pounds of sweet-but-useless blonde. Damn. I couldn't toss the girl overboard.

Could I?

"Melanie!" The wind stole the last two syllables, but Melanie started toward me, bent against the bluster.

Great, the girl would blow away. Then I'd be responsible for two deaths. I waved her back, the rushing wind filling my cheeks as I yelled. "Go get help."

The life preserver clamped under one arm, I turned back to the railing and clumsily pulled myself up, my toes scrabbling against the plexiglass barricade that offered little in the way of footholds. Why the heck did they make these things so hard to climb, anyway? Oh, yeah; so nobody climbed them.

I threw my leg over the top rail, straddling the fence. Then lurched forward. My cheek crushed against the metal bar, I clung to the way-too-flimsy security like a baby koala. The liner plunged into a trough. A surge of vertigo yanked my stomach into my mouth, and I squeezed my eyes shut. The wind shrieked with glee, salty fingers trying to tug me from my precarious perch.

What the hell had I been thinking? Totally shit idea. No way was I going to loosen the grip of either my hand or my thighs.

Forcing my eyes open, I glanced down into the black maw of the waves. I had to be about—*no*. I didn't want to calculate how many feet above sea level. Despite being on the lowest deck, even if I managed not to belly flop, slamming into the waves from this height would hurt like a slap from a frozen fish.

Melanie had struggled closer despite my shouted plea. Her face lit with questions, mouth working soundlessly, she probably thought I was trying to top myself. It'd be a pretty lame attempt, considering I clutched the life preserver to my chest with the same desperation I'd hung on to a donut the week I tried Jenny Craig.

HAWAIIAN HURRICANE is available online and at all good bookstores

NOTE FROM THE AUTHOR

Hi! If you've enjoyed this taste of the tropics, I'd love if you could leave a rating or review on Amazon, Goodreads, Book-bub...anywhere good books are found. Reviews are an author's only true feedback and help us decide what to write next!

Drop by and say hi on social media — I'm generally hanging out and posting pictures of my menagerie here:

Twitter@LaneyKaye1
Email: leehotline66@gmail.com
Facebook : LaneyKayeAuthor
Instagram : laney_kaye_author
Goodreads:Laney.Kaye
Bookbub: laney-kaye
Website: www.laney-kaye-author.weebly.com

Thanks for reading!

Laney x